When Mary Rose married Gabe,
she never expected to share him.

Enter the riveting world of the Brides of Gabriel.

Mary Rose is a young Mormon convert
of aristocratic English blood.
Bronwyn is a beautiful young widow with a baby.
And Enid, Gabe's first love, holds a secret
she's never revealed . . .

Other Novels by Diane Noble

The Sister Wife
The Veil
When the Far Hills Bloom
The Blossom and the Nettle
At Play in the Promised Land
Heart of Glass
The Last Storyteller
Tangled Vines
Distant Bells
Through the Fire
Angels Undercover
The Missing Ingredient
Home to Briar Mountain
A Matter of Trust
The Master's Hand

Written as Amanda MacLean

Westward
Stonehaven
Everlasting
Promise Me the Dawn
Kingdom Come

Novellas/Stageplays

Come, My Little Angel
Phoebe

THE BETRAYAL

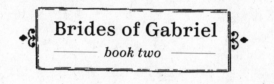

Brides of Gabriel
book two

DIANE NOBLE

AVON
INSPIRE

An Imprint of HarperCollinsPublishers

Published in association with the literary agency of Alive Communications, Inc., 7680 Goddard Street, Suite 200, Colorado Springs, CO 80920. www .alivecommunications.com

HarperCollins books may be purchased for educational, business, or sales promotional use. For information please write: Special Markets Department, HarperCollins Publishers, 10 East 53rd Street, New York, NY 10022.

FIRST EDITION

Library of Congress Cataloging-in-Publication Data has been applied for.

ISBN 978-0-06-198094-7

11 12 13 14 15 OV/RRD 10 9 8 7 6 5 4 3 2 1

I dedicate this series to the One who walks beside me
through life's valleys and leads me to the high places;
to the One who never fails to show me
the breadth and depth of His tender mercies;
to the One who fills my heart with an abundance of grace
and wraps me, flaws and all, in a love so strong
that nothing I do can ever change how He feels about me.

I also dedicate this series to those loved ones
who have given me the gift of better understanding
this story and its characters
because you are living examples of God's amazing
forgiveness, grace, and compassion.
I celebrate you and thank God that you are in my life!

O, how this spring of love resembleth
The uncertain glory of an April day;
Which now shows all the beauty of the sun,
And by and by a cloud takes all away.

—Shakespeare, *The Two Gentlemen of Verona*

THE BETRAYAL

PROLOGUE

Nauvoo, Illinois
June 1842

Bronwyn twirled in front of the mirror in the brides' room, checking the back of the elegant gown loaned to her by Brigham's wife Mary Ann. Pale blue with ivory lace, it set off her sapphire eyes, her luxurious ebony hair, and skin the color of the finest porcelain—though she would never admit to thinking of her physical appearance in such romantic terms.

She almost laughed as she twirled again, enjoying her image in the mirror, skirts and petticoats billowing. She leaned closer to the mirror, pleased to see the sparkle of merriment in her eyes, the glow of anticipation in her expression. After all, it was the day she would be sealed to Gabe for eternity. Why not think of herself with a romantic notion or two?

A twinge of guilt pressed against her heart, but she turned her thoughts to Gabe and the look she hoped to see in his eyes as they knelt, facing each other, and said their vows . . . which made the feelings of guilt return.

Mary Rose. Her dearest friend in the world. How could it be possible that she was about to become Gabe's second wife when she loved his first wife like a sister?

She pinched her cheeks until they were the hue of wild roses, thinking about the plan she and Mary Rose had devised to please the Church leaders, keep Gabe in good standing, and allow her to remain part of the family—just as she and Griffin and Little Grace always had been.

It would work, she told herself, drawing in a deep breath. It had to. For Mary Rose's sake, especially. It worried her that Mary Rose hadn't seemed well earlier that morning, and she planned to pull her aside and reassure her that never would she try to supplant her in Gabe's affections.

She only hoped that Mary Rose would arrive with Gabriel well before the ceremony started so they could spend those few moments alone.

She backed away from the mirror as other brides arrived to ready themselves. As the door opened and closed, the jangle and rattle of horse-drawn carriages and the low bursts of chatter carried toward her. After a moment, it became apparent that the excited voices that had drifted in from outside came from the grooms, not the brides. Most of the women appeared subdued, some of the younger ones even frightened.

As the time neared for all to have arrived, Bronwyn went to the door of the meetinghouse and peered out at the street. Carriages and horses lined up, empty of their passengers, but there was no sign of Gabe and Mary Rose.

One of the brides, a sad-looking young woman with red-rimmed eyes and trembling hands, spotted Bronwyn and slipped away from a group of three brides.

"I heard you're marrying Brother MacKay," she said.

Bronwyn couldn't help the little smile of pride that tugged the corner of her lips upward. She nodded as the woman continued. "I've noticed him before. He's a fine-looking man."

"'Tis true." Still standing at the door, Bronwyn let her gaze drift away from the woman's probing scrutiny back to the street, thinking about Gabe, how she'd admired him from the first moment she saw him, long before he and Mary Rose fell in love.

That first moment . . . the day they boarded the *Sea Hawk* in Liverpool and Coal climbed the topmast. He'd perched there, frightening the wits out of every passenger and seaman on deck. Gabe had climbed up after him as if he'd been born with all the strength and humor needed to rescue errant boys.

She could never have imagined how their lives would intertwine. Griffin, the man she would love forever, had been at her side, and they were expecting their first child. She didn't imagine then the loss that would soon break her heart. Neither could she have foreseen that one day—this day—she would become Gabriel MacKay's bride, his second. And that his first wife, Mary Rose, would have become the dearest friend she'd ever known.

Oh, Mary Rose, hurry! . . . She couldn't walk down the aisle without her. She hadn't asked, but she wanted Mary Rose to walk with her to Gabriel, their hands clasped in a silent agreement of sisterhood and faithfulness to their plan.

"Where is he?" The woman interrupted Bronwyn's thoughts. "Your Gabriel, I mean," she added, noticing Bronwyn's confused expression. "Shouldn't he be here by now?"

She snapped back to the present. Her Gabriel? "He . . . he should have been here . . . He felt things were getting awkward with Mary Ro— with his first wife and that it might be easier if . . ." Taking a deep breath, she began again. "Brigham came for Little Grace and me, and his wife Mary Ann helped me dress for the wedding at their home. She's keeping Little Grace for me while I—" She stopped to listen as she heard another carriage round the corner.

She flew to the door and stepped outside, just in time to see it rattle by without stopping.

Brigham came up behind her, his forehead furrowed. He had no need to ask the obvious question. Bronwyn shook her head. "I don't know what's keeping Brother Gabriel."

Brigham pulled out a pocket watch. "It's not like him to be late." He gave Bronwyn a piercing look. "I suggest you return to the brides' room and await your groom. We'll start as soon as Brother Gabriel and Sister Mary Rose arrive."

"I'll need a few minutes to talk to Sister Mary Rose before we begin."

"Not unless they arrive soon." He smiled. "There will be plenty of time afterward for sister-wife talk, believe me, Sister Bronwyn."

He took her elbow to guide her back to the meetinghouse, reached for the door and opened it so she could enter.

Bronwyn stopped just short of entering.

Mary Rose.

It took only a half heartbeat for Bronwyn's mind to whirl with the possibilities. The pregnancy. The swollen, distraught look of Mary Rose that morning. The sounds of weeping in the night.

What if . . . ? She didn't complete the thought, remembering the weariness like unto death itself the morning before Little Grace was born.

Bronwyn took a step backward, almost knocking Brigham off balance; she turned, gathered her full skirts, and hurried toward the street. "I'm going to find them," she called over her shoulder. "You can start without us."

She didn't bother to stop to ask for approval—or even to see what was surely a look of stunned disapproval on Brigham's face. Instead, she turned her attention to the unattended carriages and wagons lined up in front of the meetinghouse.

She made a beeline toward a lone horse tethered to a hitching post just beyond the last carriage—a gleaming black beast with an arched neck, sleek head, and intelligent eyes. As she placed a foot in the stirrup and swung her leg over the hand-tooled leather and silver saddle, her dress bunching up to her knees, she swallowed a smile. She would have laughed if she hadn't been so worried about Mary Rose. In the old days, she and Mary Rose would have giggled together over such a sight.

She heard a familiar voice shouting from the front of the meetinghouse. Without a glance toward the man, she leaned close to the horse's neck. "Go, boy," she cried, pressing her heels into his flanks. She hoped the beast would respond to the voice of someone other than his master's—especially since it was his master doing the shouting, commanding him to halt.

But the horse—the pride of Brigham's stables—appeared to be quite content with Bronwyn on his back. He took off like a fox after prey, and as soon as they were on the open road, she let him take the lead. He seemed to sense the urgency and galloped with hurricane force toward the MacKay farm.

As they raced along, Bronwyn leaning low over the horse's neck, she watched the road ahead, hoping to see the telltale dust of a carriage coming toward her. She had no desire to return to the meetinghouse to go through with the marriage, but she wanted to know her friend was well. Right now, that was all that mattered.

They rose to the top of a small knoll, and in the distance lay the farm. She slowed the horse and took in the scene, searching for anything that seemed amiss. The landscape was bathed in sunlight, just as it had been earlier that morning. Even with the warmth of the sun on her shoulders, a shiver traveled up her spine.

Something was wrong. The house was too quiet. Where were the children? And Cordelia, who'd offered to watch them during the marriage festivities?

Her mouth went dry, and her heart thudded with fear for her friend as she urged the horse to a gallop once more.

Gabe must have heard the thundering hoofbeats. He ran from the house, and even before she reached him, she could see his pale, disheveled appearance. And the blood on his shirt.

Bile rose in her throat as she drew back hard on the reins. The beast halted and reared. She patted his neck to calm him and then dismounted. Gabe ran to her and grasped her hands. His expression told her more than words ever could.

"Mary Rose?" she whispered.

His voice choked. "How—" His gaze shot to the horse, then back to her. "How did you know to come? She needs you . . . We need you."

"Is she upstairs?" She didn't want to cry, so she kept her focus on his eyes instead of his blood-stained shirt. "How bad is it?"

"Go to her. Quickly." He squeezed her hands before letting go. When she glanced at the panting horse, he added, "I'll take care of him. Just go to her, please."

Lifting her skirts, Bronwyn raced up the front steps.

Mary Rose's face was the same shade of white as the pillowslip beneath her head. Her closed eyelids didn't flicker, and her soft breathing was almost inaudible.

Bronwyn bent over the bed and gently took Mary Rose's face between both hands. "Dearest one," she whispered, "can you hear me?" No response. She embraced her friend, kissed her cheek, and whispered again. "Mary Rose, it's Bronwyn. I'm here."

"She fell," Gabe said from the doorway. "She's been unconscious since. I don't think she even knows about the . . ." His voice choked, and he walked across the room. "I did the best I could . . . but the infant was so small, so delicate. He couldn't even take his first breath. I tried . . . I even tried to clear his throat with my fingers. Breathe air into him." He had reached the bed and came around to kneel beside it opposite Bronwyn. He reached for Mary

Rose's hand, kissed it, and, still holding it, dropped his head.

His voice was ragged as he whispered, "Forgive me, my love. I brought this on you . . . on us. Our baby . . . Too much to forgive . . . Oh, Mary Rose . . ."

Behind him, in the cradle he'd spent weeks working on in the barn, lay the baby's body, wrapped in a soft patchwork quilt that Bronwyn had sewn to celebrate the child's birth.

Bronwyn left Mary Rose's side and moved toward the cradle. She sat down beside it, her soiled and wrinkled skirt billowing around her. She gathered the baby into her arms, bringing its still warm body close to her heart. For a moment, she just knelt there, at first rocking and humming a lullaby from her childhood, and then covering the baby's face with kisses, just as she knew Mary Rose would do.

The sting of tears rose in the back of her throat. Mary Rose had been there for her to help save the life of Little Grace, but while Mary Rose lay suffering, while her baby tried to make its way into the world, Bronwyn was primping in front of the mirror in the brides' room. She dropped her head and wept silently.

She opened the blanket, and holding the wee child in her lap, she touched each finger and toe, and gently smoothed the baby's head, and examined his tiny seashell ears.

"I'll need a pan of warm water," she said to Gabe after a few minutes. "And some clean rags. It's time to prepare him."

Still on his knees, Gabe turned to her, his expression raw with grief. "I was so busy, first trying to save him, then so afraid I would lose Mary Rose," he said, "that I didn't get a good look at him."

She swallowed hard. "Would you like . . . to hold him?" She found the answer in his eyes and laid the child in his arms.

Gabe drew in a shuddering breath and drew the child close. He bowed his head, touching his forehead to his son's. His sobs seemed to come from someplace deep within his being, a sound almost unbearable to hear.

Bronwyn moved closer and wrapped her arms around him, her embrace encompassing both father and son. She laid her head against Gabe's heaving chest and found unexpected comfort as he leaned into her arms.

September 1842

Bronwyn walked along the creek, her hands clasped behind her, trying to find peace somewhere within the muddle of thoughts and feelings. Outwardly, no one could have known the war that waged within her heart; she made sure of that. She went through her days with her usual smiles and laughter, lightening the load where she could for Mary Rose and Cordelia, taking on more than her portion of housework without complaint, teaching the children their lessons, reading to them, singing to them . . . but always aware of Gabe's presence when he was near.

Tonight, the household had fallen quiet, the children were in bed, and upstairs Mary Rose sat at her desk, probably writing in her journal. The last crickets of summer sang, and here at the creek, frogs croaked in unison with the babbling of flowing water.

The stars were just beginning to throw their spangled glory across the sky when Bronwyn heard the back door open and then close. The crunch of footsteps came toward her, and even before he spoke she knew it was Gabe.

"There you are," he said, making his way through the foliage. Though she'd taken to coming to the creek each night to sort out her feelings in peace, this was the first time he had followed her.

She turned as he came toward her.

"I'd hoped to find you here," he said. A slow smile took over his face.

"Did you talk with Mary Rose?" Bronwyn met Gabe's liquid

gaze, trying to keep that tender place in her heart from melting. "Did she give her permission?" She disliked the way her hands shook and her heart pounded as she awaited his answer.

He took a few steps closer, tucked his crooked index finger beneath her chin, and tilted her face toward his. What the starlight didn't accomplish, his touch did. She blinked and tried to step back, but her feet remained rooted to the ground. There was a time when she might have run in the opposite direction, but tonight his eyes, his touch, kept her from moving. She was sorry when he withdrew his touch from her face.

"Mary Rose is fragile, her feelings barely under control. I wanted to speak with her this afternoon, as the prophet suggested," he said, "but when I saw again the toll that grief has taken on her, I couldn't find the words. I intend to speak to her tomorrow. Hard as it may be, she needs to be reminded of the prophet's teachings, the good in it for us all. Individually, we are weak. Together, we are made strong. He sees the need for our family to be united in every way. Not just now, but through eternity. It will bring us all great joy to increase our family." He smiled.

"United, aye," she breathed, not taking her eyes from his. "What happens if we are not?"

"I don't think we need to worry about that. Mary Rose will understand and accept what needs to be done. In fact, I think she has already."

"She hasn't spoken to me about it."

"She wouldn't. She may have a difficult time at first. Many of the men have told me their experiences. At first, it is a shock, especially to a first wife, but eventually they get over it, and actually begin to enjoy the thought of having a sister wife to share the family's work, their joys, and even their sorrows. Even a baby's birth is cause for the sister wives to rejoice, each as glad as if the babe were her own. Because you and I are married in the sight of God and the Church, we're meant to share everything as husband and wife." He smiled and touched her face again. "Everything. We are meant to bring God's spirit children to earth through our bodies."

She felt her cheeks warm and scarce could breathe for the thought of his meaning. Was the prophet right in this? Could she trust her emotions when she gazed into her husband's eyes? Was it love she felt? She'd never once felt this way when she looked into Griffin's eyes, or melted in quite the same way when he touched her.

Gabe, her husband!

How her heart wanted to sing the words. How could loving each other physically as husband and wife be wrong?

If she truly believed the prophet's teachings, she could gladly welcome Gabe into the marital bed, knowing it was right and holy in the eyes of God.

But if she remained true to her promise to Mary Rose, she could not. And that meant she would denounce, at least in her soul, all she had come to believe about the prophet and the truths he taught. She too could be accused of apostasy.

"And she must understand about the baby," Gabe said. "She must do everything possible to make sure we spend eternity together, that our families are not torn asunder by apostasy."

"If she doesn't allow this . . . our . . ." Her thoughts flew around her mind like a wild bird in a cage. "Are you saying that if she doesn't say yes, you will not call her into heaven?"

He shook his head. "I love Mary Rose. That hasn't changed. I will not hurt her by suggesting such a thing."

"But you believe the prophet's words are true."

"It is his teaching . . . teaching that he receives directly from the Heavenly Father." He paused and when he continued, his voice was hoarse with emotion. "I don't like it, but I believe it to be the truth." He furrowed his brow and looked away from her, toward the house to the second floor where through the foliage a light flickered in Mary Rose's bedroom. From behind them came the soft, plaintive call of an owl, only to be answered a moment later by another near the barn.

A breeze teased a lock of Bronwyn's hair from its plait, and she reached up to tuck it behind her ear.

"Mary Rose," he said. "She's hurting, yet. I grieve for our baby as much as she does. I want us to be together through all eternity." He turned back to her, and she saw the sheen of tears on his cheeks. "Our baby . . . my part in his death. All of it, the memory of holding his lifeless body. The feelings ripped into me like some sort of ragged sword. They left a raw wound that will not heal."

She reached out to him then, first drying his cheeks with her fingers, then she gathered him close and held him, much as she did the day his baby died. He wrapped his arms around her waist, holding tight as if her solid warmth might cause life to flow again through his veins.

After a moment he pulled back. "Sometimes when I think about where we are, what has happened to us . . . to Mary Rose, our baby . . . my part in it, I can't . . ." His voice was thick with tears.

She touched his lips with her fingers. "There's no need to explain. I understand."

He cupped her face with his hands, and for a moment, just stood there, searching her eyes.

The tender place inside her melted again, and when he lowered his head toward hers, for a half beat of her heart she thought about pushing him away. But instead, she tilted her face upward and caught her breath as his lips touched hers, softly at first, and then with a hunger that frightened her even as it turned her blood to warm honey. As she experienced the fullness of his kiss, all thoughts of the promise she'd made to Mary Rose faded as surely as the dusk faded into the night darkness.

She reached for him, and when he pulled her close she wrapped her arms around his neck and melted against him.

He pulled back only long enough to kiss her again. And then once more.

She rested her cheek against the rough cloth of his shirt as he stroked her hair. She felt his breath on her ear when he spoke. "I'll talk to her tomorrow," he said. "We must do as the prophet says."

"Aye," Bronwyn breathed, "let it be."

The following night, Bronwyn lay awake, staring at the ceiling. Beside her, Gabe snored softly. Tears trickled from the corners of her eyes, rivulets of regret, of known betrayal, of disappointment in her weakness.

He'd whispered no words of love, no endearments. Rather, he spoke of her great beauty as he caressed her, as he outlined her face, letting his fingers trail down her forehead and nose, across her parted lips, her chin, her neck.

His eyes seemed to glow in the dim light, but not once did he tell her he loved her. But surely he did! Otherwise, the thought of what they'd just done was too terrible to consider.

She blinked back her tears, attempting to rid her mind of sorrow as heavy as a thousand large stones. Not because of the words he didn't say but because of Mary Rose, her friend.

How could forgiveness be possible?

She drew in a trembling breath. Unable to endure the agonizing guilt, she thought back to what Gabe had said the night before.

And she forced herself to remember that Gabe was her husband. She had obeyed him, just as the prophet said a good wife must. She had obeyed the prophet's words, spoken to him from God himself about the sanctity of marriage. The holiness of their state. The prophet himself had chosen her for Gabe above all others.

Chosen. Shouldn't that mean something? Shouldn't it take away the feeling that she'd committed a troubling, soul-deep wrong?

She let out a ragged sigh. If this marriage was God's plan for her salvation, why did it hurt so much?

She turned her head and considered the man sleeping next to her. She couldn't deceive herself; she'd wanted him as passionately as he seemed to want her.

Did he really feel the same way?

Or had edicts of the Church just been convenient or, worse, welcomed.

Gabe stirred in his sleep and reached for her hand. She withdrew it, afraid he would turn toward her and pull her into his arms once more. And crushing guilt would again enter her heart.

The bedclothes rustled and the corn-husk mattress shifted under his weight as he rolled over. She waited, almost afraid to breathe.

One touch, and she knew she would again melt into his embrace.

He did as she knew he would. Her heart raced, and she squeezed her eyes shut, trying to block out what had just happened between them. Maybe if he would just say the words of love she longed to hear . . . maybe then her heart would leap with joy and sorrow—and guilt would flee.

But the words he whispered spoke again of passion, not love, of her beauty, the soft feel of her skin, the shape of her lips.

"I can't . . ." Tears closed her throat, and she couldn't finish.

Gabe breathed heavily as she pushed away from him and moved to her side of the bed.

"Just one more kiss," Gabe said, his voice gruff. He caught her hand and moved closer.

"I can't . . ." Her words were lost as he covered her mouth with his. Before sinking into the velvet darkness of his kiss, her last thoughts were of love.

Surely, he loved her. If not, he wouldn't desire her so . . . would he?

As the sun streamed through the window and fell across Bronwyn's face, she bolted upright in bed. Then thoughts of the previous night filled her, and for a moment she relived each detail. Smiling, she stretched lazily, unwilling to let go of the memory. Though Gabe withheld the words she longed to hear, the second time they made love, his passion spoke louder than words ever could. She was certain he loved her.

Outside the open window, sparrows sang, and downstairs the children giggled and laughed and carried on as usual. She hummed a little tune as she washed and then dressed.

A few minutes later, she stood at the top of the staircase, hoping to catch Gabe's eye. But without a glance in her direction, he busily played with the children and helped Mary Rose and Cordelia set the table. He ruffled the twins' hair, grinned at Coal, bounced Little Grace into the crook of one arm, and, still holding her, moved toward Mary Rose. He circled his opposite arm around her, drawing her close, and then nuzzled her temple as if to show her all was well between them.

He looked into his first wife's eyes, and said, "I love you."

Bronwyn's daughter circled one chubby arm around Mary Rose's neck, the other around Gabe's. "I love you too," she crooned.

Bronwyn thought her heart would break.

February 1846
Crossing the Frozen Mississippi

Wrapped in heavy buffalo blankets, Bronwyn, Mary Rose, and Cordelia sat on the wagon bench of the big Conestoga. All the children were in back, tucked beneath their own buffalo blankets. A canopy of stars glittered in the clear midnight sky; temperatures had been dropping since sundown, and had been for days. The Mississippi River was frozen solid—at least that's what the lead scouts claimed.

Bronwyn shivered as she watched Mary Rose sit forward in readiness, reins in hand. At the signal, they would cross behind the lead wagon. Gabe, as captain of the first brigade of wagons, rode alongside the train from the rear, coming steadily closer to the MacKay wagon.

Bronwyn didn't have to turn to look to know his eyes were on her as he drew closer. The sound of a second horse, riding hard to catch up with him, carried above the sounds of creaking wagon wheels and the shouts of the wagoneers.

Though Mary Rose kept her unblinking gaze on the frozen river, Bronwyn turned. Enid now rode beside Gabe, her chin lifted high, her shoulders back, her red hair gleaming even in the dim light. As always, her demeanor was regal.

"We're getting married!" Enid's smile was joyful and triumphant. "Gabe and I are getting married as soon as we reach Winter Quarters. Mary Rose has finally agreed that it will be the best for us all."

Bronwyn's stomach clenched tight, and for a moment she couldn't breathe. She stared at Mary Rose, seated next to her and Cordelia on the wagon bench . "You didn't . . . you couldn't have."

Enid's laughter rang out, and the thud of her high-stepping horse's hooves drummed as if in rhythm with the sound. "She did, bless her, she did." She looked as if nothing could quench her joy.

"Dearest," she said as Gabe rode toward her. "I've just let everyone know our good news."

Gabe's eyes went to Bronwyn's first, and then to Mary Rose, who kept her gaze on the backs of the oxen. She popped the whip harder than she had before, frightening the beasts even though the leather tip didn't touch them.

The children had fallen silent as mice in the back of the wagon.

He rode closer, his gaze now on Bronwyn's again, searching her face as if looking to her for permission to love another. The look was so fleeting, she thought she had imagined it, but before he could speak, Enid rode up beside him.

"We'll discuss this later," she said to the three women, "and what it will mean to the running of our household." She flashed them another smile before riding off with Gabe.

"The running of our household?" Cordelia laughed heartily. "Methinks if she tries, she'll have quite a time of it, considering the likes of us." The older woman had come to live with them right after Mary Rose's grandfather's death. Though not married to Gabriel, she had become the matriarch of their family, full of love and laughter and spunk.

Bronwyn paid little attention to Cordelia's words or even to the rollicking laughter from the back of the wagon as Little Grace perfectly mimicked Enid's parting words.

She was too busy thinking about Gabe, too filled with wonder at his expression when his eyes met hers, too surprised at the strange stirring of her heart. The look was different than any he'd given her before. His passion for her was unmistakable. But could it be that he at last loved her? *Really* loved her?

Why now? She fell back against the wagon bench, trying to take in the jumbled emotions. Why just as he was going to take another wife?

She'd accepted that he loved Mary Rose and didn't love her—at least not with the same kind of love. She craned to look back at Enid and Gabe riding toward the back of the wagon train, silhouetted against the orange sky of the burning city of Nauvoo.

Mary Rose looked over at her. "Are you all right?"

"I think so," she said.

"I'm sorry I couldn't tell you," she said.

"Why now? You said you would never give permission for him to marry her."

Mary Rose swallowed hard, and her expression softened. "It had to be now." She handed the reins to Cordelia and turned sideways on the seat. "I couldn't wait."

"You still haven't answered my question."

The wagon wheels creaked in the snow, the oxen snorted, and behind them, the voices of the other travelers could be heard. Finally Mary Rose spoke. "It's because of you."

"Me?"

"Because you are falling in love with Gabe. And he with you." Mary Rose gave her a small smile. "I've seen it in his face long before tonight."

They fell silent again, and then Mary Rose circled her arm around Bronwyn's shoulders. "I gave my permission for him to marry Enid to save you from the heartache of loving Gabriel MacKay."

PART I

We are not born all at once, but bit by bits,
the body first and the spirit later. . .
Our mothers are racked with the pains of our physical
   birth;
we ourselves suffer the longer pains of our spiritual
   growth.

— Mary Anton

ONE

Wedding bells tolled, mixing with the sound of distant thunder.

From her hiding place in a stand of willows, Bronwyn gazed at the road leading to the temporary meetinghouse. For as far as she could see, farm wagons snaked alongside the river, kicking up dust as they rattled and swayed in the ruts, wheels creaking and horse hooves thudding. Filled with more brides than grooms, dressed in their celestial wedding garb, the mood was lively. No one seemed to notice the darkening skies and distant rumbles of thunder off to the east.

A low whistle caught her attention, and she glanced over to a sandstone outcropping near the river. Twelve-year-old Coal grinned at her and then gestured to the line of wagons before ducking again behind the sandstone embankment.

It should have been a sunny and happy late summer morning, the children chasing each other around the MacKay campground, the twins picking wild daisies to weave crowns, Coal reading a book, the little ones chattering and laughing as they chased butterflies.

But instead, Coal was here with her, about to help her carry out a daring plan—a plan, that if it failed, would mean a heartbreaking change for their family. It was difficult enough for the adults to accept Enid, but for the children to accept a new mother, and possibly lose to cholera the one they loved deeply, Mary Rose . . . She didn't want to complete the thought. Instead, she focused on the lead carriage that headed toward the meetinghouse and the woman who sat tall on the driver's bench. Enid literally glowed, an aura visible even at this distance. Her red hair caught what was left of the sunlight that streamed between the thunderheads, and with shoulders back, and smile set, she drove the prancing team with grace and power.

Beside her sat one of Brigham's many wives, her face as expressionless as Enid's was animated. Fanny Stenhouse was a favorite and often chosen by the prophet to help ready the brides on their big day.

A gust of wind whipped Bronwyn's hair, and she pulled it back from her face as Coal stood again and nodded toward the train of farm wagons, which were nearer now, close enough for her to see the wagon just three behind the lead: the James wagon, filled with a passel of young ones, or "a quiver full" as Brigham so often referred to the blessing of many children.

If all went according to plan, the storm would be the least of the troubles for the brides and grooms, especially for fourteen-year-old Sarah James who was about to marry an apostle, four times her age.

Bronwyn squeezed her eyes shut, trying not to think about what the child would face should her plan fail.

Opening her eyes again, Bronwyn saw Enid's carriage slow as it reached the meetinghouse, passing in front of Bronwyn and no more than ten yards away. Even her profile spoke of an inner strength that made Bronwyn's heart twist with envy. She watched as Brigham himself came out to meet the carriage and helped first Enid, and then Fanny, from the bench.

Head tilted upward, Enid strode into the meetinghouse, Brigham and Fanny following.

Bronwyn heard the crunch of boots on rocky soil and looked up to see Coal creeping through the willows. Just as fat drops of rain began to fall, he ducked under a large leafy branch.

"How long do we wait?" he whispered loudly.

She put a finger over her lips. "Just until everyone is inside."

"The wagon's ready over yonder." Still grinning, he swept his hair back with his hand. "You think it will work?"

She smiled back at him. "How can it fail with a team like us?" A jagged streak of lightning shot through the sky. A loud clap of thunder hit immediately, almost shaking the ground. Horses shied and bucked and empty wagons tilted precariously.

A few more jagged strikes. Another rumble boomed. Bronwyn caught her breath, and then laughed.

Grinning, Coal turned to Bronwyn. "You scared?"

Bronwyn winked. "Not a bit. You?"

"Not a bit," he said, his voice shaking. He swallowed hard. "Is it time?"

She gave him a confident smile, though she wasn't feeling so confident on the inside. Determined to disrupt the wedding, she again tried to push aside her doubts. Before she fell ill, Mary Rose had accepted the idea of Gabriel taking a third wife. She'd given her permission back in Nauvoo, telling Bronwyn it was for her own good: she would know only heartache and sorrow if she fell in love with Gabe.

No matter Mary Rose's desires, Bronwyn planned it anyway.

Perhaps she could fool herself into believing her plan was only altruistic, but in her heart of hearts she knew it wasn't true. As desperate as she was to save little Sarah, she was equally desperate to stop Gabe's marriage to Enid.

"It's time," she said to Coal.

In a small side room just off the meetinghouse vestibule, Enid dismissed Brigham's wife Fanny. As soon as she was alone with her thoughts, she ran her fingers through her hair, shook it out, and then tossed her head back, letting her long red hair flow wild and free. She touched the necklace above the lace at her bodice, a pearl choker with a cameo pendant at its center, its image of the goddess Diana mounted on gold filigree, a tiny diamond on either side. She smiled. Gabriel had chosen it, he'd said, because the likeness was so close to hers; even the carnelian shell gemstone matched the lighter hues in her sun-streaked hair. She wondered if he'd stopped to consider that the goddess Diana would be considered pagan. If not, she didn't plan to tell him.

A fitting wedding gift for a cherished bride. He'd not given his other wives such a fine gift. When he'd presented it to her that morning, his eyes held the promise that her long sought-after standing would be honored. She'd never liked having anyone give her orders, and she wasn't about to start liking it now. The first wife ruled the roost, so she'd observed.

Though he'd taken two brides before her, they would be required to move aside after the ceremony as she stepped into position of first wife in the MacKay household and in the community of Saints. She'd also made certain Gabe understood that when the family moved to their new Zion, she expected him to build her a home in town.

Gabe was set on another ranch and had even allowed Mary Rose to choose the name—the Blue Sage. Enid had determined the first time she heard the name, she would live there no longer than necessary. "All things in good time," he'd told her.

She briefly considered Mary Rose's illness and how she would take the news, once she'd recovered, that the planned wedding had at last taken place. She quickly dismissed the thought. She wanted to keep her sympathies for Mary Rose and her illness at a distance. Besides, dealing with Bronwyn's obvious affections for Gabe—and the doe eyes she constantly made at him—brought her enough trouble.

This was her wedding day, and she would allow no dark thoughts to enter her heart. She'd claimed Gabriel MacKay with jealous ownership since they were children together in Nova Scotia. Perhaps not with true love, a romantic love, but a deep affection almost as if they were family.

She had her doubts about the teachings of the prophet and his successor, Brigham Young. But for now the teachings of polygamy worked in her favor. She had one goal in mind: to make Gabriel MacKay hers.

She sensed his hunger for power and suspected Mary Rose and Bronwyn had yet to become aware of that part of him. She smiled and fluffed her hair again. She would help him climb to the highest rank on earth and that in heaven—if it existed—as well.

She touched her cameo and lifted her chin. Oh, yes, she would make him proud. Taking a deep breath, she opened the door and stepped into the vestibule.

More than a dozen brides waited in line along one side of the unadorned pale green wall. Some wore white, others wore calico; some wore broadcloth dresses adorned with flour-dusted aprons. Many of the brides were young, some too young, but Enid didn't want to think about what that meant. Some were old enough to be her grandmother. Their hushed voices hinted at feelings of fear, of boredom, of excitement and in some cases, of relief.

Enid had chosen a pale creamy green for her wedding dress, well aware that the color brought out the emerald flecks in her eyes. She took her place at the front of the line and then turned to seek out the one who she was certain already dominated the room: Gabriel MacKay.

He turned to her, his eyes warm as he assessed her head to toe. She gave him a slight nod, her lips curving into a wider smile.

It seemed they were the only two people in the room as he walked toward her and took her hand, kissed her fingertips, and leaned toward her ear. "Are you certain you want to do this?" Then he pulled back, and she imagined longing and hope in his eyes. "I've never been so certain of anything in my life," she said.

Gabe squeezed her hand gently once more. "It won't be easy, coming into a household that isn't yet ready to accept you. It will take love and patience."

Enid drew in a deep breath. "I never thought it would be. Easy, I mean." She again touched the cameo pendant at her throat. "It never has been for us."

A shadow seemed to cross his face before he smiled and lifted her chin with his fingertips. "We do have a history," he said, looking deep into her eyes. Again, as if searching.

"That we do."

"And a lot of time to make up for." This time she thought she detected a hint of sadness.

"Indeed, we do."

Out of nowhere, Hosea's image pushed its way into her heart: his rugged face, his sea- and sun-bronzed hair, wild in the wind and spray of the ocean, the look of him standing in his sea captain's uniform atop the quarter deck. She blinked back tears and swallowed hard. It seemed Hosea was telling her something, or she was remembering something he'd said long ago. Just as quickly the image washed away. She shivered, and for a moment she couldn't breathe. "Are you all right?" Gabe whispered. "You've gone pale."

She drew in a deep breath. Pushing aside Hosea's memory, she met Gabe's worried gaze and smiled. She was doing the right thing. Of course she was. Gabe was hers and had been since they were children. She lifted her chin. "Yes, Gabe, I'm quite fine. Truly."

Brigham stepped to the double doors that led to the main room of the meetinghouse.

Gabe cocked an eyebrow. "Are you ready?"

She nodded. "I am," she said, and with an affectionate look, he stepped back in line with the grooms—at the head of the queue, just as it should be.

Bronwyn and Coal sloshed through the pouring rain and took cover just outside the entrance to the vestibule. Coal's jitters had lessened visibly and now his grin spread ear to ear. She resisted the urge to ruffle his hair. For one thing, he'd almost grown too tall; for the other, he'd made it clear that he was getting too old for such gestures of endearment.

Lightning lit up the sky, and a loud clap of thunder rumbled from a ways upriver.

"The sound will cover our entrance," he said. "Make our plan easier to carry out."

"You're much too wise for your age, young man," she said. This time she couldn't resist and reached to ruffle his damp hair just as she had aboard the *Sea Hawk* when she'd been hired as his nanny. He ducked away, and ran his fingers through the mop to straighten it. The gesture, so like Gabe's, made her want to cry.

"Okay, then. Ready?"

He nodded. "I would do anything in the world for Sarah James."

"Yes, Sarah James," she said. "Especially for her."

"Aye," he said, his voice softening into the dialect they once spoke. "Aye, 'tis for her, especially."

Bronwyn heard the strains of a hymn floating through gaps in the rough-hewn board of the meetinghouse. "They've begun."

"We'll take 'em by surprise, that's for sure," Coal said. They smiled at each other.

"Aye, that we will. I daresay there will be no wedding for the Saints this day." Bronwyn lifted her weapon. Gabe's image danced before her, and the memory of their first night together filled her heart, quickly followed by an image of another night of lovemaking . . . only this time Enid was the wife sharing Gabe's bed.

Bronwyn shook the thoughts away, gave Coal a brisk nod, and led the way to the door.

TWO

Gabriel held Enid's hand as they stood with the other brides and grooms, lined up in front of Brother Brigham. The prophet's voice reverberated throughout the room, even above the racket of the hard rain on the roof, as he spoke eloquently of the virtues of celestial marriage, the joys of being united in eternity forever, families together without separation for all time.

"This commitment is from this day forward, not just for your days on earth but throughout eternity," he said. "This holy union cannot be put asunder by anyone here on earth or by all the powers in heaven." He paused and chuckled. "At this point in a Gentile ceremony, a minister would ask if anyone has reason that these brides and grooms should not marry." He laughed heartily, and the congregation tittered.

Just then, the vestibule doors flew open at the back of the room. Gabe spun and gaped.

Bronwyn stood in the open doorway, looking wild and beautiful, Coal at her side. Her usually well-coifed dark hair had sprung loose from its braid. She wore men's boots—his, he would swear—and a man's leather duster that draped to her ankles. Also his.

Everyone in the congregation turned to stare. Bronwyn lifted her rifle. Gabe couldn't be sure, but she seemed to be aiming right at his heart.

"I'm here for Sarah James," Bronwyn said. "She needs to come with me. Now."

From the corner of his eye, Gabe saw Brigham nod to the girl's soon-to-be husband, apostle Hyrum Riordan. Sounds of shifting along the creaking floorboards told him the brides and grooms might be trying to hide the girl.

"Now!" Bronwyn's expression said she meant business. Gabe knew, and the rest of the Saints did too, that she was an excellent shot. As good or better than most men. Her father had been a gamekeeper on a large Welsh estate, and, as his only child, she'd learned everything he might have taught a son.

No one made a move toward her, but at his side, Enid muttered. "If I had a weapon . . ."

Bronwyn waved the barrel toward Enid. "I'm sorry, you were saying . . . ?" She smiled.

Enid had the wisdom to keep silent.

"I've come for Sarah James," she said again.

The skinny young girl finally moved out from behind the blockade of brides and grooms. A wide smile overtook her freckled face. "Sister MacKay," she said, happily. "And Coal MacKay."

"It is indeed," Bronwyn said. "We've come for you if you'd like to go with us."

Coal nodded vigorously, grinning ear to ear. It came to Gabe in a flash as bright as the lightning outside: the boy was infatuated with Sarah James. That's why he'd allowed Bronwyn to influence him to take part in this ridiculous travesty.

Brigham stood behind him, expecting Gabe to do something.

Just what, was the question. He had about as much a chance of controlling Bronwyn, or Mary Rose, for that matter, as jumping over the moon.

He drew in a deep breath, gathering his thoughts, and then stepped forward. "Bronwyn, I order you to put down the rifle this minute. You are interrupting a sacred ceremony. You're in grave danger of going too far—"

"She already has," Brigham growled behind him.

A loud thunderclap caused Gabe to start, as did most of the congregation. Except Bronwyn, who stood as still and composed as a wild Briton woman warrior from centuries earlier. Her smile never wavered. He had a hard time equating the winsome Bronwyn, nanny and maid aboard the clipper, with this striking image before him. He wanted to rush to her, gather her into his arms, lead her away from danger, but the prophet watched his every move. He willed his feet to stay put.

"I want you to walk down the aisle toward me," Bronwyn said to Sarah James. "Unless, of course, you truly want to marry a man who's old enough to be your great-grandfather."

Sarah James ran down the aisle toward Bronwyn, neither looking to the right, where her mother sat, nor to the left, where her father, half-standing, glowered. Coal reached for her hand, and the two disappeared through the double doors and out into the rain.

Bronwyn kept the rifle trained on a place just above Brigham's forehead and imagined what it would be like to actually shoot a man. She knew she could never pull a trigger—this one or any other. The last time she'd aimed at a human being—if she could call even one of them that—had been that night in Nauvoo. The same night those thugs shot Griffin. She'd shot over their heads to frighten them. She wondered what she'd have done if she'd known the folly they planned once they finished taunting Mary Rose's grandfather and burning the family barn.

As soon as she heard Coal's signal, she backed slowly out of the meetinghouse, moving the rifle barrel from one shocked groom's face to the next. She couldn't help smiling at the brides' expressions. They appeared ready to leap to her defense should anyone try to stop her.

She winked at Gabe, gave him a quick curtsy, and then she stepped into the vestibule, letting the doors close behind her. Heart pounding, she pushed open the outer door and nearly catapulted into the farm wagon Coal had driven to the front of the building. Coal shouted to the team, popping the whip above their heads. They lurched forward in the mud. Gradually, the horses found their footing and the wagon wheels creaked to a faster pace. It seemed to take forever to reach the curve at the end of the street.

Bronwyn looked back just before they rounded the corner.

Gabe, Brigham, and some of the other men were slogging through the mud in utter confusion, staring at their horseless rigs. The women, most of them brides, were giggling off to one side. Bronwyn glanced at Coal, whose shoulders shook with laughter.

"You didn't . . ."

He grinned at her. "I know it wasn't in our plan, but it seemed like a good idea."

"Where did you hide them?"

"I didn't have time for that. Just unhitched a few, slapped their rears, and told them to trot on home."

"Which ones?"

"The important ones, of course. Brigham's, some of the other apostles."

"And your father's."

"I admit my folly. I have sinned greatly and pray I will be forgiven." His eyes sparkled. "Yes, Father's too."

Bronwyn didn't know whether to laugh or cry. "Something tells me there won't be a wedding today after all."

The two young people laughed, but Bronwyn didn't join them. Worry churned her stomach as she considered what lay ahead, the madness of their actions.

Billowing clouds were all that remained of the summer storm. Across the wet and glistening prairie grasses bars of sunlight shone through the shadows of the clouds. Shading her eyes, she stared up a thunderhead towering in the distance, backlit by the sun.

"For you, Mary Rose," she whispered. "I'm doing this is for you." Even as she breathed the words, she knew they were a lie. Of course, she'd done it for her and for Sarah James. But she'd also done it for herself. Coal popped the whip over the back of the team, and her heart trembled as she thought about the anger in Brother Brigham's eyes. No one she'd known had dared to go against him.

Until now.

What had she brought down upon their heads? Not just upon hers, Coal's, and Sarah's. But upon all she loved so dearly: Little Grace, her five-year-old daughter born that miraculous night aboard the *Sea Hawk*; Joey, her toddler son born of her one-time union with Gabe; Spence, Mary Rose's and Gabe's toddler son; Pearl and Ruby, the nine-year-old twins, Coal's sisters, and beloved as much as if they were born into the family.

What had her actions wrought for them all? She shuddered to imagine it.

As soon as they reached a prearranged hiding place in a canyon a few miles from Winter Quarters, Bronwyn saddled one of the horses. She warned Sarah and Coal to stay in the hideout and await her return. Her intention, and she hoped for good success, was to talk some sense into Sarah's mother and father, and hope of all hopes, get other mothers to join her in protest against older men taking young brides.

She looked back only once. Coal and Sarah sat on a large boulder, swinging their feet and talking. She could hear their laughter ring out across the prairie. Above her, wide patches of blue sky showed between a froth of clouds, turning the prairie into a mottled patchwork of sunlight and shadows.

It took her less than a half hour to reach the outskirts of Winter Quarters, which seemed unusually quiet. Curious, she slipped from the saddle and led the horse past the meetinghouse to the MacKay campground. The silence sent a chill up her spine. No sounds of children playing and singing, not even the murmur of Cordelia fussing over Mary Rose.

Her heart froze. *Mary Rose.*

What if her condition had worsened since morning?

When she entered the doorway of the MacKay women's tent cabin, even in the dim light, she could see Mary Rose lying on the cot, her eyes closed, with the ever-vigilant Cordelia at her side. The children sat, silent and wide-eyed, around her bed, as if waiting for Mother Mary Rose to sit up, arms open wide, and gather them into her arms.

Her eyes fluttered open as Bronwyn walked toward her. She gave her a feeble smile. "Tell me," she whispered. "Don't leave out anything." Even the effort of speaking those few words seemed too much for her. She lay back on her pillow, her complexion pale.

Bronwyn nodded to Ruby and Pearl, giving them a silent signal to take Joey and Spence from the room.

Mary Rose managed a small smile. "Every detail," she whispered again.

Ruby and Pearl each grabbed a toddler, and with Little Grace reluctantly trailing behind they skipped through the doorway.

Before Bronwyn could answer, a voice carried from the doorway.

"Every detail?" Enid laughed, a short bitter sound, as she entered the room. "The wedding didn't happen, if that's what you want to know." She still wore her wedding dress, and her red hair flew about her face as she strode toward Bronwyn. "If that's what this is all about, you can congratulate yourself. Your plans were a roaring success."

Mary Rose exchanged a glance with Bronwyn. She coughed and then closed her eyes as Cordelia swabbed her forehead with a damp cloth.

"Stopping the marriage of a child to an old man was our intent. And I'd hardly call it a success, at least not yet."

Enid said, "You haven't wanted me to marry Gabriel from the beginning. You've both resented me, knowing that I held his heart first, and will to the last." She stepped closer. "Don't you realize what you've done to Gabriel? Don't you realize you've shamed him in front of the entire community?" Her eyes flashed, even in the dim light. "Did you stop to consider what this would do to him—to have you come barging in carrying a rifle like some outlaw wildcat?"

Behind her, Mary Rose let out a weak gasp. "You took a rifle?"

Cordelia snorted. "Now, that must've made those Saints sit up and take notice."

Enid surprised Bronwyn, surprised them all, by laughing. "Actually, it did. You should have seen Brother Brigham's face. He turned several shades of red before turning purple."

Bronwyn looked at her in wonder. "You're not angry?"

"Of course I am. But ladies"—she frowned as she looked from one to the other—"you must understand that this won't stop me. I intend to marry Gabriel MacKay." She stared at Mary Rose, whose eyes remained closed. "You gave him permission to take a third wife, specifically to take me as that bride. I know you as a woman of honor. I know you wouldn't go back on your word."

She turned her fiery gaze on Bronwyn. "But you acted like a brazen hussy today. Unforgivable. Surely, you knew that neither I nor Gabe were aware someone as young as Sarah James would be among the brides.

"You're right about one thing. She shouldn't marry until she's older; and she should marry someone nearer her own age. I may agree with many of the prophet's edicts, but his decision to marry off a child bride to an old man isn't one of them."

The room fell silent, and then Bronwyn spoke. "Stopping your marriage to Gabe was incidental—"

"Ha!" Enid stepped closer. "I would say that was your primary reason for doing what you did. Stopping the child bride's marriage to the apostle was incidental."

"He belongs to Mary Rose, his first love. I was there. I saw how they fell in love."

Enid laughed again. "I see the way you moon over him, how you take delight in his presence—how you try your best to be alone with him. You flutter those long lashes, smile secretive smiles, blush when he's near. You don't think anyone else notices?"

Bronwyn willed the wood-plank floor to swallow her up. Her cheeks flamed, for there was an element of truth in the accusations. She hadn't acted on her heart's longings since leaving Nauvoo, but she didn't think anyone else had noticed. She couldn't bear to look into Mary Rose's eyes.

Enid laughed again, only this time the sound was laced with bitterness. She turned to Mary Rose. "You no longer want him anyway. I'm right about that as well, correct?"

When Mary Rose didn't answer, Enid turned again to Bronwyn. "And you dare to criticize me? You, Mary Rose's dearest friend, married her husband and betrayed the pact you'd made about allowing him to bed you."

Her crass words made Bronwyn blush again, and when she spoke she couldn't help the stammering quiver that crept into her voice. "I was wrong in what I did. I've asked Mary Rose to forgive me . . ." Even as she spoke she wondered how Enid could have known such an intimate subject. It had to have been Gabe who told her. The troubled place in her heart twisted once again. She'd thought that what went on between them was private.

Enid lifted her chin. "The point is, no matter what imagined romantic notions either of you carries in your heart for Gabriel MacKay, neither of you is willing to be his wife, to *know* him, if you want to put it in biblical terms, as a real wife should, to bear him children, to be a first wife to him and help him be the best father, husband, and Church leader he can be." She paused. "Have you considered that someday there will be another prophet and president of the Church? What if that chosen one is Gabriel? Have you thought about that?"

Mary Rose wearily opened her eyes.

Cordelia cackled. "What? Gabe MacKay, a prophet?" She shook her head. "I would venture to guess he doesn't believe half of the edicts of the prophet Joseph Smith or Brother Brigham."

"It's evident that none of you believe in him," Enid said. "It's also evident that neither of you 'wives' want anything to do with him. That, in my thinking, leaves me to take care of all his needs." She stared at them a moment longer then said, "Now, if you'll excuse me . . ."

But before she reached the doorway, Bronwyn heard Gabe talking to the children outdoors. His voice was low and solemn as he asked if they had seen Mother Bronwyn.

A moment later, his frame filled the open doorway, backlit by the sun, his face shaded, his expression unreadable.

Bronwyn swallowed hard and waited for him to speak. Mary Rose reached for her hand.

After a moment when it seemed to Bronwyn that every living creature on earth quit breathing, the thud of hoofbeats carried toward them. Above the shouts of the posse, the thud of horse hooves, the squeak of leather and jangle of tack as the men dismounted, was the distinct timbre of Brother Brigham's voice.

"You must come with us," Gabe said to Bronwyn. "The prophet's orders."

THREE

In a clearing outside the tent-cabin, Brother Hyrum shoved his face in Bronwyn's. As he spoke his skin turned the color of the ruddy end of a turnip, the contrast with his snow-white beard giving him the look of Father Christmas with yellowed teeth. "Where have you taken my bride?"

Bronwyn shivered. Coal and Sarah remained in their hiding place on Bronwyn's orders to stay put until she returned.

The other men, Brigham among them, formed a barricade around Bronwyn. Gabe stood at her side, though whether to protect her from the other men or keep her from bolting, she couldn't tell.

"I will tell you as soon as I have your word that you'll give her a few years to grow up before marrying her," Bronwyn said. She kept her voice soft and gave him a cool smile as she spoke, more to show she was unafraid than to show any softness of heart.

He made a snorting sound and looked first to Brigham and then to Gabriel as if expecting them to do something.

"You have enough wives to secure your place in the holiest, highest heaven," Bronwyn said. The hue of his complexion deepened. He drew himself up taller, lifted his snowy jaw, and then turned his back to her. "I trust that you will handle this in the appropriate manner," he said to Brigham, and then turning back to Gabe, he added, "And sir, this is your wife. I would have thought you would have taught her to know her place as a woman, and as a good Saint." He shook his head in disgust. "You, sir, should be ashamed."

Gabe drew in a deep breath. After a moment he reached for Bronwyn's hand and clasped it tight. She took comfort in the hope that he meant it as a gentle gesture, not to keep her from running. "Brother Hyrum," he said, his voice calm. "I will handle this situation with my wife. I'm sure she meant no disrespect."

Brother Hyrum sputtered. "No disrespect? She entered a holy place with a loaded rifle. She pointed it at the prophet's heart, waved it around at the rest of us, abducted my bride. Disrespect?" He thumped Gabe on the chest with his forefinger. "You, sir, do not know the meaning of disrespect if you excuse her for this behavior . . . if you do not punish her for every crime against God and the Church, from disrespect to apostasy."

"It wasn't loaded," Bronwyn said. Even as she spoke her mind whirled with the escape plans that she and Mary Rose talked about late at night when everyone else slept. Take the children and Cordelia, make off with horses and a wagon full of food to see them back to the States, or to Mexico . . . any place where they could be free.

The hairs on the back of her neck stood on end as she considered that she might not ever have that chance.

What if she were accused and convicted? She would be shunned, made to leave without the children, even the two who were hers by blood— Little Grace and Joey. Panic welled in her throat.

"We had no way of knowing it wasn't loaded." Brigham held up a hand and stepped forward. "Let's make no more rash accusations until we have a hearing. We need to listen to Sister Bronwyn's side." His piercing eyes met Bronwyn's. "You may not know, my dear, the seriousness of your offense. Charges of apostasy may indeed be brought against you."

"I have not spoken out against God or Church."

"Excuse me, gentlemen." The voice was so weak it almost went unnoticed.

Bronwyn turned to see Mary Rose leaning against the doorway, pale and thin, her face gaunt. Cordelia stood by her side, her arms wrapped around the younger woman to keep her upright. Even so, Bronwyn could see Mary Rose's knees trembling beneath her dressing gown.

Mary Rose met Bronwyn's eyes and smiled.

She swallowed hard and bit back her tears. Her betrayal of Mary Rose had been laid open once more, as surely as if Enid had sliced open her torso and yanked her heart out for the world to see. Yet here was her friend, radiating love and forgiveness in her gaze.

"Gentlemen," Mary Rose said. "I am the one to blame, not Bronwyn. She was carrying out the wishes of a dying woman. I had my reasons, and my sister understood them well." Mary Rose clutched a rough wood that made up the doorjamb.

Bronwyn rigidly held her tears in check as Mary Rose defended her.

"You all know Bronwyn's gentle nature," Mary Rose said in a hoarse, low voice. She coughed hard, closing her eyes. When she caught her breath she continued. "Left to her own devices, she would never have thought of or, more importantly, deemed it possible to carry out such an act." She tried to take a step forward and almost fell. The frail and aging Cordelia nearly went down with her. Gabe let go of Bronwyn's hand and raced to Mary Rose's side.

"I can't let you take the bla—" Bronwyn began, but Mary Rose narrowed her eyes in warning. The very moment Gabe reached her, Mary Rose went limp in his arms. If Bronwyn hadn't known better, she would have thought Mary Rose had planned it that way.

"Your valor in standing up for your sister wife is noted," Brother Hyrum said. "But it's obvious that because of your friendship, you are attempting to take the blame for her act."

Foley Gunnolf, head of the prophet's police force, stepped forward. "I say we go ahead with the trial." He fixed his small eyes on Gabe. "You should be one of her accusers. Your sacred ceremony was interrupted. Not only is your wife Bronwyn a bad example to the other women, she could have hurt or killed any one of us, including Brother Brigham."

His expression turned wild as he looked around at the curiosity seekers that had gathered, Saints all, women, men, and children. "You all remember how Brother Joseph was gunned down in the Carthage jailhouse. The same could have happened to Brother Brigham this morning." A corner of his lip twisted into a snarl as he turned back to Bronwyn. "By one of our own."

There were grunts of agreements among the men and worried whispers among the women.

"You're wrong about Sister Bronwyn," Mary Rose said, her voice weak. Gabe still held her close, his arm around her shoulders. "You all know her. She's gentle and kind. There's not a sick one among us who hasn't known her ministrations. She teaches our children, loves them all."

Mary Rose met Bronwyn's gaze and smiled. "She's a friend to us all. Don't you see what she tried to do this morning? She tried to save a girl from marrying too young." She looked across the men in the posse, then stared straight at Foley Gunnolf. "Is that a crime? If it is, then I am guilty too." She shook off Gabe's arm, and took a step forward.

"And so am I," Cordelia said. "I was in on the planning. No young girl's going to marry a man twice *my* age as long as I'm around."

One of the men snorted. "Twice *your* age?"

"As if you're some sort of spring chicken," someone else said, though his voice was lighthearted.

Some of the others laughed.

"You tell them, Sister Cordelia," one of the women shouted. "I'm with you." A few others joined in.

Bronwyn couldn't help smiling as the tension seemed to melt away. Then she saw Brigham's flaming eyes. The tension may have dropped, but the danger wasn't over.

The men drifted away from the MacKay campsite after Gabe agreed to escort Bronwyn to the prophet's quarters the following morning. "And you'd better have Sarah James with you," Brother Hyrum called back to Bronwyn as he hobbled along with the others. "The punishment for apostasy is something you don't want to learn about firsthand. If you return my bride, we will take that as a sign of your repentance."

After Gabe carried Mary Rose to her cot and tucked her in, Cordelia moved her rocker closer to watch over her patient. Gabe pulled up a chair beside Bronwyn. Enid, who'd taken the children away from the fray, returned to join them, obviously considering herself part of the family.

"I can understand why you acted as you did," Gabe said to Bronwyn. "But did you stop to think about the outcome?" He heaved a deep sigh, and then dropped his head into his hands. "Couldn't there have been another way?"

"I had to take everyone by surprise," she said. "And I can't let Mary Rose take the blame. It was my idea from the beginning."

"You may have thought of it first, but I helped with the details," Mary Rose whispered from her cot, her voice weaker than before.

"I was the one who thought of the rifle," Cordelia said, grinning as she rocked.

Gabe shook his head. Enid pulled up a chair beside him, reached for his hand. She visibly squeezed his fingers and gave him a look that said she understood him better than the others did. Then she turned her gaze to Bronwyn. Because she sat to his side and slightly behind him, Gabe couldn't see her expression. But Bronwyn could. Enid's face took on a look of confidence, strength . . . and victory.

Bronwyn bit back her irritation. "I'm sorry if my actions shamed you." She leaned forward earnestly. "But better you shamed, better me accused of apostasy, than Sarah James be given to that old man."

Gabe met her eyes. They were dark with emotion, but she couldn't read what was in their depths. Anger? Understanding? Resignation? Gabe was a proud man. She was surprised he let Brother Hyrum, apostle or not, get away with thumping him on the chest.

"I must talk to Sarah's parents," she said. "I'm sorry, Gabe, for bringing all this on you—but I'm not sorry for stopping this young innocent girl from being bedded tonight by Brother Hyrum. What happens to me is of no concern. What happens to Sarah is of great concern."

"Saint Bronwyn," Enid muttered under her breath.

Bronwyn wondered if any of the others heard the verbal slap. If they did, they didn't react.

"You're wrong, Bronwyn," Gabe said, looking into her eyes. "What happens to you is of great concern—to me and to our children. Don't ever think otherwise." His expression warm, he leaned in closer to her. "Especially to me," he said.

The room seemed exceptionally quiet. A dark shadow crossed Enid's face.

"I'll go." Gabe sighed and stood. "It will be too dangerous to take you along." His gaze remained on Bronwyn.

"No, I'm coming too," she said.

"If you do, it will only make matters worse," Gabe said. "I know you meant well, and I'll explain that to the Jameses. I'm sure they'll forgive you."

Bronwyn withdrew her hand. "Forgive me? How can you even utter those words? They should thank me."

"They made an agreement with the prophet," Gabe said.

Enid surprised Bronwyn by speaking up. "What are they getting in exchange for their daughter?"

Gabe held up both hands. "I'm not the culprit here. I'm merely guessing. I do know that the Jameses have struggled. They had barely enough food supplies to make it to Winter Quarters. When Sarah marries the apostle, the family becomes an extension of his. They will all be cared for, each of Sarah's brothers and sisters, her mother and her father. Her parents probably think that giving her to the apostle is a way to keep the entire family from starving."

Bronwyn drew in a deep breath. "First of all, shouldn't we all join together to help them? We're all struggling. It took us longer to get here than we planned. Our food supplies are miserably short. We have little, but I'm willing to give up a portion of our supplies to save Sarah from a monstrous sham of a marriage. Can't we all help so she doesn't have to sacrifice herself on behalf of her family?"

Gabe squinted at her, his expression unpleasant. "Now you are skating very close to the edge, woman. The prophet mentioned apostasy. When you refer to an apostle's sealing to a new bride, you are referring to a holy union, God ordained. I agree that the bride is young, but in the end, it's the word of God to the prophet that will decide the matter." His tone softened. "And would you allow our children to starve to 'save' a girl from what will someday be her honor and glory?"

"Honor and glory? I'm not talking about the hereafter. I'm talking about the here and now. What if it were Ruby or Pearl . . . or Little Grace?"

"We aren't talking about them." He grabbed his hat, started to the door, and then turned. "When I get back, you'll lead me to Coal and the girl—and that's that."

"You're wrong, Gabe."

He stared at her.

"You're not going alone." She stepped closer. "Don't try to stop me. If Sarah's mother can be convinced to act on behalf of her daughter, it will probably be another woman who will do the convincing." She grabbed her shawl from a hook by the door, and shoulders as erect as a young soldier's, she marched out ahead of Gabe.

She stopped outside the door and turned to him. "And another thing, Gabe. You're wrong about something else too. You're wrong about me leading you or anyone else to where they're hiding. Unless the marriage is called off, Sarah's not coming home."

Taking a deep breath, he said, "You're forgetting why they made their decision."

"If you mean the 'decision' that in exchange for their daughter's marriage to Brother Hyrum, they'll be fed and clothed during harsh times, I don't believe it. They don't have to make Sarah a sacrificial lamb."

He stared at her, his lips forming a straight line.

"I'm not forgetting anything, Gabe. I'm especially not forgetting Sarah's wedding night."

FOUR

Hosea Livingstone leaned against the railing of the *Dixie Queen*, looking out across the gently swelling waters of the Mississippi just south of Nauvoo. A wharf jutted into the river dead ahead, and he watched the crew prepare to dock. The riverboat swayed as the captain called out an order to turn starboard to miss a sandbar. Gasps escaped from a few passengers standing near Hosea.

Memories flooded into his mind as the pilot shouted more commands to his crew. He lifted his face to the sun, closed his eyes, and felt the spray of the water, letting his mind drift back to the *Sea Hawk*, the last ship he captained out of Liverpool. It had been a magnificent ship, faster than any he'd ever served as master and commander. He'd been proud of her, especially of the way she so elegantly sailed into Boston Harbor, setting the speed record for crossing the Atlantic.

"Been to Nauvoo before?"

A sandy-haired man with a pleasant face interrupted his

thoughts. Hosea studied him for a moment before answering. He'd preferred keeping to himself since leaving Nova Scotia, but this man interested him. He was a mix of good taste and travel-worn shabby, and his fingernails were dark, ink dark, as if he spent a good deal of time dipping a pen into an inkwell. Though his clothing was rumpled, he appeared to have had a recent hair-cut and beard trim. Likely in the last settlement where they'd stopped to take on passengers. His hat, even its tilt, said that he likely hailed from a city, perhaps New York or Boston. Even his shoes held a shine, unheard of in these parts.

Finally, Hosea said, "Never set eyes on the place, though I've heard plenty about it."

"First trip here myself," the man said. "I overheard you asking the captain about the Mormon exodus, so I thought maybe you knew something about the group."

"Idle curiosity, I suppose." Hosea shrugged. "Especially about the religion of the people who used to live here."

"Religion?" The man scoffed. "If you can call it that. I say it's more like one man's grandiose folly."

"You mean that of Joseph Smith?"

"Yes. But come to think of it, I could also be speaking of their new prophet and president, Brigham Young. Smith, him, and a dozen others like him." He laughed. "Pay no mind to me. I'm a newspaperman investigating the phenomenal rise of these fringe religious groups—the Shakers, the Campbellites, the Mormons, the Oneida group all out of Upstate New York—same place young Joseph claimed to have found the golden plates." He laughed. "I'm starting with the Mormons, plan to follow them west and find out what's happened since the exodus. I'm looking under every rock and bush to find out what's crawling underneath."

"Will make for interesting reading," Hosea said. "Why are you so sure you'll find something 'crawling' under their rocks and bushes?"

Instead of answering, the man stuck out a hand, and as Hosea shook it, he said, "Name's Andrew Greyson."

"Hosea Livingstone. Glad to make your acquaintance."

Greyson turned to look out at the river, leaning against the railing, ankles crossed. "Fine place, Nauvoo," he mused. "Too bad they were chased out. Some twenty thousand so-called 'Saints' have now made their way west."

"You didn't answer my question . . ."

Laugh lines crinkled at the outer corners of his eyes, telling Hosea that easy laughter was part of his character. He couldn't help liking the man. "That's true. I didn't." He turned back to Hosea. "I sometimes come on strong when I've got preconceived ideas," he said. "I try not to do that. After all, it's not the mark of a good reporter."

"Sounds like you've already sniffed around under those rocks."

"I can't go by hearsay, though there's plenty of that around, believe me." He sobered as he continued. "One bit of hearsay I am paying attention to is the rumor of the resurgence of a Mormon secret militia led by Brigham himself. Hard to pin down. Sometimes the group is called the Avenging Angels or Destroying Angels, other times the Danites, probably taken from the Old Testament Book of Daniel 7:18: *"But the saints of the most High shall take the kingdom, and possess the kingdom forever, even forever and ever.*

"What we do know for certain is that the group once served as a death squad in Far West. Once they moved to Nauvoo, supposedly it was disbanded, and its members became bodyguards to Joseph Smith or policemen for the town. At least they told as much to outsiders."

A chill traveled up Hosea's spine. "It sounds like there's more."

"After the assassination of Smith you can bet they revved up the effort to exact revenge. Nothing much has been officially reported, but there've been disappearances."

"Of those who were in on Smith's murder?"

Greyson didn't answer.

Hosea watched the rolling water for a few moments. "If they've moved from the area, there's no longer the threat from outsiders," he said. "Why would there still be need for a secret militia? Why now?"

"Even in Far West it wasn't formed to exact revenge on those who persecuted them. It was formed to, in the militia leader's own words, 'remove the salt that had lost its savor.'"

"Remove the salt?" Hosea had followed the man's reasoning until now. "Salt? What did he mean by that?"

"The militia leader was a right-hand man to Smith, and when preaching his famous 'salt sermon,' it was understood that dissenters, apostates, wouldn't be tolerated by the church."

"So they would be chased out."

Greyson shook his head. "That, and worse. He said they should be 'trodden under the foot of men.'"

Hosea's thoughts went to Enid, her headstrong, outspoken ways. How could she possibly have become a part of this group? And Gabe? He thought he'd known his friend well. Obviously, he hadn't. Gabe proved that fact aboard the *Sea Hawk* when he told him about his relationship with Enid.

"So, they've all moved on?" Hosea stared at the river, attempting to keep his disappointment from showing. "I heard some church leaders stayed behind to make sure they all got out before the governor's protection expires." He'd held out hope that Gabe might be one of those leaders.

Greyson studied him with greater scrutiny. "There may be some folks still waiting to leave from outlying areas, but not many. Brigham Young treated this exodus like a military operation. The first groups left in terror, then he sent an emissary to plead with the governor on their behalf. He got a reprieve of a few months, some say up to a year, to get the rest out of the state. After that, locals are expecting full-out war against this group."

Hosea drew in a deep breath. "Why war? What have they done to deserve that kind of treatment?"

Greyson glanced at Hosea before turning to watch the approaching wharf. "All the New York groups have their idiosyncrasies but none of the others formed militias. That tends to make neighbors very nervous. The situation with the Mormons is complicated. There were financial scams involved—at least that's what the neighbors called it when they felt they'd been tricked into investing and lost a great deal of money. They didn't stop to consider that it wasn't the fault of the Saints—the entire country was going through financial woes in those years."

A faint memory came back to Hosea. It happened on the *Sea Hawk,* dinner perhaps. He remembered the fervent apostle, Brigham Young, dining with him and others in the captain's quarters. "I know about those early years," he said. "I heard about it firsthand." Images flew into his mind, faces of long ago: Lady Mary Rose Ashley; her grandfather, the earl; Griffin the Welshman; and Gabriel who had eyes for no one else in the room but the lovely Mary Rose. He remembered how Gabe challenged Brigham's beliefs with a powerful argument, almost scoffing at the apostle's naïveté.

Greyson turned to him, his expression curious. "Why do I think you know more than you're letting on?"

Hosea laughed. There really was no reason to keep his circumstances a secret. He doubted he'd ever tell anyone every detail. Too much heartbreak. But as long as the man didn't print it up in his newspaper, he saw no harm in telling him at least part of his story.

Still chuckling, Hosea held up both hands. "You're almost correct, though my knowledge about the group is limited to a couple of firsthand accounts told to me by Brigham Young when he was a missionary apostle. Things have changed a great deal since then." Behind him, the pilot called out orders and the deckhands scurried to set anchor as they came alongside the Nauvoo wharf.

"My wife may be among them," he said, quite sober. "And a man who I once considered a friend as close as a brother."

Greyson studied Hosea for a long moment and then said, "And you suspect your wife may have become your friend's second bride?"

"I can see why you're a good reporter," Hosea said. "Yes, that is my fear."

"But she's already married . . ." He looked puzzled. "Not that it makes much difference to many of the Saints who are set on taking more wives than one."

Hosea turned away from Greyson as the riverboat docked. "My wife thinks I'm dead."

FIVE

Mary Rose watched Cordelia fuss around the small room. She opened windows to let in fresh air, shook the blankets outside to rid them of dust, fluffed her pillows and added one of her own, and finally, as Mary Rose requested, she placed her pen and ink and diary on the bedside table.

"What would I do—would any of us do—without you," she said.

The dear woman gave her a weary smile as she sat in the old rocker and closed her eyes. "I wouldn't have it any other way," she said. "Makes a person feel needed."

"You stayed by my bedside day and night. It's all pretty hazy, but it seemed like every time I looked up, you were there."

She glanced at Cordelia, who, still smiling, snored softly.

Mary Rose reached for her journal and tenderly leafed through the pages. She'd poured out her feelings with the utmost honesty nearly every night since leaving Nauvoo, recording the many deaths and injuries, trail stories of families in the wagon train. The adventures of the older children.

The entries that touched her heart now were those more personal, sometimes poetry or short stories, sometimes just random thoughts, but most often her deepest feelings—from joys to heartaches to fears. In the beginning she focused on the many acts of kindness she observed among the Saints.

But her fears too often, especially recently, touched on the rigid dictates of the Church. In her writings, she openly criticized unfair acts of punishment for those who didn't agree with their leaders. As Foley Gunnolf rose to power, she feared the cruelty she and others saw in him. Even back in Nauvoo, when he was appointed head of the police force, she felt something dark and sinister resided in his being.

Rumors spread that a second police force had formed—a secret force that carried out acts of revenge. Many of the men on the regular force were also called upon at night to be "Avenging Angels" or "Danites." Now those rumors had turned to truth, and she recorded every detail. Someday, if she ever had the chance to escape, she would take her journals with her.

What she would do with them, she didn't know. What she did know was that they followed next in line, after her children, in importance to her entire being.

As Cordelia slept beside her, she dipped her pen in the inkwell and began to write.

August 7, 1846

*But the child's sob curses deeper in the silence
than the strong man in his wrath.*
　　　　　　　　　—Elizabeth Barrett Browning

I lie here sick and helpless, trying not to weep. But it doesn't help. My tears drip from my chin onto this page, smearing the ink.

I survived cholera, but I didn't get well soon enough to help my friend . . . or my son! My heart is so heavy I almost cannot breathe.

I think of the boy and how he couldn't be more of a son to me if he was my own flesh and blood. Perhaps because I'm bedfast, memories of him keep coming . . . the first time he raced like a whirling dervish into the manor house, teasing his sisters, and raising havoc for Grandfather and me. His ready grin, his mop of straw-colored hair, the mischievous twinkle in his eyes . . . won our hearts within minutes.

I weep as I write this, missing him so. If I could give my life in exchange for his, I would gladly.

And dear little Sarah. I weep for her, for what I fear lies ahead. We tried to save her, hoped that other mothers would join us, but from all accounts none stood up with Bronwyn. Do they realize the next young bride might be their own daughter?

The very idea of it makes me sick, makes me feel worse than cholera ever did. Sarah is a child. The man who Brigham says God told him she must marry is Hyrum Riordan. He's ancient, with yellow teeth, a beard long enough to catch in his trousers. Dear Sarah is the youngest bride to be chosen for what the prophet calls the greatest privilege bestowed on womanhood.

Greatest privilege? Hogwash, as Cordelia would say.

If people would stop for a minute and consider what they know to be right, regardless of what the prophet says, they surely would see the cruelty in such a forceful act.

As I write this, I fear Bronwyn will not escape punishment. Many convicted of apostasy are expelled from the Church, the family, the community. I've seen it happen before, though not to a woman.

It's heartbreaking for the family and friends when the accused is made to leave our presence. How can we let that happen without raising a fuss? Without trying to stop it. If it happened to any in my beloved family, I would fight tooth and nail to save them. I wouldn't let them go alone, even if the prophet himself ordered me not to go.

One night I watched as a young man, a father and husband, was made to leave our campsite. It was cold and dark and he had only the clothes on his back. I listened to wolves howling sometime around midnight, and I somehow knew it was because they'd found easy prey.

I wept that night till dawn. Early the next morning I visited his wife, and though her eyes were swollen and red she never once mentioned his name. It was as if he never existed. And then she told me the prophet was giving her in marriage to someone else before the day was out.

Chattel! Is that what we are?

Is no one willing to speak out? To tell those in power over us how we feel? Are they so powerful that all we can do is cower when told what we must do? Who we must marry?

What Bronwyn did today took courage and cunning. I am in awe of her as always. It seems there is nothing she cannot do when she sets her mind to it. An hour ago, a mob appeared at our door. Brother Brigham was among them, also Apostle Hyrum Riordan, who shouted that Bronwyn should be tried for apostasy.

Even in my illness, I felt the ire inside me flash to the surface. If I'd not fainted, I was ready to do verbal battle . . . yea, I may yet!

I love Bronwyn as much as a sister born of the same parents. She is my friend, and no matter what happens, I will always stand by her. If she is tried for apostasy, I will stand with her. If she is punished, I will join her in her punishment.

I helped plan this daring raid to save Sarah James, and I will shout it from the mountaintops that this practice of old men—nay, any men—taking such young brides is wrong. It is a sin!

I read in my family Bible before the cholera overcame me that Jesus Christ Himself said that if anyone causes harm to these little ones of His, better a millstone be hung around his neck and he be drowned in the depths of the sea. I believe that applies to even the prophet, though if anyone knew I accused him of such sin, I would likely be tried and convicted of apostasy, myself. For the one I accuse is revered as if God himself.

I grow weary from my illness, and cannot write much more. But my heart is troubled by what I see in Bronwyn's eyes when she gazes upon Gabe. It is even more disturbing when I see what's in his eyes. She is looking for someone to love and treasure her. She, in all her beauty, presents him a challenge because she will no longer give in to what he believes to be his marital rights

Do I love him? A question I can't answer. Once I did beyond all human understanding, but I didn't know that loving him would end in such heartbreak, would require me to turn against all the things I most cherish.

I'm just learning about forgiveness and mercy as I read my dear mother's Bible, but I have so far to go.

I will end with a long-treasured verse from Elizabeth B.B.,

> *First time he kissed me, he but only kissed*
> *The fingers of this hand wherewith I write;*
> *And, ever since, it grew more clean and white.*

Now, my hand is frail and white, and trembles even as I write. But God help me, I remember Gabe's first kiss, and I weep.

I hear the approach of horse hooves. I pray it is Gabe and Bronwyn with good news about our son and young Sarah James.

SIX

Gabe's thoughts were as bleak as the landscape as he studied the ground for signs of Coal and the girl, Sarah James. Though Bronwyn rarely changed her mind about anything, this time her worry over the young people took precedence, and she agreed to lead Gabe to their hiding place. Once Gabe and Bronwyn discovered they had left the wagon and were missing, he'd then convinced Bronwyn to ride back to Winter Quarters for help with the search.

Instructing Bronwyn to do anything these days did about as much good as telling one of the ravens circling above to drop manna from heaven. Not only had his rifle-toting wife interrupted a sacred ceremony, she'd made off with Coal and one of the brides, dared reenter camp without them, insisted on accompanying him to the James' tent cabin—determined to get them to call off the wedding, which only increased their ire against her.

When it came right down to it, more than likely it was her fear for Coal and Sarah that finally spurred her to go for help. Nothing he said.

The situation had gotten out of control. He almost laughed, albeit bitterly. When had his wives been under control?

His second wife was about as malleable as a hedgehog. He wondered if she'd always been like that, or if life on the harsh frontier had changed her. In reality, he hadn't known her well when they married. He'd been attracted to her physical beauty— blinded by it—long before her husband Griffin died. She had spent much time in his household. Mary Rose was her dearest friend, and Griffin, Gabe's closest friend. The four had taken to the new religion and Nauvoo itself with growing conviction that their friendship was God-ordained, that meeting on the *Sea Hawk* was more than coincidence, that they would be together on their new journey from earthly time on through eternity. Even Griffin, a man of few words, grinned from time to time, socked Gabe on the arm affectionately, declaring they were friends closer than family.

Even back then, he'd had no illusions that he was immune to the feelings Bronwyn stirred in him. He couldn't help his attrac- tion to her, the way his heart drummed in her presence, or his hope that when she entered a room, her eyes would seek his first.

Sometimes they did; more often, they did not. That alone stirred his heart to craziness.

Gabe moved farther away from the wagon, and then stooped to examine hoofprints on the trail; they were deep, obviously made by a horse carrying at least one rider. He hoped it was the same horse Coal had earlier hitched to the getaway wagon. A Dakota campsite was nearby, not more than a few miles, and Gabe's stomach twisted at the thought of Coal and Sarah on the back of that horse, wandering too near the camp. Some of the Indi- ans the company had come in contact with were curious about the Saints, sometimes wanting to trade or steal. Still others were openly hostile. Brigham taught that they were the dark-skinned descendants of the Lamanites, one of the lost tribes of Israel, and that Mormons were to follow his lead and treat them fairly and with respect.

Right now, that didn't matter to Gabe. He knew of the atrocities that native people had carried out against those invading their land. Some tribes might return the respect Brigham preached, but others likely wouldn't from what Gabe had heard from other travelers. Right now, all that mattered was finding Coal and Sarah before the Dakotas did.

He straightened and gazed out over the prairie, now dusk gray. Barely visible were buffalo and Indian trails through the tall grass, bare traces of others too, perhaps made by wolves. As the sky darkened and stars began to appear, he returned to the saddlebags for a lantern and his telescope.

He lit the lantern, and then he inched his way along the trail, looking for signs of his son and his companion.

Coal was like a son to him. He couldn't love the boy more had he been his own flesh and blood. The best decision he and Mary Rose ever made was to march Coal and his little sisters out of their great aunt's house in Boston, taking them in to raise as if they were their own. He couldn't imagine the heartbreak Mary Rose would feel once she found out the boy had disappeared.

Mary Rose.

His thoughts turned to those early days of their love and marriage. She was all he'd ever wanted, all he'd ever dreamed of. But then came Bronwyn. . .

How had things become so complicated? He didn't have to ask why Mary Rose had turned against him. He knew why, knew the exact day and time, and too often he saw the sorrow in her eyes when she turned to him. The first wave of sorrow came when he married and later made love to Bronwyn; the second wave came when he told her that he was taking Enid as his third wife.

She'd borne it all with her head held high, adopting a regal stature that made him proud. She'd taken her own sweet time, but eventually she gave her permission, as all good and saintly wives were encouraged to do.

Never again did she look at him with love—and trust—in her eyes. If love was there, it was buried beneath a veil of sadness and disappointment. And trust? She'd made it clear that she would never trust him with her emotions again.

Only once after he married Bronwyn had Mary Rose allowed him to love her the way a husband should love his wife. Miraculously, a child resulted from that union, their son Langdon Spencer Ashley MacKay. Everyone called him Spence, and just looking at him made a person smile. He had reddish brown curls just like his mother's, a sprinkle of freckles, and a dimple in his chin. Gabe often thought, especially during the nights when he longed for Mary Rose to cuddle next to him and whisper and laugh and talk till dawn the way they once did, that the only reason she'd lain with him after Bronwyn became his second wife was to have something of her own to love: a child. Someone to love who would never break her heart.

Maybe someday he would make it up to her. After all, he'd taken a second wife to ensure their place in eternity as a family. They would be together forever. God had decreed it; who was he to dispute the word of God as given to the prophet?

Bronwyn's image, in all its exquisite beauty, drifted into his mind. He almost laughed. Reasons of theology . . . or *lust*? Who was he kidding?

An escarpment lay dead ahead. He climbed to the top and peered into the growing darkness. The gray-green sea of prairie grass was as empty from this vantage point as it had been from below. Squinting, he caught a movement in a stand of trees silhouetted against the sky. For an instant he followed the shadowy image, which seemed to be a horse without saddle or rider, then he pulled his telescope from his pocket, extended it, and lifted it to his eye. But before he could get a bead on the animal, it had disappeared into the darkening sky. He blinked and stared again into the scope. This time there was no sign of the horse.

It could have been an Indian pony. Or Coal's horse. Whichever it was, it carried no rider.

He stood, surveying the landscape. Off in the distance he saw riders heading toward him. Pinpoints of lights bounced along with them as they galloped. Lanterns. He breathed easier. Not Dakota. Bronwyn had indeed done as he asked. Men from camp were on their way to help.

A breeze kicked up from the west, whistling as it sailed across the grass.

Frowning, Gabe cocked his head. Above the distant thud of horse hooves and frog song, almost as if riding on the wind itself, rose the sound of someone crying.

He heard the shouts of the men on horseback now, calling for him as they rode to the site of the empty wagon. Gabe didn't answer. Instead, he called out in a soft voice, "Sarah . . ."

The sobbing stopped.

"Coal . . . Are you there? Sarah . . . ? I'm here—it's Coal's father, Brother Gabriel. Can you hear me?"

Only the night sounds of crickets and frogs met his ears. That, and the shuffling of the dismounted riders moving around the wagon.

"Sarah?" he whispered, this time louder. "Is it you? Do you need help?"

He waited. The men were moving upstream, closer to where he squatted near the water. A voice of warning from somewhere deep inside told him not to give away his location. Perhaps it was because he recognized, among the cacophony of voices, that of Apostle Hyrum Riordan, who, judging from his tone, was most anxious to find his young bride.

For a moment Gabe didn't think he could breathe. The reasons for the daring deed that Bronwyn and Mary Rose had planned and Bronwyn and Coal had carried out flashed through his mind in sickening clarity. "Stay here," he wanted to say to whoever was hiding. "I'll come for you later and see that you're given safe passage."

Before he could think through his reaction, Brigham climbed into view on the creek bank above Gabe. He swung his lantern out, gathering into its stark and blinding light the muddy creek bank, flowing water, every stone and blade of grass—and the hollowed-out cave across the creek with a small human figure curled up inside.

"There you are," the prophet and president of the Church boomed, his steely eyes on Gabe. "Find anything?"

"Thought I heard something down here," Gabe said, standing and brushing himself off. He straightened, shrugged, and started up the creek bank. He hoped Brigham wouldn't spot the girl.

"There, look over there," Brother Hyrum said, now standing beside Brigham. "On the far side of the creek. I see Sarah. Oh, my lovely, lovely Sarah."

The old man started down the bank, half stumbling, half falling, as he searched for footholds down to the creek bed. It took him only minutes to reach the weeping girl.

He tenderly gathered her into his arms, whispering soothing words as if to a child. "Now, now, dearest. It will be all right now. I've found you. That's all that matters." She was so small, even at his advanced age, Hyrum had no trouble lifting her as he stood and carried her across the creek.

"Thank you," he said to Gabe. "You're quite the hero. You found her. The little lost lamb has been found." Triumphantly, he carried her up to where the other men waited. He heard her say that Coal had just ridden off without her and she didn't know where he went.

Brigham hadn't moved from where he stood with the lantern. His piercing eyes seemed to slice through to Gabe's heart. His expression said he knew that Gabe had come close to hiding the girl from the apostle.

"Did you find your son?" Brigham said finally.

"No." Gabe started back up the incline.

"We'll ask the girl what happened, son. Maybe she knows more than she let on." Brigham threw his arm around Gabe's shoulders, and they walked back toward the other men.

The warmth of his manner calmed Gabe's soul. He'd expected a reprimand; instead, he received understanding and, he supposed, a surprising mercy. "I know what the boy means to you. We'll leave no stone unturned until we find him." He halted before they reached the others. "Today, he acted through no fault of his own. I suppose you could say he used poor judgment, but he fell under the influence of Sister Bronwyn. I think a strong warning will likely keep him on a better path."

"Thank you, Brother."

"Once he's back, however, I want him to live with the boys taking care of the herds. Learn what it is to work hard morning, noon, and night."

Gabe frowned as the impact of the prophet's words settled. "He's a scholarly one, Coal is. He's smart, smart enough to go to any university of his choice. He can't get enough of his books and writing. I don't think he'll take to working on a ranch from sunup to sundown."

"Unless his excess energy and imagination is channeled, he'll never be one of us. As for university studies, they aren't needed among our people. The world's end is coming soon, so we can't waste time with such things as formal educations." He lowered his voice. "I recognize that young Coal is exceptionally quick. I want him groomed for Church leadership. Yes, he'll have book learning with the best minds of our converts. But first, he must learn obedience. You'll soon see. Working the herd will leave him little time for anything else—especially time to plan the abduction of a celestial bride."

"What about Bronwyn?"

"You're hoping she will not be brought up on charges of apostasy, of course."

"Of course."

He studied Gabe, his face full of wisdom and strength. His was a face a person could trust. Gabe knew this to be true from his work with him in Nauvoo, on the trail during their exodus, and here in Winter Quarters.

He surprised Gabe by chuckling. "There are those who would rush to judgment, but I'm not one of them, at least in this case. The situation bears watching, however. I suggest you take charge of her every activity, monitor who she sees, what she does. You might speak to Foley about how to handle this. He's an expert in such things. I daresay he would tell you to give her charge of the household chores, even the most menial—emptying the chamber pots, scrubbing them until her knuckles peel, beating the rugs until she can no longer hold up her arms. Though I might think it harsh, Foley will tell you himself, that you will see good results. He would say to keep her too busy to think. Watch her constantly. Perhaps even have her followed. Discreetly, of course. She's going against our ways . . . we can't let that continue. We can't let other wives follow her example."

"I disagree," Gabe said, fighting to keep his voice even. "I couldn't treat someone I care about in such a manner. Foley is wrong—"

Brigham took a step closer, his eyes piercing. "There's been more than one instance. After her behavior this morning, Foley talked to some of the sisters. He found out she's quite open about her discontent with celestial marriage, especially when husbands take younger brides."

Gabe forced himself to breathe. He couldn't get Bronwyn's image out of his mind—the image of Foley's punishment, turning the beautiful Bronwyn into an old crone, aged and used up, before her time. His fists clenched just thinking about what he'd like to do to Foley's face should the man ever suggest it.

With great effort, he forced his attention back to what Brigham was saying.

"He also found out that just a few days ago she told the children in her charge that there is more than one way to reach heaven, that there is more than one true church. It seems she's telling our impressionable children much of what she was taught in her native Wales—I daresay a mix of the heresy taught by the Church of England mixed with the truth of our beloved first prophet and president, Brother Joseph."

He paused. "She is a woman of great beauty. But I believe she has the capacity to use her beauty as a weapon. I can't put this strongly enough: Sister Bronwyn cannot be trusted. After the report Foley gave me just hours ago, I've concluded that Sister Bronwyn can no longer teach our children."

"That will hurt her deeply."

"She brought this upon herself." Brigham met his gaze. "Perhaps this will ease the pain for her. Let her know that her punishment is light because of you, Gabe. I plan to bring you into my celestial family as my adopted son. Bronwyn is your wife. I want to give you—and her—every opportunity to join me in eternity, all of us, in one delightsome family."

Gabe was stunned. For a moment he couldn't speak. He'd heard of this practice among the Quorum of Twelve, the Church's governing body patterned after Christ's twelve apostles, and the prophet's closest advisors. It was an honor of the highest order . . . especially so, when he was about to be adopted by the prophet himself. He couldn't help the smile that took over his face.

He had been devastated when, many years ago, his earthly father had died at sea.

Brigham seemed to read his thoughts. "Sometimes, the greatest rays of light and hope come in the dark despair of our souls. Sometimes, when our families disappoint us, or godly men with their feet of clay let us down, our Lord sends us messages of hope from unexpected places."

Gabe's heart lifted at the prophet's words.

"One last word of advice," Brigham said. "Keep your beautiful young wife busy with babies. Her own babies." He gave Gabe another wise smile. "One right after another. I daresay, she'll not have time to think of anything else. This is God's way, not man's. It is your wife's God-given duty. She needs your godly council as head of the household, as father to her children, and as a priest. Let her know that obedience is a godly virtue, required of a Mormon wife in good standing, and with you, who have been given the godly and honorable position of ruling over her. If then she does not respond, her trial for apostasy can commence at any time I say, and excommunication will follow."

"I'm sure that won't be necessary."

Gabe tried to absorb the impact of all that Brigham had said. For a moment, he simply stood and watched the scene before him unfold: the prophet returning to the group of men, the young bride standing trembling in their midst, the old apostle smiling as though the pearl of great price had been placed in his hands.

Gabe finally urged his leaden legs to move, and walked over to Sarah, who looked up at him wide-eyed, the sheen of dried tears on her cheeks. He took off his jacket and wrapped it around her shoulders. "Tell me where Coal is," he said, keeping his voice low. "Why did he leave you alone?"

"He hid me," she said, her voice trembling. "He said he had to. We heard someone coming. He thought it might have been the Dakota, but I don't think it was. I think he thought you all were coming for us. He hid me and then was going to make a false trail.

He said he'd come back for me when it was safe to come out. But I got scared after it got dark." She shivered again.

"A false trail?"

"Yes sir," she said. "So nobody would find us ever."

Brigham came up to stand beside him. "Remember what I told you, brother. He'll come back. And I guarantee you, he'll never run away again."

"What will happen to him?" Sarah said, starting to cry again. "He's my friend. He wanted to help me."

Before either Brigham or Gabe could answer, Hyrum hobbled up to stand beside his bride. "I want us to be married right here," Hyrum said, "right now."

Sarah was openly sobbing now. "Please, I can't." She looked up at Gabe. "Sister Bronwyn said—"

"What Sister Bronwyn told you doesn't matter," Brother Hyrum said.

Brigham gestured expansively. "We've had celestial marriages in homes, in the outdoors, in wagons. The place doesn't matter, for this is God's world." His arms took in the sweep of prairie, now shining silver beneath the starlit sky. "And this couldn't be a better time or place."

He gave Sarah a proud and gentle smile. "Dear girl," he said, "it is God's will for you. Do you dare to question what glories he has in store for you through this blessed union? That will last through all time and eternity?" He softened his voice. "Dear one, unimaginable blessings await you the moment you say these holy vows and pledge your troth to this godly, honorable man.

"You may be frightened now, but if you will let go of your fears, forget the lies told you by those who are instruments of the devil himself, you will be elevated to the highest heaven. Your children and grandchildren will call you blessed. You will be honored throughout eternity."

"I don't want to question the glories to come. I believe them with all my heart," she whispered. "But must I really say them now? Tonight? Can they not wait?"

The old apostle took both her hands in his. "Dearest, it is important that you agree. It is God's plan. And should you disagree, you will not be called into heaven's highest realm when your time comes."

She bit her bottom lip. "But surely someone else mi—"

"Let us not tarry," Brigham said. "The marriage meant to be fulfilled this morning will happen now. We are God's chosen people, and you, dear Sarah, are chosen for the great honor of being joined in holy matrimony to this good man. Dare I say, one of the best among all Saints."

Hyrum grew bright as he looked down at his bride. But Sarah didn't meet his gaze. Instead, she kept her eyes on Brigham. "I don't care about the secret name," Sarah said to him. "I thought I did, but I don't. Not really." She backed away from the group, now looking wildly around as if for Coal . . . or anyone who might help her. Finally, she fixed her gaze on Gabe, her eyes watery and pleading. "Tell them," she said. "Tell them I don't want to do this. Tell them that surely God doesn't require it. Tell them that I should be able to say, yes, I want to or, no, I don't. Tell them. Maybe they'll listen to you. Brother Brigham always listens to you. Can't you help me?" When Gabe didn't answer, her lips trembling, she said, "Do you not have any compassion in your heart for me? Please, help me."

"Many brides are nervous at first, my dear." Brigham said. He gave Hyrum a nod, and the old man stooped to whisper into his young bride's ear.

"My secret name?" she said, looking at the apostle. "Is that what you just said? I couldn't quite hear you. Is it—?"

He put a knobby arthritic finger over her lips to shush her from speaking it aloud, whispered into her ear again, and then pulled out a kerchief and dabbed at her tears. "The name that I'll use to call you into heaven," he said, smiling. He touched her cheek gently, and then reached for her hand and kissed her fingertips. "You'll soon see that this life is what God intended all along. You'll be happy." He laughed lightly. "As my youngest wife, you'll be a pet among the others. It will be like living in a family with more loving sisters and even mothers than you can imagine."

She gave up a shuddering sigh. "But it's forever," she said. "That's what scares me."

"It is indeed," Brigham said. "That's the wonder and the glory that God has in store for you."

She smoothed her torn, muddy skirt, and still weeping, stared at Gabe expectantly.

Gabe swallowed hard. God's will? Could this truly be God's will?

Brigham was God's representative on earth. Polygamy represented the full restoration of the only true church, complete with the restoration of the Old Testament patriarchs' marriage to multiple wives. It might be hard to understand, but God's ways, he was learning, weren't always easy to understand.

This girl's marriage was from God. It had to be.

Minutes later the ceremony was over. With his arms wrapped around Sarah, who sat sidesaddle in front of him, Hyrum led the group of men away from the empty wagon.

For a long moment, Gabe watched their lanterns bounce across the prairie. Shouts of congratulations and the laughter of celebration carried on the wind back to where he stood. He shuddered when he thought of what awaited this innocent girl tonight. Gradually the voices faded, and the pinpoints of lights disappeared as if swallowed by the darkness.

Still holding the lantern, he retraced his earlier steps looking for evidence of Coal's trail. He found none.

Finally, he wrote a note, telling his son what had transpired; and taking a small chest from the back of the wagon, tucked it inside and left it near where Coal had parked the wagon so the boy could find it, should he return. His heart heavy, he hitched the horse to the wagon and started back across the prairie.

He tried not to think about the horse without a rider that he'd spotted just as dusk fell. But the image kept returning to his mind. Could it have been Coal's? And did the Dakota have anything to do with his disappearance? Something must have happened to keep him from returning for Sarah.

Even as he popped the whip over the back of the horse, his thoughts remained with Coal, the boy who had won his heart from the first time they spoke—atop the mast on the clipper ship before it left the Liverpool harbor.

He blinked rapidly and looked up at starlit sky. Images of Mary Rose and Bronwyn whirled in his mind. How could he return home to them without the son they loved?

SEVEN

That night, long after the others were asleep, Bronwyn stared at the ceiling in the women's tent-cabin, which she shared with Mary Rose, Cordelia, and Enid. She could hear the soft sighs of the children sleeping in the adjoining room. When Gabe and some of the other men put up the temporary structures, made of oiled canvas and rough-hewn planks of wood, the children had been thrilled to have their own quarters. The twins, now nearing ten, to their delight, had been put in charge of the younger ones—Bronwyn's Little Grace, now five; and Joey, her toddler fathered by Gabe; and Mary Rose and Gabe's toddler, Spence.

The men's tent-cabin was usually occupied by Gabe and Coal. But it remained empty this night, with Coal missing and Gabe having ridden off without telling anyone where he was headed. Enid was gone too, and Bronwyn winced as she wondered if they were together.

She fluffed her pillow, and closed her eyes. But the images of the day kept her awake—and the worry over Coal.

She could not bear to think of what any of them would do

without him, the boy so quickly growing into manhood with his lopsided grin, the fuzz on his jaw he couldn't wait to shave, the gangly legs and feet too big for the rest of him.

"You still awake?" Cordelia whispered from the cot next to Bronwyn.

"I'm worried about Coal."

"God's got him in His great big hands."

"I wish I could believe that." She felt tears trickle from the corners of her eyes and into her hair. "I shouldn't have involved him."

"Once he found out about the plan there was no stopping him. Besides, you both were doing it for Mary Rose."

"Mary Rose gave her permission for Gabe and Enid to marry. I wasn't doing it for her."

"Quit talking about me behind my back," Mary Rose whispered from her cot. "I gave my permission, but that didn't mean I was happy about it."

"You told me the night we crossed the Mississippi you'd done it to save me from falling in love with Gabe."

"Did it?" A rustling came from the direction of Mary Rose's cot as she shifted beneath her bedclothes.

Tears came to Bronwyn's eyes as she thought about him, about how no matter how hard she tried, he filled her thoughts.

"Gabe will always love Mary Rose," Cordelia said gently before Bronwyn could answer. "He may not realize it right now, caught up as he is in this celestial marriage business. He's like a little boy at the candy counter at a mercantile. They all are. The teaching that the more wives a man has, the higher his place in heaven . . . ?" She cackled. "Folderol. Made-up rules supposedly from God almighty to bed as many women as a man could want in a lifetime. That's all it is. Folderol."

"The prophet says it's to take care of our widows and older orphaned girls, the poor who have no one else to bring them into a marriage covenant," Bronwyn said.

"How many proposals of marriage do you suppose I've had?" Cordelia laughed again. "Not counting my only true love, the earl. Am I not a needy widow?"

Bronwyn knew she was right. She suspected that Mary Rose did too, though neither said.

After a moment, Mary Rose turned to Bronwyn. "Don't take all the blame. No matter what we thought about Gabe and Enid's union, we thought we could save Sarah."

Cordelia cleared her throat. "By the way, where is Enid?"

"She should be finished out at Nellie Nesbitt's," Bronwyn said. "Either things were worse than first thought or she was needed somewhere else." She kept her suspicions about Gabe and Enid to herself.

"She's good that way," Mary Rose said. "Helping others, I mean. No matter what time of night or day, or whatever she'd rather do—she goes beyond what you might think is necessary to help those in need, animals or people."

"She has a healing touch," Cordelia agreed. "No doubt about it."

"But do we want her as a sister wife?" Bronwyn said, mostly to herself. "She wants to be first in the eyes of the community, first in all our lives. She feels entitled."

The women fell quiet for a moment, and then Mary Rose said, "She saved my life, you know."

"The cayenne potion," Cordelia said. "I thought so."

"No one else was here when she forced me to drink it. I thought it would kill me." She laughed. "Even Enid said . . ."—she imitated Enid's Nova Scotian-Scottish brogue—"'This will either kill you or save you so drink up and let's see what happens.'" She laughed again. "For the first time since she arrived in Nauvoo, I could have hugged her."

Cordelia laughed. "She sneezed all afternoon. That's how I knew she'd given you her potion." Her blankets rustled and her cot squeaked as she turned toward Bronwyn. "We're all in this together. We'll protect you, just as you would, and probably will have to, protect us."

"That's what Gabe said—just after he told me about the prophet's plans to set me on a straight and narrow path. He said he'd protect me as best he can." Gabe had met her at the cookfire earlier, and while he ate the meal she'd kept warm for him, he'd told her that when he returned, Coal would have to work as a cow hand and that she would no longer be welcome to teach the children. She related all he'd said to Mary Rose and Cordelia. The room fell quiet as they pondered this news.

"Gabe wasn't even there that night," Cordelia said.

"What night?" Bronwyn said.

"The night I found out you could shoot."

"The night you saved my grandfather's life, and mine," Mary Rose added. "The night the ruffians burned the barn and likely would have put us inside to burn with it, if they could have."

"The point is," Cordelia said, "I was shooting from inside the house downstairs. Didn't have a clear shot. We'd have been goners if it hadn't been for you."

Bronwyn couldn't help smiling as she remembered the night. It was the latter part she couldn't bear. "I was aiming over their heads. Just wanted to scare them off." Now she knew she should have aimed lower.

"No matter. You're more than a pretty face," Cordelia said. "Don't ever forget it."

But Bronwyn barely heard her. Her mind couldn't help but turn to what happened later that night. After the ruffians had gone. When Griffin was killed, heroically protecting Brother Joseph.

That night for the first time Gabe had gathered her into his arms, and they had clung to each other in their mutual grief.

She didn't know then the heartache that lay ahead.

And now she didn't know what new grief might come.

EIGHT

Bad things happened on nights when the moon spilled its tears on the earth.

That's what the village crone in Wales told four-year-old Bronwyn the night her mother died. Decades of moons had come and gone since then, but Bronwyn never forgot the old woman's words. Or the squeeze of her heart when she remembered her loss and wondered at the unfairness of heaven's tipped bowl of tears.

Such a sliver of moon hung in this night's sky, causing a tremor to travel up Bronwyn's spine as she urged her mare up an incline. There she halted the horse and looked out over the sweeping landscape, deep gray in the pale moonlight. A wind from the west kicked up and she felt it lift her hair from the back of her neck. Ordinarily, it would refresh her; now, it merely brought on another chill.

When sleep did not come to her, she slipped from her bed and headed silently to the corral. She didn't bother to saddle her horse, but as was her preference years ago in Wales, she mounted bareback and rode away from Winter Quarters.

Her heart was troubled, and she wondered if she would ever again find peace. After what happened to Sarah, the growing urge to flee with her family away from this community beat as strong in her mind as her heart did within her chest.

Had Mary Rose not fallen ill, they might have escaped. But it seemed with each day that passed, they grew more entangled with the hierarchy of the Saints, the beliefs that she was unsure of, and the actions of the leaders, the prophets.

The horse whinnied and danced sideways. Bronwyn stared up at the night sky.

If there was ever a time to leave, it was now. Her heart beat faster as she considered the thought. They would need to leave soon, before winter set in. If they could make it to the Oregon Trail and fall in with other wagon companies, no matter which direction they were headed, the family would have the protection of others. Their food supplies weren't adequate for a journey across the continent, but she could outshoot any man and if need be, she could pull down a buffalo.

Despite her dire thoughts, she almost chuckled. A buffalo? Her? What would she do with it after she shot it?

It was just a dream anyway. Mary Rose remained on the precipice of danger, and the journey from Nauvoo had weakened Cordelia's constitution. She put on a blustery front, but heading west with a wagon full of women and children would be the last thing that her aging body could handle.

And what about Coal? What if he returned to find his family gone?

She looked up at the sky again, thinking about England, Wales, and home. Before she fell ill, Mary Rose had shown her the deed to her estate in Salisbury and told of her desire to return.

Then cholera struck, and for days she lingered close to death. She had been one of the fortunate ones; most who fell ill with the dreaded disease died within days.

Besides Mary Rose's illness and Cordelia's failing health, another problem of greater magnitude faced them. They were in the middle of a harsh continent, surrounded by those who would block their every effort to escape, even if they had the means. Not only that, if caught, she and Mary Rose would be tried for apostasy and their children taken away from them . . . and then they would be expelled from the community.

Shunned in this life . . . and throughout all eternity.

Without bidding, words and phrases from her childhood came back to her, words her father taught her to say when nightmares filled her head. Or when her longing for her mother's love became too much to bear:

Keep watch, dear Lord, with those who . . . weep this night . . . give your angels charge over those who sleep. Tend the sick, Lord Christ; give rest to the weary, bless the dying, soothe the suffering . . . shield the joyous; and all for your love's sake. Amen.

She remembered how he spoke of God's love and held her close as she wept for her mother.

He said that the old crone had been wrong. The bowl of the moon was not to hold heaven's sorrows; it was to hold its joys—but you had to believe in the One who would fill your heart with those joys, and to believe in His loving kindness no matter what happened in your life on earth. Believe in the God who loves you, child, he'd said, as if you are the only one in the world to love.

Bronwyn stared up at the moon again and drew in a deep breath. Her father's words . . . *the One who loves you as if you were the only one in the world to love* . . . enveloped her as if on the wind that waved the tender grasses of the prairie.

Oh, God! her heart cried out. Are You there? If You are, show Yourself. Come to me. Please, I beg of You. Make Yourself known to me—if You are there.

Only the sounds of the prairie night met her ears, the late summer frog song from the creek, the singing of the tall grass as the breeze passed over its tips, and in the distance the low gurgling of the swift-moving water. God remained silent.

Her world seemed to be unraveling, day by day, leaving only the coarse threads of resentment toward Enid's lofty attitudes as she chattered on and on about her marriage to Gabe—at least, she had done so until this morning. Beside these were the threads of sorrow and regret over betraying Mary Rose. She hadn't stayed true to their agreement that she would not share her bed with Gabe. The knowledge that the feelings of attraction to him were as strong now as they'd ever been filled her heart with shame. The memory of their night together taunted her always.

The sound of hooves pounding the dirt road signaled that a rider headed toward the MacKay camp. Moments later, Gabe's horse climbed the rocky cliff, small stones skittering behind him. The horse, high-spirited and gleaming even against the night sky, nickered and danced sideways.

Her heart caught at the look of Gabe in the starlight.

NINE

Even in the pale starlight Bronwyn could see concern in Gabe's expression. "Has there been any news of Coal?"

"Nothing," she said.

He held her gaze, his brow furrowed with worry. "Can you stay with me and talk a while?"

She tried to say no, and hesitated for a heartbeat, but the look of him, standing there in the moonlight, his gaze riveted on hers, grabbed at her heart. When she nodded, he reached up to help her from the horse. He kept his arm around her as they both looked up at the starlit sky.

"I know you're as worried about Coal as I am," he said. "I've just been out searching for him again."

"You were?"

"Yes, Enid rode with me. I saw you here and told her that I needed some time alone with you. She encouraged me to talk with you."

"So this was her idea—"

He chuckled. "Do I detect a note of sister-wife rivalry?"

She gave him a sharp look. "This is not a laughing matter. You act as though sharing a husband is a normal state that we should embrace. We're taught that it's God-ordained. But if it is, why does it hurt so much?"

"God's ways are not always easy."

"Those words sound like they're from the prophet's mouth, not yours. Not from the man you used to be."

"The prophet . . ."

"Don't say it."

A breeze floated over the prairie grasses, its fragrance so sweet, it made Bronwyn want to weep.

"When are you marrying her?" she whispered, wishing it didn't matter so much.

"Tomorrow."

"You were childhood sweethearts."

"Yes."

"You fathered her child . . ."

"That has nothing to do with our marriage now. Enid and I . . . let our emotions . . ." He drew in a deep breath as he stared into her eyes. "I'd just found out that my parents died at sea. The comfort I found in her arms turned into something neither of us expected . . . or wanted." He sighed deeply. "I didn't know about the child, his birth or his death."

"She was in love with you," Bronwyn said.

Gabe studied Bronwyn for a moment before answering. "When she married Hosea, she loved him with all her heart. She followed us to Nauvoo after he was lost at sea and she was certain he wasn't coming back to her."

The breeze kicked up again, lifting strands of Bronwyn's hair from her forehead. She didn't realize her tears had spilled until her eyes stung in the wind. Her emotions whirled, unsettled as ever. Again she thought of the God of her childhood. What was it she longed for? And why did it always seem just out of reach?

Gabe misunderstood her tears and gathered her into an embrace, rested his cheek on the top of her head and tightened his arms around her. After a moment he pulled back to look her in the eyes again. She waited for him to kiss her, her thoughts doing battle. Wanting him to kiss her. Hoping he wouldn't, for if he did, she was afraid there would be no turning back.

He touched her lips with his fingertips, outlining them gently. He stooped to kiss her. For an instant she remembered the velvet soft feel of his lips on hers that night in Nauvoo . . . Then taking a deep breath, she pushed away from him. "Don't," she whispered, her voice hoarse.

Gabe moved closer, moved his hands to the sides of her face, now lightly caressing her lips with his thumbs. Butterfly-wing light. She shivered as she saw the heat of passion in his eyes.

His voice was husky with desire when he spoke. "You are my wife," he said, "bound to me for this life and through the next. Why do you push me away when our coming together as man and wife is ordained by the prophet? Ordained by God?" The entire time he spoke, she was aware of the rough warmth of his hands on her skin, the gentle touch of his thumbs on her lips.

He bent and covered her mouth with his. Gently he kissed her and then pulled away, his gaze never leaving hers. He kissed her again, this time his lips lingering on hers. She circled her arms around his neck and strained to melt into his embrace.

Then she stepped back, her heart pounding. What had she done?

He reached for her again, but she simply stared into his eyes. With every fiber in her being, she wanted to melt into his embrace. To again feel his lips on hers.

"No," she said, pushing him away. "I can't . . . I can't do this."

Gabe stepped back, breathing hard. "I care about you, Bronwyn. You are my wife. How can you do this to me?"

She drew in a deep breath, willing her heart to stop its wild beating, her knees to quit their trembling. She blinked, took a second breath, and nodded. Her voice shook when she spoke. "You must not do that again."

With a half-smile, Gabe assessed her words. For several long moments he didn't speak, then he said, "Somehow I don't think you mean that. If you weren't my wife, I might abide by your request. If I didn't see a desire in your eyes as strong as my own, that too might deter me. But my dear . . ." He stepped closer again, and tilting her face upward with his fingertips, he stared into her eyes. "My dearest Bronwyn, the truth is, you are my wife in the eyes of God and the Church. And I see a desire in you that makes your words meaningless." He traced her lips again with his thumb, and then stepped away from her.

"Tomorrow at dawn," he said, "I want you to gather the family to tell them my news. Have them come to your quarters. I'll give each of you a blessing, and pray for Mary Rose's healing, as is my priestly duty. We will celebrate tomorrow's wedding, and pray for safe journey. Will you call everyone together at daybreak?"

"Safe journey? Whose?" Was he taking Enid on a wedding trip? That was unheard of among the Saints. And why would he leave now, after what had happened with Coal?

"If we don't leave by week's end, we'll be caught in winter's snows. We have a long journey ahead."

"We?"

"Brigham and a few men he's chosen to accompany him west."

"I knew Brigham and some of the others were going, but you've said nothing about it." She folded her arms and lifted her chin. "I, for one, am glad you're going."

He laughed lightly. "After that kiss, I thought you might implore me to stay."

Her tone was biting when she spoke. "We face a winter without enough food supplies. Many of our men joined the U.S. Army battalion to march west, so we'll have little protection. Does that matter to you?"

She considered the suffering their friends and neighbors might face with so many of the leaders away. Who would hunt for food for the hundreds encamped at Winter Quarters? Who would protect them from Indian attacks?

She gave him a bitter laugh. "We don't need you, Gabe. Go with Brigham. Find our promised land. Do what you need to do for the Church. We'll keep watch over the Saints here, those ill, those who may be starving."

"You speak with much audacity, my dear. It's not like you, not at all like the Bronwyn of old."

"The Bronwyn of old was Mary Rose's servant and nanny to her wards as we sailed to America. Is that how I should remain, sir?" She gave him a curtsy. "I thought I was part of this family."

"Perhaps if you were a proper wife to me, you would be."

They stared at each other for a moment, then he shook his head. "I'm sorry, I shouldn't have said that. But you must admit, you've taken on more spunk or, as Cordelia would say, more spit and vinegar."

Her mind flew back to what he'd told her about traveling west. "The marriage tomorrow, a wedding night or two, and then the journey." She did a quick calculation. "And then you'll return in time for your baby's birth—nine months or so, I would guess?"

He rolled his eyes to the starlit heavens. "Yes," he said. "As always, it seems you know me better than I know myself." He fell quiet, and after a moment said, "That's why this moment, this night, there is nowhere else on earth I'd rather be than here with you."

"Here with me . . ." she whispered, wanting to believe him. "Then don't marry Enid," she said, "don't leave us. If that's truly the way you feel, don't go."

"Say yes to me tonight," he breathed. "I'll do anything in the world for you, if you'll come to me now"—he reached out to her—"if you'll be my wife in every sense of the word."

"And in the morning, will the wedding bells still toll for you and Enid? Will you still love Mary Rose?"

He stared at her without answering.

"Do you love me, Gabe?"

"There are many emotions I feel. You have to understand the complexities of plural marriage . . ."

"What about love?" A hot sting of tears burned the top of her throat as she awaited his response. "Can you ever love me as if I'm the only one in the world to love?"

"That's not our way," he finally said. "You know that, and still you reach for something you cannot have." He glanced up at the thin bowl of a moon, ready to spill its sorrows on the earth.

"You said you'd do anything in the world for me," she said softly. "But that must not mean love." *Perhaps the only one in the world you can love is yourself.*

He mounted the tall stallion, and rode back down the hill.

PART II

Earth's crammed with heaven,
And every common bush afire with God:
But only he who sees takes off his shoes.
                              —Elizabeth Barrett Browning

TEN

I don't know any gal worth her salt who'd want an old vagabond like me," Greyson said as he stoked the campfire. "I can't stay in one place long enough to set down roots. Don't know that it's in my makeup. Or ever will be. That's why the newspaper business suits me fine."

Hosea laughed. "For one thing, you're not old. You've got a long life ahead of you if you don't get eaten by a griz."

"You sound more like a mountain man every day." Greyson left the fire and settled against his saddle with a heavy sigh, looking up at the night sky.

"There's something about being around the folks in these wagon companies," Hosea said. "They seem to have a particular way of speaking. Colorful and hard not to pick up."

"I'd call it a peculiar way of speaking," Greyson said, "not particular. Most sound like they're from the mountain country or the deep South—even if they hail from outside the country."

"With the exception of the French Canadian trappers."

"Can't understand a word they say either," Greyson said with another laugh. "But they do make good pemmican. Anyway, love's not in the cards for me."

Hosea sobered, thinking of Enid . . . just as he did a hundred times a day. "You might be surprised what God's got planned for you. One thing I've learned in my lifetime is to expect the unexpected."

Greyson threw back his head and laughed. Hosea didn't think he'd ever met anyone who laughed as easily and heartily as this man. Made him pleasant to be around. "I believe you, my friend. Get washed off a ship and end up in the belly of a whale."

"Not quite. Washed up on shore. A very rocky shore."

"You told me you don't remember much after the wave took you. Only that you thought you were a goner."

"True."

He gave Hosea a sly glance. "So who's to say you weren't in the belly of a giant fish?"

"True again."

They fell silent for a moment, and then Greyson said, "You're a born storyteller. First time you told me what happened, I could see every detail in my mind's eye. I felt I'd been right beside you as you learned to walk again and learned what life was all about— especially the simplicity of loving God and being loved by him— from Giovanni and Cara. And your Enid . . . you've described her with such detail, I think I'd know her if I saw her."

He turned to Hosea again. "I could have used hearing your story once a long time ago. I could easily have been a man who let himself be taken by the wave."

Hosea studied his friend for a minute, letting the information settle. "I'm not a writer. I can picture things in my mind, feel the emotions, but I've never been one to write that sort of thing on paper, not even in a letter. Never good at expressing myself in person either, especially to Enid. I don't know if she ever knew how much I loved her."

"Love her," Greyson corrected.

"What?"

"You say you once loved her, but for weeks now all I've heard is you talking about her, telling me every detail with what's an obviously loving and tender heart. You still love the woman. You may finally get the change to tell her when we get to Winter Quarters."

The thought both terrified and excited Hosea. "Sometimes I wonder about the change of heart I had when I was with Giovanni. I remember the anger and betrayal I felt, and I wonder how that bitter heart could have changed to one filled with love." He stared up at the sky, the moonrise behind the pine branches, the silhouette of the needles against its glow. "I also wonder if the love will still be there when I see her again." That was the thought that terrified him.

The prairie wind kicked up, a low hum coming from some nearby hills, and grew louder as it approached—a sound that never failed to sooth Hosea's soul. It was the very breath of God. He smiled to himself. This was a good place to be. Near the warmth of the fire, stomach full of pan-fried trout, in the company of a good friend.

The pain of his injuries never left him, but he found them easier to bear when he thought of the good things in his life. He had no riches, only enough to get by—a good horse, a wagon, some good boots, and a walking stick. He found the condition more freeing than any he'd ever experienced.

"You said you could have easily been the man who let the wave take him," he said. "You've felt that kind of desolation?"

His laugh lines disappeared. "Lost love. Truth be told, it was probably unrequited love. I was young and foolish, let a good thing—a good woman—get away."

"If you could have let a wave take you, that's serious love, lost or not." He reached for his walking stick and then rolled to one side to lessen the pain when he stood. With great effort, he pulled himself up and made his way to the fire to stoke it. Embers shot into the night air like hundreds of orange fireflies. A small moment of beauty, a ritual he enjoyed. At first Greyson tried to take over the physical labor at their campsites, but soon learned it was Hosea's desire to do as much as he could muster without help.

"We met when she stopped into the newspaper office," Greyson said. "She was a fiery one, straight from Ireland. Her name was Shannon O'Hara. Had the greenest eyes I'd ever seen." Hosea could almost hear the smile in Greyson's voice. "She wanted a job, said she wanted to be a writer. I'm not proud of the way I treated her. I said she could clean our offices, help me set the type, that sort of thing. The whole time I was being a dirty, rotten fool, I was falling in love with her. Teased her about her way of speaking, the comical turns of phrases she used. She gave it back at me, matching my wit with her own—though, in that glorious brogue, calling me an '*eejit*,' and tossing that mane of curls over her shoulder. What I didn't know was, the girl could write." He shook his head slowly. "She had talent, but by the time I'd discovered it, by the time I discovered I loved her, she'd been hired by the competition on the other side of town and was being courted by her boss."

"Did you go after her?"

"I tried to talk to her once, but it didn't go well. Ended up making a fool of myself. Told her that the only reason she was hired was because her boss had his eyes on her. As you can imagine, she became indignant, even when I tried to apologize. So I wrote her a letter, declaring my love. She tore it up into tiny pieces and had it delivered to my office. She'd written one word across the envelope."

"Let me guess," Hosea said. *"Eejit."*

"That's it," Greyson sighed. "I heard she married the editor of the newspaper not long after."

The fire died to a steady lick of flames, and the conversation stopped, each man lost in his own thoughts.

"Tomorrow, we'll be in Winter Quarters, if we travel the miles we plan," Hosea said. "They say thousands of Saints are in the campground, resting before continuing their journey west. Should be plenty of material for your stories."

"What I've sent my editor so far is hearsay," Greyson said. "I'm champing at the bit to get some firsthand accounts. From what he says, folks can't get enough of what I'm writing. They're fascinated to read that these folks who call themselves Saints have set up their religion so it's actually an edict from God to take more than one wife."

"Polygamy piques one's curiosity," Hosea said. Bile rose in his throat as he thought of Enid with Gabriel . . . could she have married him? He was already married to Mary Rose.

And Gabe. What about the man, his friend, the one he'd sailed with, made the world's clipper ship speed record with, the one whose wedding he officiated?

What would he feel when he encountered Gabe?

"And perhaps we'll find your Enid," Greyson said.

Hosea's chest tightened at the thought. "Maybe," he said. He looked up at the spangle of stars, drew in a deep breath, and prayed that God would help him through whatever he might find tomorrow.

Especially, if he found Enid.

He stared into the heavens, remembering the night they wed. Their lovemaking had been passionate and tender, wild and satisfying, and lasted well into the dawn. Afterward, she'd touched his face, cuddling close, and whispered words so loving they made his heart ache with joy.

"I pledge you my love from now until forever. I will love no one but you." She'd traced her fingertips along his jaw as if trying to memorize the shape of his face, and then she met his eyes and seemed to almost drink in the love she saw in his soul.

Her eyes had filled with tears. Tears! This from a woman who never cried. She let them fall unashamedly, dripping down her cheeks onto his. He tasted the salt on his lips as she wept. She bent to kiss the tears from his lips, and smiled to see his eyes had filled.

"Aren't we a pair," she'd said. "Strong, invincible, and so much in love it hurts enough to cry."

He'd touched her face, and she caught his hand with hers. "Don't ever leave me," she'd said. "You can sail the world because I know that's what you love. But please, my dearest captain, please promise me this one thing. . .

" . . . that never, ever, no matter what happens to either of us, you will never leave me . . . that you will always come home to me."

Still holding his face between her gentle hands, she bent to kiss him. A deep velvet kiss that seemed to hold all her heart's love for him.

He blinked up at the stars, the ache in his heart almost unbearable.

That was exactly what he'd done. He'd left his beloved Enid.

ELEVEN

Hosea flicked the reins above MacDuff, the horse he'd won at an auction after finding out it was on its way to a glue factory upriver. MacDuff—a swayback with big yellow teeth and a coat the hue of a mouse dipped in mud—seemed to understand his good fortune. He held his head high..

They reached the top of the hill, and Hosea halted the horse. Grabbing his walking stick, he eased himself down from the wagon bench. Greyson had arrived before him, dismounted, and now squinted into the horizon.

"That's got to be Winter Quarters." He handed his telescope to Hosea. "What do you think?" Reaching into his vest pocket, Greyson pulled out a small hand-drawn map and studied it while Hosea lifted the telescope to his eye.

He scanned the landscape, focusing on the village. There had to be thousands of tents, cabins, and wagons. People everywhere, children playing. Men working crops, perhaps alfalfa.

Brigham Young's fanaticism showed. They'd heard he wanted

everyone to be prepared for the next leg of the journey. The first to arrive a year ago planted crops for those still to come. They left in staggered groups so there would always be some Saints remaining to take the newcomers under wing.

"Looks like he's done what he set out to accomplish," Greyson said. "It's a beehive of activity down there. We've heard about it, but to see it firsthand . . ." He let out a low whistle. "The man is a genius. The U.S. government should be watching his planning abilities. Seems they could learn a thing or two for moving troops."

Hosea collapsed the telescope and handed it back to Greyson. "This is no encampment. It's a small city. I wonder how I'll ever find Enid—if she's still here."

"From what you've told me about your friend Gabe, he'll be found with the leaders. Most folks know who their leaders are. That's where we'll start."

Hosea stared at the place for a moment then nodded. "Let's go. One way or the other, I need to know." He turned to head back to the wagon.

Greyson caught up with him. "There's a chance he could have left when Brigham did."

Hosea and Greyson heard snatches of information about the Mormons as soon as they set foot on the Oregon Trail at St. Joe. The big news was that Jim Bridger, the well-known trapper and explorer, had run into Brigham somewhere west and told him about a location that might suit their needs—a great valley in the west, with a lake as big as the Red Sea, and just as salty.

It was reported that he warned Brigham that the land was arid and unusable, but with those words, apparently Brigham gave the trapper a big smile and thanked him heartily. "That's just the place for us," he'd said, and then nodding to the others, he knelt on the ground. His men did the same, and they praised God for leading them to Bridger, and asked for God's continued guidance.

Hosea hoisted himself up to the wagon bench and sat back, looking down at Greyson.

"You going to be all right?" Greyson adjusted his hat, turned the brim down against the sun. "About Enid, I mean?"

"If I can get my heart to keep beating, I'll be fine." He chuckled.

"Then let's see if we can find your wife, my friend." Greyson swung onto the saddle of his bay, and led the way back down the incline. Hosea chirked to MacDuff, who rolled a bloodshot eye at him and then turned slowly forward again to pull the wagon down the hill behind Greyson.

They trundled along the main road leading into town. People seemed to know they were outsiders. Or was it his imagination? Hosea nodded to a couple of men walking along a boardwalk and attempted to look friendly. But neither tipped their hats or nodded back.

How could they tell he and Greyson weren't Saints? He tried to ignore the eerie feeling that traveled up his spine and caused the hair on the back of his neck to stand up straight.

Greyson slowed the bay and waited for Hosea to catch up with him.

"Do you get the feeling we're being watched?" Hosea glanced toward a roughhewn wooden building. A lace curtain shifted like someone was behind it.

"I just saw a couple of men hurry into the livery, glancing back at us every few steps," Greyson said. "Couldn't tell if they were afraid or defiant. Maybe a little of both."

Now the street seemed emptier than before. Hosea watched as mothers gathered little children and hurried them inside a shop or home. Again, curtains moved as if someone was watching them ride by, and he thought he saw the glint of a gun barrel.

The town grew unnaturally quiet. Above, ravens called out their haunting cries as they circled, and along the empty road, the wagon wheels creaked and the horse hooves thudded.

It was a relief when he noticed a building that loomed larger than the others. "Looks official," he said to Greyson. "A meeting place, maybe?"

"Let's see what we can find out." Hosea hoisted himself from the bench again, then led MacDuff to a hitching post as Greyson did the same with the bay.

They entered the building and looked around. A round woman with pink cheeks and a tight gray bun bustled toward them, a mop in one hand, a dust cloth in the other. She frowned.

"Brother Brigham's made it quite clear that unless we're having a meeting—"

Greyson removed his hat out of respect. "We don't know your customs, I fear. Please forgive us if we've wandered someplace we're not supposed to be."

Her cheeks turned brighter. She blinked, and then smiled. "You're Gentiles, then?"

"I suppose so, according to your way of thinking, ma'am."

Her smile grew. "Well then, that's wonderful. We don't get many folks who just stop by for no reason."

Hosea pondered her friendly ways. Her attitude wasn't in keeping with the strange behavior of the others outdoors. He stepped forward. "Actually, we do have a reason." He ignored Greyson's warning look. His friend wanted to get as much information as possible before the woman went on the defensive.

"We're looking for someone," Hosea said.

She studied him, her eyes filled with compassion as she took in his face with its broken nose and cheekbones, the scars that showed above his beard, the lopsided smile. "Who is it you need to find?"

"I have a friend who is with you. His name is Gabriel MacKay."

Her smile widened. "You know Brother Gabe? Why, laws-a-me. I know him. So does everyone else in Winter Quarters."

Brother Gabe? He exchanged glances with Greyson. "You're hoping to see him again, then. That's why you're here?"

"Partly, yes. That's why." He took a deep breath. "Can you tell me how to find him?"

"You're about three months too late, I'm afraid. Brother Gabriel rode with the prophet to find our promised land a year ago. Then he returned to lead his family and others to the place they'd found."

Hosea tried to breathe, but it seemed the air had been sucked right out of his lungs. He could barely get the words out. "Left for the Salt Lake Valley?"

She nodded. "Yes. They're headed for our new promised land, for our New Zion." She lifted her chin. "The prophet has already chosen Deseret. It's in that disputed territory of Mexico, you know."

"We're aware of that," Greyson said. "However, if the U.S. wins the Mexican-American war, Deseret will be part of the United States, not Mexico."

The woman's face clouded. "That's not going to happen," she said. "We've been run out of Kirtland, Ohio; Far West, Missouri; and Nauvoo, Illinois. Terrible things were done to us. Brigham is taking us to a place where no one will ever molest us again. God's spoken to him about it, and that's that." She placed her hands on her hips.

Greyson broke the tension with one of his ear-to-ear smiles. "Well, ma'am, if the other women among the Mormons have even half your gumption, I don't think you need to be worried about being run out of our New Zion."

She laughed. "Our family leaves next week. My husband's been chosen as captain. It's nearly too late in the season to make the journey, but he says God will be with us, and we'll make it fine."

"It's a long journey," Greyson said, solemnly. "Winter will set in before you get there."

"We've known hardship before, Mister—"

"I'm sorry, we should have introduced ourselves earlier. I'm Andrew Greyson . . ."

Hosea stepped forward. "And I'm Hosea Livingstone."

She nodded. "I'm Sister Amanda Riordan. My husband, Brother Hyrum Riordan, is one of the prophet's closest advisors. He's one of the twelve apostles. Sometimes they're called the Quorum of Twelve." She pulled her shoulders back in pride.

"Glad to meet you, Mrs. Riordan," Hosea said, and Greyson murmured the same.

"You can call me Sister Amanda," she said pleasantly. "Now, is there anything else I can do for you boys? I need to get on home. Our newest sister wife is, well, indisposed. She's just a little slip of a thing and scared silly, so the rest of us are taking turns sitting by her side."

It took Hosea a moment to realize that Sister Amanda meant one of her husband's wives was about to deliver a baby. He flushed slightly, glad for once that his face was mostly covered by a lengthy beard and mustache. "Only one more question," he said.

"What's that?"

"Brother Gabe?"

"Yes?"

"How many wives does he have? Or, maybe I should say, how many did he have when he left Winter Quarters?"

She surprised him by laughing. "Three. Though that last one was a challenge to get down the aisle. He had two to start with—Sister Mary Rose and Sister Bronwyn—and if Sister Bronwyn'd had her way, the number would have remained at two. She tried to stop the wedding between my husband and Sarah, the young bride I just mentioned. Caused quite a ruckus during the ceremony. Carted her off and hid her away, hoping to stop what God ordained. Said she was too young."

Hosea tried to take in the information. Bronwyn was married to Gabriel too? He remembered her well from the *Sea Hawk*—and that she was married to a man named Griffin. Happily, it seemed. Snatches of memory came back to him. They had a baby during a storm. People thought it a miracle that Bronwyn had lived through the ordeal.

"How old was she?" Greyson asked. "The young bride."

"She had just turned fourteen."

Greyson looked as shocked as Hosea felt.

"And she's with . . ." Hosea couldn't get the word out.

Not one to mince words in most instances, Greyson finished for him. "She's having a baby?"

"It's God-ordained," Sister Amanda said firmly. "The greatest blessing a woman can have bestowed upon her. Bearing a child as one of God's chosen."

"The name of the third wife," Hosea said, his heart ready to thud through his chest. "The wife that Brother Gabe was going to take before the ceremony was interrupted."

Sister Amanda smiled. "Nice woman who has a healing touch. She works with animals mostly, has brought many back from death's door. She's from Nova Scotia, I believe I heard someone say. I heard she studied medicine in Scotland, and that's why she's so good."

Hosea felt the blood drain from his face. He leaned hard against his walking stick as his knees went weak. In less than a second, Greyson was by his side. "From books," he whispered. "She learned how to be a veterinarian by corresponding with a doctor in Scotland. It was her dream to go there in person, but I don't think she ever made it."

"You know her, then?" Sister Amanda's face folded into worried lines. She brought him a chair, and he gratefully sat.

"The woman you describe is my wife."

She drew in a deep breath. "You mean she was already married?"

Hosea wanted there to be no mistake. "Her name . . . ?"

"Enid," she said, and then as realization hit, her jaw dropped. "Enid Livingstone."

TWELVE

North of Winter Quarters

Hosea landed on his back in the roiling waves, unspeakable terror overtaking him as the frigid waters sucked him into their depths. He fought to get to the surface, but the dark foaming waters mixed with black-green sheets of rain. Which way was it?

Something in the shape of a serpent circled him, watching, waiting, as the currents tossed him like a child's plaything. He kicked to reach the water's surface, but it remained just beyond reach . . . or maybe he was kicking himself deeper into the water's depths, not toward life-giving air. His brain was muddled, his body broken and weak.

Lungs bursting, strength ebbing, he gave in to the ocean's power.

Let it take him. Wasn't that what he wanted anyway? Wasn't that why he stood too long on deck? Stood where any master and commander worth his salt would never go, especially during a storm?

The sea monster circled closer. And closer. He felt it brush against his face. And then his arm. Wasn't that the way of sharks? Of killer whales? They examined prey to see if it was worth the trouble to kill. He waited for his arm to rip from his torso, blood blackening the dark water. He'd seen what these giants of the sea could do to a man. He prayed death came quickly.

The thing grabbed him. Shook him. Hosea waited for pain. For blood. None came. Obviously, he was numb from cold and sightless from salt water. Or maybe he was already dead.

His lungs screamed for air, telling him he wasn't. He struggled to kick loose, but he might as well have been a mosquito compared to the sea monster's size and strength. He hit at it with his fists.

No use. No use at all.

A strange calm came over him. In the same instant, the monster propelled him through the water . . . to the surface. Hosea felt frigid air blast against his skin and then fill his lungs. Stars filled the black sky directly overhead, though sheets of water raged out of storm clouds around him. It seemed the monster had surfaced in the eye of the storm.

He gulped the air, but not nearly long enough. The sea monster dove downward again. Then all went black, a deep velvet black. As Hosea felt himself falling deeper into the darkness, he thought the monster's shape seemed more like a hand, a giant and gentle hand, that had wrapped itself around Hosea's broken body.

Hosea woke in a cold sweat. A screech owl hooted from a sycamore overhead, and a wolf howled in the distance. The coals from their cookfire cast a red-orange glow across the pallets where they slept.

Greyson snored softly, his head on his saddle. The horses stood peacefully under a sycamore a short distance away.

Hosea sat up to move his aching body before settling into a new position. As he did, the dream that woke him returned in vivid clarity, just as always.

The monster he remembered from the sea hadn't taken him in death. It had delivered him to life. To a rebirth upon the rocky shore of Maine. Or as Greyson liked to put it, he'd been vomited out of the whale's belly right in front of two people sent from God to give him directions to Nineveh.

He'd wondered many times about the hand he thought he'd seen. It was clearer in his dreams than it had been the night he almost drowned.

He looked over at his friend. Greyson had decided to return to Winter Quarters, "ingratiate" himself—Greyson's word—to the apostle, Hyrum Riordan, and travel with the wagon company the old man was captaining to the Great Salt Lake.

Hosea saw no sense in doubling back. Or in putting up with what might be open hostility to the "Gentiles." Greyson had argued the wisdom in joining up with a larger company of travelers. Greater protection with greater numbers, he'd said. But in Hosea's thinking, it would also take him longer to find Enid. Gabe's family already had a three-month head start. He wanted to close the distance between them, as many miles a day as his body could take.

The thought of seeing Enid married to Gabe sickened him, and he struggled with the myriad emotions that filled his heart, mind, and soul. It had been years since he last saw Gabe, ordered him off his ship, and out of his life, but the old feelings of jealousy and loss simmered below the surface.

He thought he understood himself better, thought he had worked through the darkness of the human spirit. He'd come to terms with his broken and crippled body. He was a far cry from the dashing master and commander of tall sailing ships. But hadn't he learned to accept life with great humility, love others with an all-encompassing love, take joy in God's creation and his creatures, do good for others no matter the cost to himself?

He'd thought the rebirth of his spirit was permanent, that his old self had been left on that bleak Maine shore, like a discarded snakeskin.

Until now.

He pictured Gabe. Handsome. Outgoing. Gracious. He'd won the prize, that one. He'd bedded Enid before she and Hosea married. He told himself again that they had been young and impetuous, that they had made love only once. But she'd secretly borne Gabe's child, not bothering to tell Hosea before or during their marriage. And now he shared her bed again. And Mary Rose's. And Bronwyn's.

His stomach lurched, and the sting of bile filled his throat. He bent over and dropped his head between his knees. *Oh, wretched man that I am,* kept playing in his mind like a discordant symphony. More accurately, a single instrument, off pitch, broken beyond repair.

Why had the dream come back to him after all this time?

With Giovanni's help he'd come to believe it had been the very hand of God that reached out to save him. The old fisherman said many times that the whole of his being had nothing to do with his broken body. The precious part of him, his soul, had been healed. It was that which the big hand had reached down to pluck from the roiling waters.

Giovanni. Cara.

His eyes watered as he thought of them, remembered that first Christmas they'd spent together. He wanted to go back, though something told him that if they were sitting beside him this minute, they would disagree. They would also tell him that God's work in him was unfinished and if he hadn't figured out what that work was, then he needed to continue on his journey until he did.

For a long while, he stared at the dying embers.

How could he go on, knowing that soul-deep healing was still needed? How could he look upon Enid's face with the same love and forgiveness that God had offered him? Was it possible?

Just do today what you must, came to him. *Tomorrow will take care of itself.* Not an audible voice. He almost chuckled, thinking about how often God seemed to speak to him with Giovanni's voice, or at least the memory of his voice. He fought a sudden longing to return to the fisherman's cabin on the rocky Maine coast, to sit in the company of Giovanni and Cara, warm himself by their fire, and soak in the peace of their presence. And God's.

He reached for the walking stick, and stood, wincing as the familiar pain shot through his back and down one leg.

"I could use that Giovanni voice in my head a little more often," he muttered with a half-grin, talking more to God than to himself. "That's the honest truth." He stoked the fire, added a few pieces of wood, and then put on the skillet.

Sister Amanda had insisted on giving them fresh supplies the day before. By the time Greyson woke, Hosea had two thick slices of ham frying in the iron skillet.

His friend stretched and scratched his head. "I could get used to this kind of food."

"You'll likely be eating like this every morning if Sister Amanda has her way. Something tells me that life for the apostles' wives might be easier than for ordinary Saints."

"Brother Hyrum's got some thirty-four or thirty-five wives. How can he feed that many?" He stood and scratched again, and then went off into the brush to relieve himself. He came back chuckling. "Can you imagine having that many wives nagging at you at the same time?"

Hosea laughed. "One was plenty for me, thank you."

Greyson sobered. "I know this is hard for you . . . traveling alone to catch up with her. Sure I can't talk you into coming back with me?"

He shook his head. "I came close to changing my mind during the night. But in the end, I know it's the right thing to do—to carry on, I mean. And the faster, the better."

Frowning, Greyson headed to the nearby creek, stooped, and splashed water on his face. When he turned back, his mouth was set in a grim line. "For weeks you've been telling me your love for Enid is so great that no matter what she's done, you'll follow her to the ends of the earth and try to win her back."

"I still feel the same way."

"I saw your face yesterday. I know what the news did to you." He sat down on a log near the fire. "You sure you want to be alone?"

"What if the Saints won't let you join them?" Hosea said. "Have you thought about that? If they find out your reason for joining them is to write about them, I doubt you'll be welcome." He raised his eyebrows. "Not sure it's a good idea to be in their company."

They both laughed. Hosea went on. "I know the news rocked me off my heels, but these Saints are making a sham of real marriage. Enid thinks I'm dead. She's been pulled into a religion built by a man, not God. She's been blinded—I owe her the truth." He shook his head. "It's the least I can do after what I've put her through."

Hosea cracked some eggs into the iron skillet, flipped them a few times, and then scraped the ham and eggs into two metal dishes. He handed one to Greyson.

"It's going to be hard to leave you, my friend," Greyson said as he shoveled the food into his mouth. He grinned. "Though you can be assured I'll miss MacDuff more than I will you."

On cue, MacDuff rolled back his lips, showed his large yellowed teeth, and snorted. Greyson shot a grin at Hosea. "If you ever need me, you'll know where to find me."

"Traveling west with hundreds of Saints . . ." Hosea said, picturing the wagon train. "I think you'll be easy to spot."

They finished their breakfasts, then shook hands. "We'll meet up in the place they call Zion. I am looking forward to stirring things up a bit with you in the kingdom of the Saints."

"It'll be a pleasure." Greyson looked worried. "You take care now."

"I started this journey knowing the dangers I'd be in. Traveling alone, I mean. Never thought I'd meet up with a traveling companion who turned out to be a good friend. In my book, I'm money ahead."

Greyson kicked the ground with his boot, following the action with his eyes. "I'm not one to voice my religious views, my thoughts about God . . ."

"I know, my friend—though you certainly have no trouble voicing your opinions about everything else on God's green earth." He chuckled.

"This is more, well, personal. Might even seem unmanly to speak of."

Hosea laughed again. "Unmanly?"

"Before meeting up with you I thought religion was for mothers to teach their little children, for women to talk about amongst themselves, or for circuit preachers to thunder from the pulpit—'fire and brimstone will be upon your head if you displease your Maker!' That sort of thing."

"That doesn't seem unmanly."

"In my way of thinking, it is. Men hiding behind fiery words instead of living what Jesus Christ taught—what you've told me about, what you've lived since I met up with you. I've watched you live what you believe—a life of simplicity and love, of forgiving even the most wicked of offenders. The worst betrayals.

"I've never heard anyone talk to God the way you do. It's like he's sitting beside you at the fire. Or riding beside you on the trail. You tell him when you're mad as hell, you tell him when you think he's painted a beautiful sunset, you tell him how you agonize over those you care about. You talk to him like he's listening. Like he cares.

"Your kind of religion isn't the same. I don't even know if you can call it religion—compared to what I've heard all my life. It's living something from the inside out, rather than letting it be something you put on like a coat."

Hosea stepped closer. He knew he and his friend shared a belief in God, but this was the most Greyson had said about his feelings.

Greyson laughed suddenly. "How'd I get into all that? What I'm trying to say is"—he looked up and met Hosea's gaze—"though I'm not one to pray out loud, especially in front of other people, or talk to God the way you do . . ."

Hosea chuckled and finished for him, " . . . you'll talk to God about me. You'll pray for me."

Greyson gave him a half-grin. "Guess I wasn't too concise— but, yes, that's what I was trying to say." He turned back to the Appaloosa, stepped into the stirrup, and swung his leg over the saddle. He looked at MacDuff. "You take care of my friend now, you hear?"

MacDuff gave him another big-lipped smile.

Greyson raised his eyebrows, adjusted his hat, and nodded toward Hosea. "Don't forget Nineveh." He turned his horse and headed toward the trail. "Don't let anything or anyone delay you," he called over his shoulder. "Remember the great fish . . . or whatever it was that started you on your quest. God's got his hand on you."

Hosea sat in the silence of the morning, staring after his friend. The sun rose behind the stand of trees, and a light breeze rattled the leaves. He bowed his head and tried to pray, but the words wouldn't come.

He'd put up a good front with Greyson and felt almost embarrassed by what his friend saw in him. But in truth, he was sick at heart. He talked about forgiveness, mercy, and love. What if, when all was said and done, he couldn't do what he knew God required of him?

From behind the dark edges of his mind came a prayer that Giovanni had taught him as he dealt with his pain, both flesh and bone and spirit:

"Lord Jesus Christ, you are for me medicine when I am sick; you are my strength when I need help; you are life itself when I fear death; you are the way when I long for heaven; you are light when all is dark; you are my food when I need nourishment."

Giovanni had said it was written by Ambrose, Bishop of Milan, who died in the fourth century. How could someone who lived so long ago have written a prayer that spoke to Hosea's heart this day, hundreds of years later?

A breeze rustled the sycamore leaves, and somewhere a robin sang. He stared upward in wonder. Could it be that prayers never died? Never disappeared? He found it difficult to let such a thought seep into his brain. A living, breathing prayer as vibrant today as it was nearly fifteen hundred years before. . .

He was still pondering the idea when a different kind of rustling caught his attention.

MacDuff snorted nervously and turned toward the sound. It came from several yards upstream. Hosea followed the horse's gaze.

There, as still as statues, stood three Indian braves, bronze chests gleaming in the early morning sun. Their spears told him this wasn't a social call.

Before he could reach for his walking stick and ease his pain-wracked body to standing, they had swiftly, silently, surrounded him.

THIRTEEN

Salt Lake Valley
Spring 1848

Standing on the wide front porch of the new farmhouse, Bronwyn swallowed her irritation as Enid rode up on a high-stepping gray. The horse had been a gift from the prophet as a thank-you for the help she'd given so many families, caring for their animals and teaching new ranchers proper care for their stock in this new, mostly arid land.

The only finer mount in the entire valley was Brigham's gleaming coal-black stallion. Enid called the mare Empress and it seemed, at least in Bronwyn's eyes, that Enid herself wanted to live up to the title.

Since the MacKays' arrival in the valley only a few months ago, much of Gabe's time had been spent with the prophet overseeing the building of the city. His experience with designing ships quickly adapted once again to the new challenge. Brother

Brigham wanted this city, the crown jewel of all Mormon settlements, completed in record time, every street laid out with attention to the minutest detail, the temple square at its center.

They spent the winter and early spring drawing out the plans, and as soon as the ground thawed, the building began.

Brigham's first concern was that families and children have shelter as quickly as possible. In a carefully organized effort, families joined each other to help with house and barn raisings, most often making parties of hard work. The women planted gardens with seeds and seedlings brought from Nauvoo, cooked, and canned food while the men did the building.

The MacKay farmhouse on a prime piece of property was one of the first finished, another gift from the prophet who'd carried out his promise to adopt Gabe as his spiritual son. The large barn went up the same day, thanks to the help of neighbors, quickly followed by an expansive fence to pen their cattle and a coop for their chickens.

Enid dismounted Empress and hurried up the porch steps toward Bronwyn. "Is Gabe here?" Inside the children were making such a playtime racket, she could barely hear Enid's words.

"He left with Brother Foley early this morning. He didn't say where he was headed."

"He promised to go with me when they raise our town house walls. The men arrived at sunup, everything is in place—but he needs to be there to oversee the construction."

"I'm sure they can manage without him. He's given them written instructions, hasn't he?"

"Of course."

Just then, Mary Rose stepped outside and greeted Enid. Bronwyn admired the way she hid her feelings. She did a better job of it than Bronwyn did. They had discussed this turn of events often, the elegant house in town that Enid had talked Gabe into building for her. She said it was because of her work in the new science of veterinary medicine that she needed a place to work on animals. The whole setup irked Bronwyn to no end, but Mary Rose seemed completely at peace with it.

"Is there a problem with Gabe's instructions?"

"Not at all." She frowned. "It's just that I know this home is extremely important to him and he wants it done right. He's said as much many times." She gave them a slightly condescending smile. "He will be spending most of his time there, I'm sure he told you."

"He hasn't mentioned it," Mary Rose said. Her smiled cracked a little as she spoke. "Though he's devoted to this family. His children are more important than any building, whether it be farmhouse, town house, or temple. I'm certain he'll be as attentive as ever to them."

Enid let out an impatient sigh and started back down the stairs. "I must get back. Our new buggy is arriving this afternoon, and I must see to its proper placement in the livery."

"Dear . . . ?" Cordelia called out inside the doorway. Enid turned as Cordelia stepped outside. She held a speckled metal pot in her hands. "I fixed up some fried chicken for you to give to the men helping you build that fancy house. I figured you probably didn't have time."

Bronwyn could see the struggle in Enid's expression. She didn't want to be bothered, but it was the expected thing to do at a house raising. Finally, she said, "Thank you. I'm not much of a cook, you know."

"I know," Cordelia said. "You just tell those menfolk that you fried this up early this morning before you got to your other chores."

Enid smiled. "Well, thank you," she said with less irritation in her expression. "I appreciate it."

"Gabe will appreciate too," Cordelia said, her eyes twinkling. Holding the pan, she walked partway down the steps. Mary

Rose and Bronwyn exchanged glances, wondering what she was up to.

"And when you get settled in," Cordelia continued, "we expect a tour. I ran into Sister Bessie at the mercantile the other day, and she was telling me how you plan to fill your town house up with fancy furniture. She told me you want to put all the rest of us to shame. She supposed you meant Mary Rose and Bronwyn. But, I said as fast as I could get the words out—and loud too, in case anyone else was listening—that you wouldn't do such a thing." She shook her head. "I didn't believe it for a minute."

Enid's cheeks turned pink and swallowed hard. "Well, thank you for the chicken. I'm sure the workers will enjoy it."

"I'm sure they will, dear," Cordelia said, trotting down the remaining steps. "I want you to take every bit of the credit for it. And you make sure to have a bit yourself."

Enid nodded, mounted, and waited as Cordelia handed her the metal pot.

Moments later, Enid, carefully holding the pot in front of her, made her way back down the road that led to town.

"That was a lovely thing to do," Mary Rose said as Cordelia made her way back up the steps.

"It brought me great pleasure to do it for her," Cordelia said. "Truly." She started back into the house and then turned. "She seems to like cayenne, so I used it instead of salt for the flavoring." She was still chuckling as she headed back to the kitchen.

Bronwyn's eyebrows shot up. "I wouldn't want to be there when the workers take their first bite." They both laughed.

Bronwyn's thoughts turned to the town house. She'd tried to rein in her emotions from the first day it was mentioned. It seemed that everything Enid wanted, Enid got. And always, it was better than that of hers or Mary Rose's. She let out a pent up sigh.

Mary Rose seemed to read her thoughts. She reached for Bronwyn's hand. "I wouldn't trade this rambling farmhouse for anything in the world. We're surrounded by our children, you and Cordelia are my dearest friends, and now we've managed to get Enid out of our hair."

"*We* managed . . . ?"

This time it was Mary Rose's eyes that twinkled. "Enid thinks she talked Gabe into the new arrangement. I admit she came up with the reasons, but Gabe didn't want to separate the family . . ."

" . . . until you convinced him."

"For the sake of peace and quiet, I told him it would be best for us all."

Bronwyn squeezed her friend's hand before letting go. "You never cease to . . ."

Mary Rose quirked a brow. "To . . . ?"

" . . . astonish me."

Still smiling, Bronwyn entered the house, Mary Rose following. "I think we need to hide that cayenne," Bronwyn said.

"Before Cordelia strikes again."

Even as she laughed, Bronwyn felt a deepening sense of foreboding. It kept her awake at night, it invaded her thoughts during the day. She didn't speak to anyone, not even Mary Rose or Cordelia, about it.

Was it this great valley, their promised land, with its stark beauty, a place of danger? Or was it the sense that she had entered a place where escape was not possible?

The following Sunday, at the meetinghouse, the strange sense overtook her again, this time adding a sense of suffocation. As Brother Foley stepped to the front of the meetinghouse, her heart pounded so hard she felt certain those in the rows around her could surely hear it.

She glanced at Mary Rose who, though listening to Brother Foley with rapt attention, had a complexion the hue of bleached linen. She caught Bronwyn's glance and reached for her gloved hand, squeezing it in sisterly understanding.

On the far side of Mary Rose, Enid sat straight-backed, biting her bottom lip. Her expression was staid, though two bright pink spots had appeared in her cheeks.

"Blood atonement," Brother Foley thundered. "It is important that you understand this new teaching. Already, we have enemies who would harm us. The Mexican-American war is over, and we are once again living under control of the United States government. President James Polk has not said he will protect us; neither has he said he will not. His spies are among us. Pretending to be Saints. When in truth they are vipers spouting poisonous words about our life, spouting lies that are carried across the country only to be enhanced with still more lies and innuendos."

Bronwyn heard Mary Rose's sharp intake breath as the head of Brother Brigham's private police force stepped to one side of the podium and, with piercing eyes, scanned the families sitting before him. He had a fierce look to him: bald on top with a fringe of hair that hung below his shoulders, a well trimmed beard, and small eyes that disappeared into his eyebrows.

The room was full—women on one side, men on the other—perhaps a hundred altogether. He had no difficulty commanding the attention of all, even the children. Perhaps that's why Brother Brigham often chose him to deliver dire news.

A Franklin stove radiated a glowing warmth in the back of the room. Even so, the Saints huddled close together, blankets on their laps and coats around their shoulders. As they breathed, white puffs appeared before their faces in the frosty air.

The winter had been harsh, and while the days were lengthening into spring, a foot of fresh snow covered the ground. Though Brigham had put each new wave of immigrants to work immediately, building houses and businesses and irrigation canals, work had ground to a halt during the stormy winter. More houses were needed, and quickly.

"Blood atonement," he thundered again. "My friends, it's time we get used to the idea that though we are a peaceable people and wish others no harm, we must go beyond an eye for an eye, a tooth for a tooth." He let his gaze move across the congregation, and it seemed he lingered too long on Bronwyn's face. She felt her cheeks redden with embarrassment. Could he guess her feelings? Know her heart was even now turning against the teachings of the prophet?

Bronwyn wanted to grab her children and run. She fought a war within herself to keep still, to keep herself poised with an agreeable comportment. No one must guess her inner thoughts. It was dangerous before the pronouncement of blood atonement; now, it was far more so. For herself. For her children. For them all.

She calmed herself, trying to find something good in his words. Everyone knew that Brother Foley liked to thunder on about persecution, both real and imagined. Wouldn't it be wiser to focus on the good things God's chosen people were accomplishing? And on the building of the city that lay ahead?

Those thoughts were wiser than any plans she dreamed of for escape. She swallowed hard, sat back in her chair, and willed her heart to slow to a natural rhythm.

Besides, they were thousands of miles away from those who wished them harm, weren't they? Her heart started to race again as she looked up and down the row of MacKays.

They took up an entire row, except for Gabe who sat with the men, and Cordelia who sat in the front row so she could better hear. Bronwyn held Joey on her lap, snuggling him close to keep him warm, and Mary Rose held Spence, who slept on her shoulder. Enid had her arm around Little Grace, who at seven thought the sun rose and set on Mother Enid, who she was sure talked to horses—and even better, sure they talked back. She said at least a dozen times each day that she wanted to be just like Mother Enid when she grew up and pestered her constantly about accompanying Enid when she visited the outlying farms to care for sick and injured animals.

The twins, Pearl and Ruby, now almost twelve, sat on the other side of Mary Rose. They were as lively as ever, but their hearts always seemed to hold a deep sadness, especially when they recounted memories of the past.

First their parents disappeared, now Coal was gone too. It had been so many years since they'd seen them, the twins didn't remember much about their mother and father, missionaries in the Sandwich Islands; but they loved their brother, and though he'd been gone for over a year, they talked about him constantly.

Not knowing what happened to him was the hardest to bear. Every day, Bronwyn wondered if he was dead or alive, if he had run for his life once he discovered what happened to Sarah, or if he had been captured by the Dakota.

After Coal's disappearance, Gabe and the other men spent three days combing sand hills and tall prairie grasses for miles in every direction out of Winter Quarters, even visiting the Dakota village with gifts to trade for him. The Dakota, through an interpreter, said they knew nothing about such a boy. They took the gifts anyway.

Gabe left with Brother Brigham a few days later, as planned, and when he returned with the news that they'd found the new Zion, it seemed that spending time with Enid, his third wife, was his only concern. Not searching for his son.

Bronwyn leaned back to listen to Brother Foley's rants about the coming end of the world and the persecution of God's chosen ones in the days to come. He predicted that the United States government would rise up against the Saints and attempt to run them out of their new land.

"We will fight back!" He raised his fist in the air. "No one will ever come up against us again!" He stepped back up to the plat-form. "Blood atonement," he said, his voice no more than a hoarse whisper. "Remember the words, for you will hear them again in the months and years to come.

"Brother Brigham has received a revelation from the Lord about the practice and has gone to him again and again, pleading on his knees to make certain he understood without error.

"You may ask what blood atonement means . . ."

Several members of the congregation looked at each other in fear. Worried whispers rose from several, though not loud enough for Brother Foley to hear. Others nodded in support, even vigor-ous support.

"Blood atonement means that our enemies must be killed if they are to receive eternal life."

Bronwyn's breath caught in her throat. She glanced at Mary Rose who had turned even paler. Enid frowned and put her arm around Little Grace, scooting her closer as if trying to protect her from Brother Foley's words.

"You see, sisters and brothers, anyone who comes against us, any apostate who turns away from God's only true church, must have his—or her—blood spilled." He paused dramatically. "It is the way of the Lord. We may not understand it in full now, but as the rev-elation becomes clear to the prophet, he will make it known to us." He raised his fist. "Let no man come against us. Retribution will be swift and sure. This is our land. God gave it to us as surely as he gave the Garden of Eden to Adam and Eve. We will never be driven from the land God has given us . . . never again."

"Now let us have a reading of the Psalms, followed by hymn number eighteen."

The Psalms were read and then the congregation stood to sing,

Ere long the vail will rend in twain,
The King descend with all his train;

The earth shall shake with awful fright,
And all creation feel his might.

Bronwyn shivered as she sang the mournful words. *Awful fright?* Brother Joseph once spoke of them as a joyous people. How long ago that seemed. She scanned the congregation, taking in the fearful faces around her. She and Mary Rose still talked of escape. They didn't know how or when, but still they spoke of being ready when the time was right.

An emotion that had simmered somewhere deep inside for a long time now bubbled fiercely to the surface. *Blood atonement?* It was an excuse to kill. She sat back, willing her breath to even out, her heart to stop its racing.

Even little Joey looked up at her with a frown. She hoped it was because of her noisy, quick intakes of air, not from wonder or, worse, from this teaching.

Children were present. Old women and men. Good, honest, hardworking people who loved their God and their families. What had they to do with such an edict? Did the church leaders want to frighten them into submission, make sure they didn't go against the teachings of Joseph and Brigham?

She felt her face go red and bit her lips together to keep from speaking out.

Blood atonement? How could such a thing be of God?

Murmurs rose around her. Several people whispered to each other behind gloved hands. She glanced across the aisle to see if Gabe looked disturbed. But he sat still and staid, looking unperturbed.

If she were a good Saint, she supposed she would ask herself completely rational questions based on the belief that the prophet's messages from God were infallible. She would wonder, as she was certain other truly good Saints did, how seriously and how soon such punishment would be carried out. If it were truly of

God, and for the eternal salvation of their enemies, shouldn't one be inclined to go along with it? It was for the greater good.

But she felt anything but rational.

Gabe had just stepped into the aisle when Brother Foley strode over and pulled him away from the other men around him. "Could I have a word with you?"

Gabe nodded. "Of course."

"You have been a nominal member of the Danites for some months now."

"That's true."

"But I've noticed that you've missed many of our meetings."

"Brother Brigham has me busy with the building plans for the new temple." He smiled. "It's not been intentional, believe me. It's just that there are only so many hours in the day. We're trying to prepare the field for planting—at least we were before the storm hit."

"I understand. But you also have your duty to God and to the church. You need to be with us, brother, especially now."

"Brother Brigham told me his thoughts about this some time ago—and his need for prayer before telling his people. I was surprised that you told all to the congregation. Perhaps this should have been well rehearsed with the priesthood first."

Brother Foley narrowed his small eyes. "Are you criticizing me?"

Gabe hesitated before answering. Of course he was, but did he want to get into it with this fiery-tempered man? "I doubt that you would speak of such a serious matter without discretion—or direction from the prophet. But, surely you realize the terror it might strike in the hearts of our families, our wives and children. I daresay, I would have spoken to the men privately first."

Foley regarded him for a moment. "You are required to become a more active member of the Danites. Brigham has ordained that as well."

"He understands my dilemma. He wants the temple design completed so work can begin as soon as the weather permits. Design is my gift, and he believes I'm using my gift well. I doubt that he would require such a sacrifice of my time."

"The announcement today was not simply a general announcement," Brother Foley said.

"What do you mean?"

He lowered his voice. "I am putting together a list of suspicious people. Hundreds of people have joined us, with thousands more expected to arrive during the summer. We must root out those who aren't with us. We must act quickly." He handed Gabe a folded piece of paper. "Put this in a safe place. It is a list of those you will be responsible for watching. Each member will be given a similar list. It's the first of those to come. Keep them in a safe place."

Not bothering to unfold the paper, Gabe stared at the man, dumbfounded. "I'm sorry. I don't believe I heard you correctly. "

Foley smiled and slapped Gabe on the back. "You heard me, Brother. Loud and clear. All of us must do what's necessary to protect our way of life." He dropped his voice. "This is not an easy thing for any of us. But we must remember what has been done to us, done to our wives and innocent little children in the past. Look at this new teaching as a means of protection, and it will be easier to understand."

Staring after him, Gabe absently tucked the paper in his pocket and headed for the door to find his family.

FOURTEEN

Bronwyn and Mary Rose waited until the children had fallen asleep and then, with Cordelia, sat down near the fireplace to discuss Brother Foley's words about blood atonement. Cordelia's chair creaked as she rocked, and her eyes snapped even before the tale was finished. "I wish I'd been braver," she said. "I would've stood right up and told him what I thought then and there. They can come after me to slit my throat if they want." She glanced at the rifle hanging above the door. "I'd show them a thing or two."

Mary Rose leaned forward. "I don't think they're talking about us. He said something about there being spies among us. I heard a rumor that someone is sending reports to a newspaper in the east about our ways, especially about our practice of plural marriage."

Cordelia laughed. "Well, that should keep folks in the States yapping about us for quite some time." Her look said she rather enjoyed the prospect.

Mary Rose sat forward and lowered her voice "What do you think about leaving, now?"

Bronwyn's heart raced. They had talked about it before, but never had she seen the other two women look so serious. Or so scared.

"I think we need to go before this blood atonement business is actually carried out," Mary Rose said. "And if by some miracle Coal does follow us here, we need to somehow leave word for him. I can't imagine how it would be for him to travel across the country in the dangerous conditions we know all too well only to find us gone without a trace." She leaned forward. "Even at the risk of someone else getting hold of the information, we must leave word with a person we trust."

"That's of utmost importance," Bronwyn said. "Leaving is one thing. Seeing to the safety of us all—including Coal—is quite another."

Cordelia frowned,. "But who can we trust?" She folded her hands and sat back in her rocker. "Perhaps one of us should stay, just in case."

"We won't leave anyone behind," Bronwyn said. "Not for a minute. We'll find a way to leave word. We'll just need to ponder the question while we make our plans."

"And pray," Cordelia said. "Especially that."

"You'll have to be in charge of that part of our plan," Bronwyn said with a laugh. "My prayers never seem to get past the top of my head."

"They don't need to, child," Cordelia said, quietly. "God reads them in your heart—just like he reads them in Mary Rose's journal."

Both women looked at Cordelia with surprise. She often spoke of her communion with God, One who seemed different than that spoken of in the meetinghouse or by Gabe when he intoned blessings for them all. Hers was a friend, someone who knew her every thought, good and bad, and loved her anyway. But this was the first time Bronwyn could remember Cordelia speaking of Mary Rose's poetry and writings being something that God might pay attention to, might consider prayers.

"Groaning of the heart that can't even be put into words," Cordelia said as if reading Bronwyn's thoughts. "That's what the Good Book says, that's what he sees in us. Those are the best kind of prayers, the most honest and deep. The Book also says he keeps our tears in a bottle. That tells me he knows our trials, our heartaches and sorrows, better than even we do. Don't ever say your prayers aren't heard. They are. Every last one."

For a few minutes no one said anything. Cordelia's words settled like a comforter, soft and warm upon them. The fire crackled and popped, and Mary Rose stood to stoke it. She put on another piece of wood and sparks flew up the chimney. Then she turned and stood with her back to the fireplace as the conversation continued.

"One thing for certain, we have much planning to do, and that may take some time," Bronwyn said. " We're closer to California than to the east coast. There's the southern route, the Old Spanish Trail that would take us into the southern part of California. Wagon companies often travel that way, but we'll be in Mormon country all the way to Mountain Meadows. We run the risk of being found out, caught, tried for apostasy." She drew a deep breath.

"Let's make a plan, tell no one, then we'll watch for a wagon company to join," Mary Rose said. "We'll blend in, plus if we need help along the way, broken axels or wheels, we'll have the men in the train to help out."

"Pshaw," Cordelia said. "We're three strong women and five feisty girls. Ruby and Pearl are almost grown. They'll be women soon with strong constitutions. We don't need menfolk. We can make it on our own."

"I hear you have to hoist your wagon up treacherous passes with rope pulleys," Mary Rose said.

"What about Enid?" Bronwyn searched Mary Rose's face and then Cornelia's. "Should she be in on this?"

"Can we trust her, that's the question?" Cordelia sat back and rocked, her brow furrowed. "I would like to think so, but . . ."

"She saved my life with that cayenne concoction," Mary Rose said. "Her heart is good when you get past the blustery surface."

"She may never trust us again, especially to season her chicken," Cordelia said with a grin.

"She loves Gabe," Bronwyn said. "Because of her devotion to him, she might tell him our plans."

"She doesn't love him," Cordelia said. "I would stake my life on that." She shrugged at their expressions. "I thought you two knew that. I think she had fairytale dreams of him being her first love, and then when her husband died, she needed someone to love her and hightailed it across the country to find him. She's filled with guilt from the secrets she kept from them both— What was her husband's name?"

"Hosea," Mary Rose said.

"The captain of our ship," Bronwyn added, "and a good, good man. His death was such a tragedy . . ."

Mary Rose and Bronwyn exchanged glances, and then Bronwyn said, "Do you think Gabe loves her?" Mary Rose turned to stare into the flickering flames in the fireplace. Even her profile showed a lingering sadness. She couldn't help the twist of her own heart. Too often Gabe occupied her thoughts, bringing a mix of guilt and shame. . .

"He felt an obligation, perhaps, to her because of their past, and because she'd come so far to find him. And then there's the prophet's unrelenting admonition about the hereafter. He practically walked Gabe down the aisle himself to marry Sister Enid."

For a moment, the only sound in the room was the crackling fire and the slow, steady ticking of pendulum on the mantel.

"The other thing is this," Cordelia said, her gaze on Mary Rose. "He's never quite gotten over his love for you."

Mary Rose turned to the older woman, her eyes brimming. "It's too late," she whispered. "Whether he has or hasn't, it's too late for us."

FIFTEEN

Gabe sat with Enid on a settee in front of the fire in the town house they'd moved into only weeks before. Her conversation was lively, but as happened so often, his mind drifted to other topics. Some nights it was the building of the temple, ideas for the layout of the city, his growing friendship with Brother Brigham, or most often, how much he missed his family, especially the children. Truth be told, sometimes he ached for a loving word from Mary Rose. Or the coquettish way Bronwyn glanced at him from beneath her long lashes. He missed their laughter and chatter when talking with Cordelia. The ranch home was full of light it seemed, light and laughter and song.

But those weren't the thoughts whirling through his mind tonight. No, tonight his thoughts had zeroed in on another disturbing conversation he'd had with Brother Foley. As Enid talked about her plans for the clinic, he remembered another of the lists that Foley handed him from time to time. He'd tucked the latest one in his new desk, without reading it. He wondered about the names that might be included.

Now the folded paper drew his mind like a magnet. But he said nothing to Enid. He considered the premonition he had about this one. There had been something dark in Brother Foley's eyes when he handed it to Gabe. Though eager to get to it, he decided to wait until he was alone. Even that was strange. Did he not trust Enid?

He turned to her, pretending to give her his full attention as she went into detail about the clinic. He'd known her since they were children. They'd made love when they were teenagers. She'd borne his child . . . and then kept it a secret from him. And from her husband, the best friend he'd ever had. That secret had destroyed their friendship. Perhaps, it had also caused her husband's death.

Secrets. It seemed she was good at keeping them. Still, he decided to wait.

"Are you all right?" Enid touched his cheek with gentle and loving fingers. "You look pale, my darling."

He caught her hand in his, drew her palm to his lips, and kissed it. "I just have a lot on my mind."

She gave him a sweet smile. "I know something that will turn your thoughts in an entirely different direction." She blushed and laughed lightly. "Though maybe my words are too bold for a proper lady to speak."

He laughed with her. "You've always been a lady," he said, "even when riding along the ocean's edge barefoot with your hair streaming wild and free. Even then you were a lady."

She looked pleased that he remembered. "We always did love each other, didn't we?" she said, almost childlike.

He kissed her hand again. "We did. And no one can take that away from us."

"Why should they try?" She frowned. "Do you know something I don't?"

He pulled her into an embrace. "It was a figure of speech, that's all." He stroked her lovely hair, and said, "Go on up to bed. I'll be there soon. I have some business to attend to first."

She went to the stairs, turned and looked back at him. "Sometimes it seems . . ." She halted, frowning. "It seems as though I don't have all of you. I don't have all your heart, even though I was your first love."

You don't have all of my heart, he wanted to say. You can't have all of my heart. You knew that when we married. You are my third wife, even though you try to be first. You will never be. It is our way. When you married me, you agreed to our way of living.

But he said none of what he felt. Instead, he smiled. "You were indeed my first love. You have my love now. That will have to be enough."

She read between the lines. He could see it in her face. With her lips pressed together, Enid turned with a slight toss of the head, and made her way up the dark stairs, holding the kerosene oil lamp in front of her.

As soon as Enid had gone, Gabe went to the mahogany Chippendale-style desk that Brother Chamberlain had delivered the previous day. The matching chair was exquisite and more comfortable than it looked. Enid had struck up a friendship with the cabinetmaker on the trek from Winter Quarters and insisted that he make the desk and chair as a wedding gift to Gabe once his cabinet shop was completed. It was to be followed by six more chairs and a dining table. She said all this would enhance his standing in the community, especially within the hierarchy of the Church.

He hadn't realized until now how much he missed the ranch house, its plain furnishings and, most of all, its occupants.

He unlocked the side drawer and drew out the paper. He unfolded it, and held it close to the candlelight. His gaze landed on the first name, and his stomach lurched as though he'd been struck.

SIXTEEN

I know those two are up to something, Gabe. They hush their voices when I enter the room—on those rare occasions that I'm actually invited to be in the same house, that is." Enid gave a bitter laugh. "Which is very seldom. Not that I mind." But of course Gabe knew she did.

Working at his desk, Gabe returned his pen to the inkwell and settled back in his chair. "I'm sure it's nothing nefarious, if that's what you're worried about." He turned back to his plans for Temple Square, dipped his pen in the inkwell, and continued writing. The list weighed on his mind, but Brigham was expecting the latest addition to his plans by this afternoon. He would think about the disturbing implications later. It was difficult enough to try to concentrate with Enid vying for his attention.

"Are you sure you wouldn't like to go with me?" She stood and went to the window, pulled the floor-length lace curtain back, and peered out at Brigham's house across the street. "It's a beautiful day. I can pack a lunch, and we can stop on the way back from the Websters'. My time there shouldn't take long. I just need to check on the purple calf that was born with two heads."

Gabe grunted something unintelligible as he went back to the plans for the temple. "You go ahead, dear. I need to finish this."

"You didn't hear a word I said, did you?"

He chuckled and glanced up again. "About the purple calf? Or the two heads the poor thing must stumble around with for the rest of its life?"

Her lower lip protruded. It was an expression he never thought he'd see on Enid's face. Strength, yes. Stubbornness, yes. Sorrow, maybe. But petulance? Never.

"I'm being nettlesome, aren't I?"

"I have been busy lately. I know you may feel ignored."

"I miss you." She walked over to him and laid a hand on his shoulder. "You've been spending a lot of time at the other house."

"They need me too." He pulled her down to his lap and circled his arm around her waist. "You knew what you were getting into when you agreed to marry me." He lifted her hand and kissed it tenderly. "Besides, I shouldn't be away from the children too long. I don't want them growing up thinking they don't have a father."

The word "children" fell like a stone between them. Enid stood and went to the window again, turning her back to Gabe. "Do you blame me?"

"What do you mean?"

"Because there are no children here. I know you expected me to be with child by now. Truly, I thought I would be too. I so hoped that . . ." Images of the baby she lost so many years ago came back to her. The pain, the blood, the shame, the hope that it would bring Gabe back to her . . . it had been his baby too. Only he hadn't known.

He stood and came over to her. Pulling her close, he said, "I know what you're thinking, but we can't allow our sin to make us feel that God is punishing us for what happened."

She pulled back and stared up at him. "Sin? Punishment? I wasn't thinking that at all. I'm concerned I might not be able to have children because of what it did to my body." She blushed, talking about such things, but it didn't stop her from barreling on. "Hosea and I tried, as you know"—her cheeks flamed again—"and something prevented me from conceiving. I always thought it was because of . . . our baby."

Tears stung her eyes, but she didn't want to weep in front of Gabe. His other wives might cry, but she was the strong one, the one he could depend on. She pushed the pain back, the memories of the tiny, perfectly formed baby that died. "Don't ever mention sin and guilt to me again," she said, her voice steely.

"I didn't mention guilt."

"Yes, you did."

He shook his head.

She thought about it for a moment, and then said, "Maybe you didn't, but it's what you meant." Her tone grew louder. "'Guilt' is right up there with 'sin' and 'punishment' in your religious lexicon. And they all point to me."

He turned pale but said nothing, and he didn't try to stop her when she ran for the door, pushed her way out, and headed to the stable at the rear of the house. Within minutes, she mounted Empress, the big roan she favored, and took off like the wind.

Gabe agonized over the edict he had received from Brother Foley. He wondered if Brigham knew of it. He dropped his head into his hands, thinking of the document he was about to sign.

Did he have a choice?

Would he be run out of the priesthood if he refused?

He read the edict again, staring hard at the twins' names and the name of the man he would pledge them to in marriage. Together, the day they turned fourteen, they would go to him, one of the eldest apostles in the Church, a man who seemed to be gathering brides, present and future, the youngest and prettiest, like pearls on a string.

His eyes blurred, and he drew out his handkerchief and rubbed them dry. Then he lifted his pen from the inkwell.

SEVENTEEN

Sitting at her desk in her upstairs bedroom, Mary Rose reached for her journal and leafed through the pages, stopping at an entry made just days after the wagon company left Nauvoo.

> *On the trail out of Nauvoo*
> *February 18, 1846*
>
> *God answers sharp and sudden on some prayers,*
> *And thrusts the thing we have prayed for in our*
>   *face,*
> *A gauntlet with a gift in it.*
>
> — *Elizabeth B. B.*

She smiled, remembering the night she penned the quotation. It had been an exceptionally trying day, physically and emotionally. Enid shouted commands to Mary Rose and Bronwyn as though she, not Gabe, were captain of the wagon train. That night Mary Rose had prayed for patience, hoping that God would somehow muzzle the woman's mouth. But instead, it seemed the very thing she prayed for had been thrust in her face—in the form of Enid Livingstone, who let it be known to neighbors, friends, and anyone else who would listen that she was to become Gabe's third wife. Not only that, but move up to the position of first wife. Mary Rose sighed, remembering her reaction. Seething was too kind a word.

Maybe God had answered her prayer. Maybe she was mellowing. Whatever it was, she was actually beginning to warm toward Enid, and to understand her better.

She bent closer to the journal and began to read. . .

> We made only two miles today, walking miles, not riding miles, through drifts of knee-deep snow. The youngest rode in the wagon with Cordelia. Coal and the twins climbed in and jumped out making snow angels and snowmen until Enid, who seems not to have the patience she needs with children, got after them and said she didn't want to hear a peep out of them for the rest of the day. That's like telling the sun not to shine. We are all too weary to sit her down and tell her how she might be better accepted by us all.
>
> Love. Respect. Humor. Acceptance. If she would but act on those four little words and extend some good will to all, she might find life easier. But with her airs and ways, I don't think we'll see much change. She's set her cap for Gabe, and that's all that matters.
>
> In spite of her rigid ways, the children are taking to her quite well. Little Grace loves her most of all. I think it's because she has a way with horses that seems almost magical. Bronwyn says nothing about

her daughter's attachment to Enid, but I can tell she is bothered by it.

Tomorrow, Gabe tells us, we will drop in elevation. It will be difficult for the wagons and wagoneers, but we will see milder weather soon.

We are hungry and cold, but I worry more about the children than I do about the adults in the family.

Mary Rose stood and walked to the window, gazed out at the wide sweep of desert, the red, sandy soil, the forested mountains in the background. The ranch was near a seasonal stream, so she and Bronwyn had already planted a vegetable garden. One crop had been harvested, and just two weeks ago they'd planted a second. The seedlings popped through the soil days earlier. For a few minutes, she watched as Bronwyn knelt in front of a row of beets, plucking weeds.

The rumble of an approaching carriage carried on the wind, and Mary Rose looked toward the sound. Gabe, riding in a fancy carriage—no doubt the one Enid spoke of earlier—halted his team in front of the house.

Bronwyn stood when she saw him, and Mary Rose saw her blush. Gabe said a few words and they laughed together, and then he touched her arm as if sharing an intimate thought, turned, and headed up the side-porch steps and into the house.

Bronwyn again knelt in the garden, and it seemed to Mary Rose her cheeks still held high color. Although, it might have been the play of sunset that turned her golden.

Downstairs, Gabe's laughter mixed with that of the children. As the sun began to make its descent, she sat down at the writing desk and lit the kerosene lamp. She dipped her pen in the inkwell and began to write.

Purple Sage Ranch, The Great Salt Lake
April 17, 1848

Girls blush, sometimes, because they are alive,
half wishing they were dead to save the shame.
The sudden blush devours them, neck and brow;
They have drawn too near the fire of life, like gnats,
and flare up bodily, wings and all.
What then? Who's sorry for a gnat or girl?
                                        —Elizabeth B. B.

Bronwyn and Gabe occupy my thoughts far too often. Is it because I love them both? Is it because I see beyond the shell of Gabe's heart and know a great and lonely abyss resides there? I fear that Bronwyn, though still holding herself back from him, will ultimately give in. I warned her once—and she didn't heed my words—that I hoped I could save her from falling in love with him, and he with her, by giving my permission for him to take a third wife, Enid.

Love? Is that what Bronwyn feels? I cannot know for certain. Perhaps my dearest friend, drawn as she is to him, convinced of his desire for her, cannot tell the difference. She has drawn too near the fire, and I fear that she too might flare up bodily, wings and all.

But what will happen once she gives in . . . the same that's happened to me? Love lost. A soul bereft.

I can't help that I still love him. I will tell no one, not even Cordelia, though sometimes I think she knows my heart better than I do. If my dearest friend were anyone else but Bronwyn, I would tell her. I would ask her advice about winning his heart again.

But that is fantasy built on listening to too many fairy tales when I was a child.

As for Gabe, he seems driven by desires for power, for love—or perhaps adoration—from all his wives. But which of us does he truly love? Or is he driven to reach still further and further for things he cannot have because he can't live with himself? Because he can't admit that what he'd led us all into is a sham?

And because he's in too deep to get us safely out.

Or is he aware of the danger we face, every last one of us? And that, like the warning of distant thunder before a storm, the power of those who rule us with God-given authority grows stronger. They bind us with fear, real and imagined.

Whispers of blood atonement echo across this bleak valley and soon will become shouts.

Am I alone in this fear of those who say they want to protect us, who say they want to see us into the highest reaches of heaven, happy on earth, and happier in heaven?

My heart breaks at the thought of harm coming to any, but the greater danger will come if we stay. We make our plans, Cordelia, Bronwyn, and I. We will bide our time, and when it is right we will take with us our beloved Little Grace, Ruby, Pearl, Joey, and Spence.

It's time to flee . . . but will we have the courage?

One thought haunts me . . . can Bronwyn leave Gabe? Can I?

EIGHTEEN

Bronwyn knelt in the vegetable garden just behind the farm-house, plucking weeds and breathing in the scent of the damp soil. It was dusk, and the children were inside the house with Gabe and Mary Rose. Lamplight glowed through the windows, and the music of their laughter floated toward her. Ruby and Pearl had their fiddles out, showing off a song Sister Sarah Riordan taught them the week before: "Three Blind Mice." They had squawked it out at least a dozen times in the last hour, and now Little Grace was begging for them to teach her.

Sister Sarah, who rode out to visit the MacKay farm nearly every day, learned to play the fiddle from Brother Hyrum's newest bride, a pretty young woman with dark ringlets and large violet eyes named Naomi, who'd told everyone she'd played profession-ally in Boston. Sarah whispered to Bronwyn on one of her visits that Naomi spent much time crying in her bedroom and playing the violin at the same time, just like Sarah did the first year she was married to the elderly apostle—only Sarah didn't have a fiddle.

Sarah had lost two babies since marrying the apostle, one by a miscarriage just weeks after conception; the second, stillborn soon after the wagon company rolled out of Winter Quarters.

She seemed to blossom when visiting with the lively MacKays in the evenings, especially in the presence of Mary Rose. Bronwyn suspected it was because Mary Rose knew what it felt like to suffer such a loss. Since the Riordan wagon company arrived in the Salt Lake Valley, Sarah spent more time at the MacKays than she did in the apostle's home.

Mary Rose came out to join Bronwyn in the garden, knelt beside her to help with the weeds, and kept her voice low as she spoke. "Sarah mentioned she heard a wagon company is coming through soon—they're just north of us, coming out of Fort Bridger. Scheduled to come through Salt Lake the week after next."

Bronwyn's heartbeat quickened. "We're not ready." She looked up at Mary Rose. "We have only begun to plan."

"We have enough food," Mary Rose said, "now that Cordelia finished drying the last of the jerky. And clothing for the children. This morning Pearl showed me the little sweaters she just finish knitting for Joey and Spence. She made two others last week."

"No wonder the dear looks so bleary-eyed at breakfast." Bronwyn stood, brushed off her apron, and stretched her back. "But we can't just ride out of here. It's impossible. Too many lives are at stake. As much as I want to go, I think we need to wait. I still think it's too soon. What does Cordelia say about it?"

"She agrees with you. She doesn't think we're ready."

They never spoke of their journey in the daylight hours, especially if the children were near, but waited until the children were in school or in bed. Tonight was the exception.

Bronwyn knelt again and sliced her spade through the soil near a cabbage plant to get at the deep roots of a milkweed. The squawks and screeches of the girls' fiddling inside the house wrapped around her heart and squeezed it tight.

"No matter when it is that we leave, the children will miss Gabe," Mary Rose said, a deep sadness in her voice. "They'll never see him again."

Bronwyn put down the spade and plucked another weed. "We will all miss him." She didn't look up to meet Mary Rose's gaze. "How about you?" she asked. "Will you miss him?"

Mary Rose let out a deep breath. "If I said no, I would be lying." She put down the spade, and rocked back on her heels. "I will always miss the Gabe who fell in love with me and married me. I ache when I see him, thinking of those days. But he's changed. I won't miss the man he's become."

Bronwyn pondered her words . . . and the knowledge that, try as she might to resist the emotion, Gabe still had the ability to make her pulse race. She patted the roots of the cabbage seedling, added a handful of soil, and tamped it down. It seemed several had loosened themselves in the soil since the last weeding.

"What about your feelings for Gabe?" Mary Rose's voice dropped to a whisper. "You said you'd miss him. Do you love him . . . love the man he is now?"

"I don't know who he is now either. I often compare him to Griffin to try to figure it out. Griffin offered me respect and friendship. He didn't talk much, even when we were courting, but he loved to hear me chatter on and on about anything and everything. Hardworking? Aye. And he did it for me. At heart he was a dreamer. Lived somewhere inside himself. Sometimes even when I was with him, I felt lonely. I longed for him to show me his feelings. His love.

"If it had been left to him we never would have left Hanmer. In fact, we never would have met the Mormon missionary, been converted, and crossed the Atlantic on the *Sea Hawk*.

"I got tired one night of sitting in our little cottage, longed to go to the Hanmer Arms and see our friends, have a pint, and talk and laugh until the wee hours of morning . . ."

She stopped, lost for a moment in reverie as she pictured that drizzly, foggy night. "Griffin knew how much it would mean to me, so he agreed. That night, one of the twelve missionary apostles was holding a meeting there. We were invited in.

"Griffin didn't want to stay. He'd worked hard all day, chopping wood for my father at the estate. I implored him to stay . . . for my sake." She plucked at another weed and tossed it aside. "He would have done anything for me. The rest you know. Once we converted, they promised Griffin the world if we came to America, starting with our first positions as your employees."

It was growing darker, and from the corral, a horse nickered. A few peeps could be heard from inside the chicken coop by the barn, and farther out, crickets chirped and frogs started up a racket of song.

After a moment, Mary Rose said, "What about passion?"

"Griffin wasn't a passionate man." Her memory drifted back to Wales when they courted and wed, to the voyage aboard the clipper, to their trek to Nauvoo. "I knew he loved me in his own way, but he wasn't able to show it."

"Gabe offers you passion," Mary Rose said. The note of deep sadness in her voice didn't go unnoticed. "The missing ingredient with Griffin."

Bronwyn didn't answer, but she knew Mary Rose was right. Instead, she laughed lightly. "If God could only create a perfect man whose heart is honest and straightforward, brave and just, one who shows his lady love respect, friendship, and deep, abiding love. Gabe is not that man, at least not to me." She looked across the few feet that divided them, her gaze settling on Mary Rose's face.

For an instant, Mary Rose's expression softened and her eyes shone, much as they had the first time Bronwyn observed her and Gabe and together on the *Sea Hawk*—he, the architect of the fastest ship in the world and close friend of the ship's captain;

she, Lady Mary Rose Ashley, elegant and beautiful, granddaughter of an earl, brought up in an English manor house. Oh, how her face glowed whenever her new love came near. And his adoration for her was palpable.

It took one's breath away to see their love blossom aboard that clipper.

Now, in the dwindling light, only a hint of that grand and glorious first love remained in Mary Rose's eyes. Something sad settled into Bronwyn's heart as she thought about the changes the years had wrought, changes none of them could have known.

"He was that love to you, though, wasn't he?"

"Once," Mary Rose said, "a long time ago."

They worked together in silence for a few minutes, and then Mary Rose said, "Isn't that what we all want? You, Enid, and me . . . to be loved by someone as if we're the only one in the world to love?" Mary Rose smiled gently. "I heard you tell Pearl and Ruby to hold out for that kind of love, that they deserve nothing less."

"The best thing we can do to assure they find that kind of love is to get them out of the territory as soon it is safe."

"When it's time, we'll make it out, even if the Danites shout 'blood atonement' from the mountains to every Saint within earshot." Mary Rose shivered visibly. "We'll speak of details later. For now, I'll go in and get the little ones to bed."

Reluctant to go inside, Bronwyn went to the barn for a lantern, brought it back, and set it beside the garden. Instantly, moths clustered, hurling their bodies against the glass chimney. Some, merely stunned, fell to the ground. Others found their way closer to the flame, and like miniature torches, flared briefly and died.

The fiddling quieted and, through the open window, Bronwyn heard Gabe give the children a blessing before they scampered off to bed. Even Sarah James stayed and received a blessing before racing out of the house, mounting, and riding toward the Riordan ranch.

Though the images were mere shadows through the flour-sack window curtains, she could see Mary Rose ascending the stairs with the children who were like stair steps themselves as they climbed. First the tallest, Ruby and Pearl tromped up, then Little Grace, followed by Joey and Spence. As they stepped into the loft that served as a nursery, Gabe said something that made them all laugh. She could still hear them giggling when he opened the door, stepped from the house, and strode toward Bronwyn with a purposeful gait.

"I spoke with Brother Brigham today," he said, "and he gave me his blessing to talk to you about a new beginning." His smile widened as he came closer.

Bronwyn dusted the soil from her hands and stood. "A new beginning?"

"For our marriage," he said.

NINETEEN

"What do you mean, a new beginning for our marriage?"

Gabe chuckled. "All in good time. First I want to say how pleased I am with the education and comportment you're teaching our children. Your work with them hasn't gone unnoticed. You and Mary Rose are good mothers."

She gave him a sharp look. "In spite of what Brother Foley and others said about my influence back in Winter Quarters?" When he didn't comment, she studied his expression. "They still hold a grudge, am I right?"

"You judge them too harshly."

She laughed. "I judge *them*?"

"They have a right to judge. Word gets out. Only recently, Brother Brigham heard about the comments you made to other women, criticizing him and others. He says you're firing up some of his own wives—especially when it comes to the topic of celestial marriage. One told him just the other day that she wants a divorce."

She bit back a smile. "Fanny Sten—"

He laced his fingers, steepling them at his lips, his disapproval evident even before he spoke. "This is no laughing matter. I've said this before, Bronwyn. You've changed. You once were sunny-spirited and easygoing, now you've got a mind of your own."

"A mind of my own?" She gave him a half-smile. "Aye, that once would have been seen by you—dear husband—as a good thing. I've told you before, I'm no longer the nanny I was when you first set eyes upon me. This place, this wild country, makes a woman tough. If it doesn't, we won't survive."

"Being strong is one thing. Being foolish is quite another. Being outspoken is downright dangerous." He paused. "He said you spoke to the ladies at the last quilting bee, telling them you advocate raising children with minds of their own. You said they need to inform their daughters—as you do ours— from their earliest years that they do not need to obey Church authority, or even their parents, if told they must marry young." His eyes bored in. "Did you realize who you were speaking to? Didn't you know the word might get back to Brigham?"

She stared at him, unblinking. "What I cannot understand is why you—or anyone else—would not stand up for those who have no one to speak for them."

He ignored her words. "They told their husbands—just as you knew they would. Your actions and words reflect badly on me, on Mary Rose, Enid—on our entire family. Didn't you consider the repercussions?"

"I didn't say anything they hadn't already thought of themselves." She stood and took a few steps away from him, leaning against the fence that divided the garden from the corral.

"You must take greater care," he said.

"What are you afraid of? That if I speak the truth, you'll lose your good standing in the Church? That you'll not be chosen as one of the Quorum of Twelve? Or that I'll be tried and convicted of apostasy and, because of me, you will lose your priesthood? Are honor and dignity and moral purpose less important?"

"You sound like you don't care what happens to us."

She stared at him for a moment. The frogs hushed in a singular voice as if an animal of prey were near. The only sound was the sizzle of moths hitting the flame inside the lantern.

"Maybe I care too much," she said.

He stepped closer, frowning. "What do you mean?"

"I will do anything to save my children—all of them—the twins, Little Grace, Joey, and Spence. Coal too, if he were here."

"You won't save any of them if they're taken away from you."

Though the air was balmy, a chill traveled up her spine. "You would never let that happen."

"There could come a time when I would have no choice." He took hold of her shoulders. "You don't realize the seriousness of this. You might as well come right out and tell me your plans."

She slipped from his grasp, a flicker of apprehension coursing through her. "What plans?"

"Brother Foley is having you watched. There are rumors . . ." He looked up into the pale sky where stars were just beginning to appear.

"Rumors about what?"

"I can't say."

"That's what your announcement is really all about. A blessing for our marriage. It's likely Foley's idea of keeping watch over me day and night to make sure I don't slip away." She attempted to laugh, but it came out in a hoarse, frightened whisper. "I suppose you plan to move back here, bringing Enid with you. You'll make up a rotation sheet—Brigham himself probably showed you how. Fanny Stenhouse, the wife who's divorcing him, told me all about how it works."

"It's nothing like that," Gabe said gently. "You know me better than that."

"I don't think I know you at all."

He ignored the barb. "Brigham trusts me more than even his closest advisors. I am to be his ambassador, his representative to places he cannot travel. I will begin a new settlement in the south of the territory. Our people are already moving there. I am to be in charge of the building of this new community. He has blessed our marriage and ordained that you will be the one chosen above my other wives to accompany me there."

For a moment Bronwyn didn't think she could breathe. "Go with you . . . ?" she finally managed. "Alone?"

He stepped closer, cupped her cheeks, and gently tilted her head upward. Captivated by his gaze, she felt powerless to move.

"You told me one night in Winter Quarters that if I would love you alone, you would be a wife to me."

Her heart raced. What was he talking about? "What about Enid? And Mary Rose? I don't understand . . ."

Still holding her face gently, he kissed her lips. "I am your husband," he breathed, so close to her ear she could feel his breath. "Our union has been blessed again by the prophet, God's representative on earth. He hears from God about these matters, and he has heard from God about us. We are being given a second chance to make things right in the eyes of God."

He kissed her again, this time lingering. And then he whispered, "I beg your forgiveness for those times I have hurt you. I also ask if you will give me a chance to prove how much I care for you."

For an instant, nay longer, she wanted to believe him. Longed to believe him. She looked into his eyes and swallowed hard.

"It will be as you've always wanted," he said. "You will have me to yourself. Brigham is having a ranch house built for us on a hillside overlooking Mountain Meadows. It will be the place of new beginnings for a marriage that will last through time and all eternity, a holy place. He has been there himself, chose it with me, his adopted son, and you, my bride, in mind."

"I can't love you . . . I don't love you. As long as you believe in plural marriage—that it's the only means to reach the highest place in heaven—I cannot. As long as you say you can love three women equally—when I know, we all know, you can't—I cannot." She narrowed her eyes. "Tell me I am your only love, that there are no others."

It took only a heartbeat to realize she didn't want to know the answer. What if he told her what she'd dreamed of hearing him say? Could she bear the pain, the guilt, the disappointment in herself for not being stronger? Of betraying her best friend? The pain of it all almost became physical as she waited for Gabe to speak.

He reached out to gather her into his arms. "Surely you know by now how much I want to be with you. You are different from the others. You are the grand passion of my heart. Brother Brigham is giving us this chance to make things right, to start all over again. He wants to bless our union before we leave."

"I can't leave Mary Rose and Cordelia. I wouldn't think of splitting up the children. No, Gabe, we can't go with you," she said. Fear tied her stomach into a knot.

"I need you to think about it," he said. "It wouldn't be forever. You will be free to come back to visit; Joey and Little Grace will be with us part-time, then we'll bring them back to visit with Mary Rose, Cordelia, and the others. I will need to make numerous trips back and forth to present reports to Brigham. You and the children could come with me as often as you like. Think of it as a grand adventure for us all, a new beginning that in the end will bring us closer."

Her mind raced ahead, thinking of the children, of Mary Rose, and Enid. "You would consider splitting up the children? They think of Mary Rose and me as their mothers. They love us both. You would force them to only have one of us? What about Enid?"

"There will be some adjustment for us all. But many men practicing the sacrament of plural marriage have moved their wives into separate houses. At least, those who can afford it. As for us, we'll of course take Joey and Little Grace. Maybe Ruby or Pearl, whichever one would like to go. One of them needs to stay here to help Mary Rose with Spence."

He looked into her eyes in that way he had, staring as if into the depths of her being, making her knees go weak. "My preference, and the prophet's, is that we spend a few months together without the children. He suggests that if we are to bring spirit children into this physical world, as good and righteous Saints, we need to spend time alone."

She thought of the implications, and her heart fluttered. But the fluttering didn't bring with it a pleasant image. Nay, it was one of a battered, dying butterfly trying to take flight, only to see the ground nearing as it fell.

"I don't believe you're telling me the whole truth. You love our children. You wouldn't put four hundred miles between them and us without a reason. You know the heartache it would cause. They're still not over Coal's disappearance. The twins, especially. How can you even consider taking one away from the other? What you suggest would be devastating for all."

He stood back and crossed his arms and, leaning against the fence, studied her. He let his gaze drift to the stars instead of her eyes when next he spoke. "Everything I've said is true."

"But not the whole truth. I'm sorry, but I cannot accept your offer. Your feelings toward me are no secret, but we're kidding ourselves if either one of us feels it's love. It's . . . it's something else. Passion, perhaps? Or the will to take what I will not allow?" She stepped closer to him, this time capturing his gaze in a way that would not allow him to blink. "I'm a conquest, Gabe.

"It's taken me a long time to figure it out, but what you feel for me is just that. You are attracted to me because you can't have me. It's been that from the day you discovered that Mary Rose and I had vowed my relationship with you would not be physical. You couldn't wait to conquer my determination to be faithful to my friend."

He started to shake his head, but this time she reached up and held his face in her hands. "You can try to convince me of this grand gesture made by Brigham or Foley, but even as you kissed me I had already figured it out. I've become too outspoken to keep near the other women. They want me away from the Saints' new Zion. They'll go to any lengths to see that it happens—from 'adopting' you as a spirit son to sending your outspoken wife as far away as possible." She laughed lightly. "And best plan of all is to keep me eternally pregnant so I'm unable to travel and can't stir up trouble."

The flicker of something in his eyes told her she was right. "That's already been mentioned, hasn't it?"

Gabe took her hands from his face and held them gently. "I've tried to protect you. As far back as the night in Winter Quarters when Coal disappeared, Brigham suggested it."

"Why didn't you press it?"

"The things he said were too . . . personal, too difficult . . . to hear about you." He hesitated before going on. "Regardless of what you think of me, I respect you too much to have carried out their suggestions."

"So now, their suggestions have turned into orders."

"You are in great danger—I've said that from the beginning. I want to save you from the consequences."

"I can't do it, Gabe."

"I didn't think you would." He gave her a crooked smile and touched her cheek gently with the back of his knuckles. "But I had to try." His waggled his eyebrows, breaking the seriousness of the moment. Bronwyn couldn't help smiling. "And you must admit, it was a pretty enjoyable attempt."

He turned to leave.

"Gabe . . ."

He stopped and looked back.

"What are we going to do?"

He drew a deep breath. "Let me worry about that." He studied her face. "About all this other . . . I promise I will honor your wishes from now on."

"Thank you."

His expression turned somber. "But, please promise me that you'll practice the utmost discretion with your words and activities. I fear for us all if you don't."

As soon as he left, she considered all he said. Had he too easily agreed with her at the end? Accepted the futility of his attempts to woo her? Was feigned sincerity his new tactic?

But could she trust him? She honestly did not know.

She fell to her knees by the garden and dropped her face into her hands. They smelled of loamy and moist soil, of decaying leaves. The lantern still burned to one side. In its light, she turned her hands over, examined the calluses, the broken fingernails, the scars made from driving the oxen and changing wagon wheels.

She straightened her fingers, tightened them into fists, and then straightened them again. The look of them, the motion, comforted her. They held evidence of what she had done. They told her that nothing was too hard for her. Not even saying no to Gabe.

She would not go with Gabe. Nothing he, the prophet, or the head of the Avenging Angels could say or do would make her.

She and the family were being watched. Escape was now the only way to keep the family together. The wagon train that Sarah told them about drew nearer each day. They would somehow get word to its captain. Her mind spun with the details of their plan, the actions that still needed to be carried out, the dangers. . .

Coyotes yipped in the distance, and a lone wolf howled. She shivered and looked to the house, the evidence of her loved ones inside, for comfort. But the windows were dark, for even Cordelia had turned out her lamp and gone to bed.

Be brave, she told herself. Think of your hands and what they've done. Put your shoulders back. She and Mary Rose had planned their escape for months. Now, finally, they would choose the time and place for a rendezvous with the wagon company.

She just needed to put fear aside.

Cordelia always said there was nothing like pulling weeds or cleaning a closet to clear the cobwebs from mind and soul. Tonight cobwebs abounded. The wolf howled again, this time closer to the ranch.

She moved the lantern closer to the garden and began weeding again, ripping out one tough fat weed at a time, ever conscious of the howling drawing nearer.

She set her jaw in a determined line and worked her way down the row of cabbages. By the time she moved to a row of beets, slicing deep into the soil with her spade, all was eerily quiet. The coyotes had apparently made their kill, and the wolf had moved on to new territory. Or sat somewhere in the wilderness surrounding the ranch, his yellow eyes watching her every move.

She had just reached the end of the second row of beets when her trowel hit something hard. Thinking it was a stone, she dug around it until she reached its edge. She gave it a yank to pull it loose.

It was larger than she expected. Frowning, she got on her knees and felt around the object with her fingers. It didn't give.

It was also wider than any stone that could have been left in the garden—just below the surface—when she and Mary Rose planted a few months earlier.

Strangely, it seemed less dense than stone, even sandstone. She knocked at it with the handle end of her trowel.

Wood? She knocked again to be sure. A wooden box?

She moved her fingers around the object, inch by inch, feeling her way along. Only soil met her probing. If this was some sort of lid, it had nothing but soil underneath it.

She stood, hands on hips, to assess the size. It was at least five feet long and perhaps two feet wide, or a bit more. Probably nothing more sinister than lumber tossed aside at their house raising. Six inches or more of soil with clumps of seedlings covered the object, making it heavier than it otherwise would have been.

She moved along its length, and then across one width, carefully removing the plants and brushing off the soil. By the time she got halfway up the opposite side, she was able to jiggle the wood. Pleased with her progress, she stood, and yanked the wood upward.

The hair on the back of her neck prickled. She dropped the object with a thud and backed away as a sickening odor filled the air.

A foul and distinct odor . . . of death.

The sheer horror of the thought of what, or who, might be under the wooden plank, twisted her stomach. She bent over the cabbage seedlings and vomited.

TWENTY

Soft whimpering cries filled the night air. It took Bronwyn a half heartbeat to realize they were her own.

She knelt near the garden, shaking so hard she could not stand. She covered her nose and mouth with her apron, tears streaming down her face from a bout of dry heaves, from the lingering stench of death, and from the acrid smell of her own vomit.

Still crying, she wiped her face again with the edge of her apron and then crawled away from the corpse, backward, half expecting whatever was underneath the boards to lift them and climb out of its grave.

Her breaths came in pants, short and shaky, as she tried to gather her wits. Something died, but was the corpse animal or human? The stench of death still hung in the air, clung to her nostrils, her clothing. The body hadn't been there when she and Mary Rose planted the garden. That meant it was placed there recently, and on purpose.

Not placed. *Buried.*

For her or Mary Rose or even one of the children to find.

She pictured Little Grace or one of the twins discovering the corpse while picking beets. Her stomach roiled, and again she doubled over, fighting the urge to vomit, the bile stinging her throat. After a moment the feeling left her, and she drew a deep breath, forcing herself to breathe easier, slowly, evenly.

She tried to grab on to a rational thought, make a decision . . . anything to keep the image of what lay beneath the board from her mind.

Why was the corpse there? Who had buried it? Was she being watched? Shuddering, she glanced around the circle of ambient light from the lantern. What, or who, crouched beyond the light?

The nausea subsided, and her thoughts came fast and clear. Mary Rose, Cordelia, Little Grace, Ruby, Pearl, Joey, and Spence—all those she loved—were in danger. The monster who left this thing in the garden for any of them to find would win if she cowered in fear, afraid to go for help.

The decision made, she tried to stand. Her limbs would not support her. Half crawling, she made her way to the side door. She grabbed the doorjamb and, clinging to it for support, drew herself up to standing. Her knees supported her weight at last.

She hurried inside, closed the door, and slammed the deadbolt across. She ran to the great room, latched and locked that door as well. Then she moved a ladder-back chair to the one side, stepped onto it, and reached for the Hawken that hung above.

Her legs now as strong as her will, she quickly moved from room to room, upstairs and down, securing windows, checking on the sleeping children, Cordelia, and Mary Rose. In her own bedroom, she slipped out of her dirty clothing, washing the filth and smell from her face and hands, and pulled on her riding clothes and boots.

The mantel clock struck midnight as she came back down the stairs and moved the ladder-back chair to a place where both doors where visible—and the garden, where she'd left the lantern burning. She then doused the indoor lamp and sat in darkness, the Hawken across her lap.

The wolf howled again in the distance. Another answered nearby. A shudder traveled up her spine.

All became quiet again. Too quiet.

Then she saw movement, no more than a shadow, just beyond the circle of the lantern's ambient light. Fear swept through her once more. She picked up the Hawken and moved toward the window.

TWENTY-ONE

Leaning back in the silk settee in front of the fireplace, Enid waited for Gabe to return. She wore her loveliest nightclothes, made of a soft gossamer cloth trimmed with lace, and had pulled her hair back and tied it with a ribbon. The fire had died to glowing embers and with it her hopes for a romantic evening with her husband.

She stood and placed a few knots of oak on the fire. The resin in them liquefied, and sparks flew up like Chinese fireworks. Sometimes she felt as though her life might fly apart in much the same way. Since marrying Gabe, it certainly hadn't turned out as she expected. Life with her so-called sister wives wasn't easy. She'd thought she could make Gabe hers and hers alone. It seemed her so-called sister wives and Gabe himself had other ideas.

As far as she could tell, each bride wanted Gabe to herself. Well, perhaps Mary Rose didn't. Once in a great while, Enid noticed a warm glow in her eyes as she watched Gabe—usually when he wasn't aware of it—but more often than not, her demeanor toward him dripped of cordiality bordering on indifference. Enid did concede that great sorrow might lie just beneath the cool surface. After all, Mary Rose couldn't have known on the day they married what lay in store for her, for them.

Bronwyn, however, too often looked upon Gabe with passionate adoration. Anyone near them could see it if they paid attention at all. And, in Enid's opinion, nothing in the world was more attractive to a man than a pretty woman gazing upon him with dreamy eyes beneath thick lashes, her complexion like that of the finest porcelain and cheeks the color of roses.

Gabe had ridden out to the ranch earlier to spend time with the children, or so he said, but suspicions filled Enid's heart as the time dragged on. He should have been home hours ago. She tried not to think that he might be in the arms of Bronwyn or Mary Rose. She pressed her lips together and decided to believe he was on Church business. But the way Bronwyn looked at him was an image that kept returning to her thoughts.

She checked the time on the mantel clock, and then stood and walked to the bookcase to pick out one of her medical books: *Treatise on the Diseases of Animals, Large and Small,* published by the Edinburgh Royal Infirmary. At least such reading would keep her mind off her jealousies and turn her thoughts to a more productive use of her time. She had never thought herself prone to such a feminine weakness, but life among the Saints, it seemed, had brought out something long dormant.

She sat down again and opened the book. Several of the farmers in the valley had reported stillborn calves. There had been too many for it to be a coincidence. The Ellises were the latest, and she planned to visit them in the morning to examine the calf's body, feed, and water.

Even as she listened for Gabe's arrival, she leafed through the *Treatice*, found the references she needed, read through them, considering how the information might relate to the dead calves.

She suspected the cause might be the water, the high-alkaline content, but she couldn't be sure. Brigham had engineers working on a canal system to bring snow water from the mountains into the Great Salt Lake Valley, but the huge project would take some time to finish. Meantime, the calves died.

She placed the book on the settee beside her, patting the cover almost affectionately, and then smiled as a memory filled her mind. What excitement she'd felt when it arrived—sent to Nova Scotia from the doctor in Scotland who'd become her mentor, one of the first to study in the field of veterinary medicine. She had written to Hosea just before his last voyage, and he had received the letter in Liverpool before the *Sea Hawk* set sail for Boston.

But his return letter had been bittersweet. He told her that he had arranged for her to see a fertility doctor in London and wanted her to accompany him on his return trip to England. She'd been dismayed, shocked, and frightened, for it was an appointment she could not keep. Her secret would be found out. The child she'd borne with Gabe.

She recalled her anticipation as the *Sea Hawk* neared harbor. Her man, her captain, was coming home from the sea! Their love had been fierce from the beginning, so fierce she thought it strong enough to withstand the harshest of storms.

Looking back, she should have told him about the secret she'd kept so long. Instead, she asked Gabe, his comrade and friend, to break the news. Her cowardice destroyed their long friendship; it destroyed Hosea's love for her.

Her eyes filled at the memory of her husband. Oh, what a sight he'd been . . . tall and handsome, elegant and strong. A commanding presence, especially when in his captain's uniform.

A sigh escaped her lips as she tried to imagine how life would be if she hadn't betrayed his trust, if he hadn't died. Would they have settled in Nova Scotia in the little cottage by the sea? Or would they have sailed together around the world, the captain and his bride, as Hosea had always wanted to do?

She stood, trying to shake his memory from her mind. Hosea was dead. Gabe was her husband now, for better or worse. With a heavy sigh, she stood and reached for a lamp, and then she made her way up the stairs to retire to bed, downhearted that Gabe thought so little of her to keep her waiting.

She lay awake for a time, listening for the beat of horse hooves, but the only sound was the flutter of leaves against her window and the hoot of an owl from a cottonwood a few houses down the street.

Her eyes grew heavy, and finally, she turned down the lamp and settled against her pillow.

As she fell asleep, Gabe's image came to her. He was a boy again, grinning at her playfully as they raced their horses along the lacy waters of the beach. He shouted that he was faster and better, but when she overtook him, riding around his horse, deeper into the water, he called out that where she was going was dangerous. "Come back," he cried. "Come back!"

But still she rode on, laughing as her horse's hooves sprayed water on them both.

She turned to see if Gabe followed, but he had halted his horse. His face was filled with fear. He seemed to be pleading with her, but she couldn't understand his words. She called to him to join her, but he kept crying, "Come back."

A wind came up, and in the distance a storm brewed. Still she laughed and danced her horse along the edge of the Atlantic. She knew Gabe still called to her, but she ignored his warnings.

And then a new voice joined his and she looked up to see Hosea standing by Gabe. He was no longer a boy, but a man, full of hearty laughter and eyes full of life's joy. They stood together on an outcropping of granite, these friends. Hosea! Her heart leapt when she saw him. His eyes caught hers, and her heart danced as surely as the mare she rode danced in the shallow waves. They laughed together, these friends. They beckoned to her to join them.

She slid from her horse and ran to them. Both opened their arms to claim her, but she ran straight to Hosea, taking joy in the rough feel of his arms around her. "You live!" she shouted. "You live!"

He twirled her and laughed when he set her down again.

Gabe ran from them, calling over his shoulder that they needed to hurry, that the storm was still coming and nearly upon them.

Hosea held her but seemed distracted by the coming storm. She turned to follow his gaze. Gabe was right. The sea and sky had turned a dirty shade of gray. The storm had circled and approached again, this time its thunder violently shaking the ground.

"We must jump," Hosea said, pulling her with him to the side of a cliff. "It's the only way we can survive." He gave her a pleading look. "I love you, it's always been you, only you. . . ."

The storm raged around them now, whipping her hair into her face. "I'm afraid," she cried, now sobbing. "How can you love me? How can anyone love me?"

Hosea touched her tears with his fingertips. "I love you," he repeated, and then he fell from the cliff backward, down . . . down . . . down . . . until he was swallowed by the ocean.

His eyes held hers even from beneath the ocean's surface. Their color, so like that of the sea with flecks of sunlight dancing on its surface, aquamarine with a scattering of jewels. How could she ever forget those eyes, so full of love they made her want to weep?

"Hosea!" she cried. "Wait for me . . ."

She jumped. . .

Slowly, she became aware of a hand touching her shoulder, and a voice . . . "Enid . . ." Shaking herself out of the dream, she opened her eyes. It was Gabe.

"You were dreaming," he said.

She reached for his hand. "I know. Thank you for waking me. It was . . ." She tried to grab snatches of it before it disappeared like smoke into thin air. "Hosea. You and Hosea were in the dream. You ran away, and Hosea jumped into the sea. He was drowning again, Gabe." She started to cry.

Gabe sat beside her on the bed, and then reached down to gather her into his arms. He gently cuddled her closer.

"You called his name," he said. "You said you wanted him to wait for you."

She nodded, taking comfort in the warmth of Gabe's shirt against her cheek. "You ran from us, though you shouted out a warning that we were in danger. You said a storm was brewing and moving fast toward us. I could see it coming, Gabe. It was dark and terrible. I knew it had something to do with losing both of you."

He tightened his arms around her. "You're safe now," he said. "You'll never lose me again."

She pulled back and tried to study his face, but the room was too dark. Even so, she remembered him in the dream and considered the child he once was, the man he'd become.

"How did we end up here?" she whispered. "You filled my dream as a child, then suddenly you were half boy and half man, and now you are fully the man you were destined to become."

She reached up and traced the side of his face, moving her fingers along his jaw. "What happened to the laughter, the innocence, the friendship between us? Between you and Hosea?" Her eyes filled. "This is a place of competition. Men competing to climb the ladder of Church hierarchy, women competing for the love of one man married to many wives.

"And the doctrine," she said. "I've tried to understand. I know there are times when I'm just being plain stubborn, but then there are those other times when I truly want to believe. But when a man—a man I consider fallible—speaks for God, tells everyone under his power that God says the more wives you take, the greater your place in heaven . . ."

"You knew about our doctrine when you said—"

She covered his lips with her fingertips. "I don't want to hear that again. Or how the Old Testament prophets, even King David himself, had harems full of wives. It can't be God's best for us. I wonder if it wasn't his best for the prophets of old either." She fell silent as the owl hooted softly again in the distance. "There's so much we're missing . . . I can't pinpoint it, but what we're doing, how we're living . . . doesn't feel right for many reasons."

"This is a harsh place," Gabe said. "The rules are different out here—for everyone, not just the Mormons."

"As Cordelia would say, 'hogwash!'" She fell silent. Downstairs the mantel clock chimed two in the morning.

"I need to go," he said after a few minutes. "I—I have a meeting . . ."

"This late?"

He stood. "Yes, it's Church business. I'm sorry." He turned abruptly, and headed through the doorway.

"Gabe," she called after him. "Wait . . ." She swung her legs out of bed and ran to the top of the stairs. "Where are you going?"

The door closed with a thud. Minutes later, she heard the low murmur of men's voices in the street below her bedroom window. She ran to look, pulled back the curtain, and watched as a posse of men on horseback thundered down the road leading from town.

TWENTY-TWO

At first light, Bronwyn pulled a sheet of paper from a small desk by the front window, dipped a pen in the inkwell, and wrote. . .

Dear Mary Rose,

I made an upsetting discovery last night in the garden and believe our family is in danger. I will explain later. You, Cordelia, and the children must remain inside with the doors and windows locked. Give the Hawken to Cordelia—I know she's still a crack shot and will protect you, should anyone threaten your safety.
I will bring help.
B.

She folded the paper and left it on the bottom step of the staircase, where Mary Rose was certain to see it. Heart pounding and anxious to be on her way, she waited until she was certain Mary Rose or Cordelia was stirring upstairs.

Then she grabbed Gabe's pistol, dropped it into her satchel, and ran for the door. She didn't bother to saddle the roan, and once mounted, rode like the wind toward town. She passed no living soul, and shuddered at her vulnerability should she meet up with those who might cause her harm.

The sun rose just as she arrived in town, and people began to mill about, crossing the road in front of her, chatting as they cleaned horse dung from the streets or swept walkways. A buggy rumbled by, and then a few men on horseback, looking at her curiously, bareback and without a male escort this early in the morning.

She slowed the horse.

Gabe's town house, directly across from Brigham's imposing home, loomed in front of her. The jitters started again, and by the time she slid from the horse to secure the roan to a hitching post near the picket gate, her knees had turned to liquid and she was trembling like a sycamore leaf in a windstorm.

Though the sun had risen, the front of the handsome two-story house was shaded by two tall trees that flanked the walkway. A single light still glowed in a downstairs window.

She opened the gate, gathered her courage, and headed toward the front door. With each step, her mind whirled with all that had happened the evening before: Gabe's warnings and advances, the discovery in her garden, and now, standing outside the house where Gabe lived with Enid.

She knocked, and heard footsteps approach from the other side. A moment later, Gabe stood there, staring at her, his surprise obvious.

Her mouth went dry. The horror of the corpse she'd seen in that split second, the stench, the sense of danger, threatened to overwhelm her.

"Gabe . . ." The word came out as a shaky cry. She brought her hand to her mouth as her stomach roiled again, and her eyes filled with tears.

She blinked rapidly, and willed her knees to stop trembling. "I need your help. It's serious. Please . . ."

He opened his arms to her, and she fell into them. No matter what had transpired between them the night before, she needed to feel their strength. "Tell me what happened," he said, resting his cheek on the top of her head.

"I-I found a corpse . . . in the garden." She pictured the sight and her stomach roiled again. "Last night . . . after you left."

"I'll go back with you. Come in while I get my things."

She stepped inside and waited in the foyer, the parlor on one side, the dining room opposite. Even in her panic, she couldn't help noticing the fine furnishings, the Chippendale furniture, the Persian rugs. The fine desk with a cut-glass lamp burning near where Gabe had obviously been working.

Gabe returned in a heartbeat, clomping down the stairs in his hurry. He went to the desk, whisked away the papers he'd been writing, placed them in a side drawer, locked it, and dropped the key in his vest pocket.

"Tell me about the children," he said, when he'd finished. "And Mary Rose?"

"When I left, the children . . . everyone . . . was fine." She stepped toward him. "I think it was human remains, but once the stench hit me, I dropped the cover. I didn't see much. But the smell . . ." She stepped closer to him, swiping at her tears. "Something is wrong. I can feel it. You told me last night that I'm being watched, that I've put our family in a dangerous position because I'm outspoken. Is this the next step for those who are watching?"

His eyes again took on the warmth and affection she was used to seeing in them. "I should have stayed last night. I—I knew, from talk around, that our family, you especially, might be in danger." He shook his head. "I had to take care of some other serious business during the night. I'll ride back with you . . . we'll get to the bottom of this, find out what it is and who did it." He fell silent for a moment, staring through the window toward Brigham Young's house, now bathed in the light of the early morning sun.

"Shouldn't we call the police, the proper authorities?"

For a moment he didn't speak. Then he said, "Of course, we will. But I want to have a look first. You said you weren't even sure the remains are human."

"Gabe, I'm scared, especially after what you told me last night. You tried to get me to leave with you. Now I understand why . . ."

He came back to her and pulled her into his arms again. "You're trembling."

"Of course she is, Gabe."

Bronwyn stepped back from Gabe's embrace as Enid descended the stairs. She was still in nightclothes, a rather immodest gauzy gown covered with a lacy duster. Her hair was pulled back and tied with a matching satin ribbon. All, a pale green that brought out the color of her eyes and set off her red hair. She looked lovely in the morning light.

She heard Gabe's quick intake of breath, but could not tell if it was from the ravishing beauty of his third bride or from the fact that she'd caught them in a tender embrace.

"I couldn't help overhearing," she said, "and I agree with Gabe. Let's not let the authorities know anything about this until we investigate it ourselves."

Bronwyn tilted her head. *Investigate it ourselves?*

She frowned as Enid walked toward her, her filmy nightclothes billowing as she walked. "Part of my training in veterinary medicine included physiology and forensics. I want to have a look before we turn the police loose to investigate."

Bronwyn glanced from Enid to Gabe then back to Enid. This

all seemed too easy, too pat. Her heart raced just a bit. Could she trust them?

Enid didn't seem the least bit perturbed to find Bronwyn in Gabe's arms, his head resting on hers.

The horror of her discovery washed over her again, and Bronwyn felt her knees threaten to give way beneath her. Gabe came to her side in an instant, caught her, and in another instant, Enid stepped to her other side.

They helped her to a wingchair, and eased her down. Enid instructed her to put her head between her knees. Bronwyn did as bade, felt blood return to her head and her strength return, and looked up, still shaking but wary.

Enid peered into her face. "Poor dear, you probably haven't had a thing to eat this morning. Let me fix something for you—hot cocoa? Tea?"

"My family . . . I—I can't be away any longer. They need me. Thank you, but I must go." She looked at Gabe, wondering if she'd made the right decision to come for him. In her fear, in her panic, had she run to the wrong person for help?

"You can stay here, if you'd like to rest," Enid said. "You're pale as a ghost."

"No, really. I'm all right. Please do come by this afternoon. I'm curious about what you might find."

A few minutes later, Gabe helped Bronwyn onto the wagon bench, climbed up to sit next to her, and then chirked to the horse. They had traveled only a short way, when Bronwyn touched Gabe's hand. "Can you tell me what's going on? You both know something . . . you've found out something you're keeping from me. Does Enid have anything to do with this?"

He kept his eyes forward.

Her heart pounded. "Gabe, what is it?"

TWENTY-THREE

The flat, arid landscape shone white in the morning sun, except where long shadows of trees crossed the trail. The wavelets on the lake sparkled like a thousand jewels, almost blinding in their intensity. The sun was at an angle that struck Gabe and Bronwyn in the face. Gabe pulled his hat low to shade his forehead, but Bronwyn had left the ranch so early she hadn't thought to bring even a poke bonnet. She shaded her eyes with her hand. Without a word, Gabe glanced over, removed his hat, and handed it to her. She smiled to herself. It took a lot for Gabe to give up his hat.

They rode along in silence for several minutes. Finally, Gabe turned to her. "There are things I know but can't speak of," he said. "Please don't ask me to tell you what they are. Trust me that they have nothing to do with your discovery."

"Trust you?" She almost laughed. "After what you attempted last night?"

"I spoke from my heart . . . about wanting to complete our marriage, wanting some time with you. Alone." He glanced at her, and she felt her cheeks warm. "You can choose to believe me or not."

"We settled that last night," she said.

"Yes, we did."

"What I found in the garden," she said, "was placed there on purpose."

"I fear you may be right." He flicked the reins over the back of the horse.

"So you can tell me that much."

"It's obvious. We don't need a crystal ball." He glanced at her again, but this time shot her a half-grin. "Bodies don't bury themselves, especially under a couple of pieces of wood."

"Think how it looks to me, Gabe. First you attempt every way possible to put me in an isolated place where I can't be near family."

"That's not at all what I proposed to you." He gave her an incredulous look as he swept his hand through his hair. "I wanted to give us some time to be alone and build a life together. You make it sound like I wanted to throw you in jail."

She turned on the wagon bench so that she partially faced him. "You can't deny that someone wants me to leave this place even if they have to scare me away. Is it Enid?"

He blinked and gave her a sharp look. "Enid?"

"She's made it clear that she would like you all to herself."

He threw back his head and laughed. "No, I can tell you, it's not Enid."

"How can you be sure?"

His voice softened. "I know her."

"Someone wants me to leave."

He drew the horse to a halt and reached for the brake. The wagon rumbled to a stop, and a cloud of dust rose behind them.

"Look, if someone wanted to scare you into leaving with me, why didn't he—or she"—he rolled his eyes—"just throw the body, human or animal, at the front door? Or leave it on top of the cabbages in the garden?" He raked his hair with his fingers again.

"No," he said. "No one is trying to frighten you into going with me to an outlying settlement, if that's what you think. What I offered you last night—a home of our own, first to occupy as husband and wife—was to make up for all the time lost when we should have been together. Then, to bring our children and create a new family unit, perhaps to become leaders south of here. We might have had that chance."

He reached for her hand. "The place is growing. Thousands of Saints are arriving each week from the east. You know that is true. Brigham has a dream, a dream that our people will settle the entire territory—from here all the way into California.

"He wanted me to be his representative, a leader with his mandate to make decisions on his behalf."

"You said 'wanted' instead of 'wants.'"

"I met with the prophet last night and told him I couldn't do it." He kissed her fingertips. "And you needn't worry. I told him it was my decision, not yours. I could have taken Enid, and made up a logical reason for it, but I don't want to leave you or the children."

"What about Mary Rose?"

He turned to look out over the horizon, and she followed his gaze to the lake in the distance, the mountains behind, the azure cloudless sky.

"Ah yes, Mary Rose," he said, his voice husky. "She's another story . . ." Without another word, he flicked the reins, and they started on their way again.

As they rumbled along, Bronwyn couldn't help noticing the way he worked his jaw as they rode. He'd made his proposal and the aftermath sound so reasonable. Trust him, he'd said, and then he'd looked at her with that way he had, as if straight through to her heart. But, could she?

He said there were things he couldn't tell her. What were they? And why not?

Little Grace raced to Bronwyn as soon as she stepped through the door. She was getting too big to lift these days, but Bronwyn swept her daughter into her arms anyway, hugging her close. Joey raced around the corner and grabbed her legs. "Mommy, Mommy!" he said, looking up at her. "Something bad's in our garden. Mother Mary Rose didn't let us go out to play." He stuck his lower lip out.

Bronwyn stooped and gathered him close. "Father will take care of it. And Mother Enid will be here shortly too."

The twins tromped down the stairs, and it seemed the entire house shook with the noise.

Gabe came in from the barn and, stooping down, opened his arms. The little ones reached him first, Joey looking up at him with adoration, Spence nuzzling under his arm. Little Grace was next and gave him a tight hug around the neck. The twins came around the corner, smiles lighting their faces as soon as they saw him.

They all started talking at once, and Gabe threw back his head and laughed. "One at a time. We'll start with the youngest."

Bronwyn kept looking toward the window, waiting for Enid to arrive so they could get through the dreadful task ahead. But she was grateful for Gabe keeping the children happy and occupied while they waited.

The look of him playing with the children made her heart ache, made it seem that what she and Gabe felt for each other was natural and right, and that she could trust him—just as the children did.

Then she noticed Mary Rose standing back, away from the others. The smiling mask that Mary Rose most often kept in place lifted for a heartbeat. In the second, Bronwyn saw clearly her deep pain . . . and longing. Not a passionate longing. But a patient and enduring longing. Just as quickly as it appeared, it faded.

"Me," Spence yelled.

"No, me," Joey yelled louder.

Gabe hugged them and set them on the ground. "Okay, since we can't decide, we'll start with the oldest."

"My brudder is the youngest," Spence said, letting out an exaggerated sigh.

Joey looked around to see if he had everyone's attention. "Well," he said, "last night a boogie man came and left something bad in our garden. Grandmother Cordelia told me so this morning."

"A boogie man?" Gabe glanced at Cordelia, who rolled her eyes.

The children continued with their chattering, Gabe now the center of attention. Bronwyn nodded her thanks to him, and then motioned Mary Rose and Cordelia to follow her outside.

When they were out of earshot of the family, she told them what she'd discovered the night before.

"I knew it must be bad," Cordelia said, "for you to leave all of a sudden like you did."

"I stayed until dawn when I heard you moving around upstairs."

"I figured as much," Cordelia said, "but you should have come in to wake me. I would've sat watch with you."

Bronwyn gave the older woman a hug. "You needed your sleep. Besides, we all are going to need our wits about us. Gabe told me last night—before the gruesome discovery—that I've been too outspoken. The word is getting around."

"We all have been," Mary Rose said. "I don't think you've said things more pointed than Cordelia or I."

"You weren't at the quilting bee," the older woman said, laughing. "I've never seen eyebrows raised so high—and on some who are the wives of Brother Brigham." She shook her head slowly. "Best laugh I've had in months."

"Enid has studied forensics and physiology," Bronwyn said. "She's coming by to see if she can determine what caused the death—if they're human remains."

"I'd say she should determine it even if they aren't human." Cordelia gave them an intense look. "If someone's trying to scare us with a dead pig or deer or something, what it is will tell us a lot. Also, we should do a count of our own livestock. I bet you buttons to biscuits it's one of our own. I once heard about a rancher who woke up one morning to find that somebody who didn't like him cut off the head of his prize pig and left it on the porch. The poor thing had been like a family pet. They'd named him Jesse, and it like to broke their hearts."

Mary Rose shuddered and held up one hand. "Let hope it's not as dire as that."

In the distance a cloud of dust rose from the horizon . . . a horse heading toward them at a gallop.

"It's Enid," Mary Rose said, shading her eyes. "I'm glad she's coming."

As soon as Enid rode in, Cordelia went back into the house to keep the children away from the windows. Gabe stepped outside, and Mary Rose and Bronwyn exchanged worried glances.

"This isn't going to be pretty," Enid said. "Are you certain you want to stay and watch?"

"Yes," Bronwyn said, lifting her chin to look braver than she felt.

Mary Rose drew a breath and nodded. "I'm ready. Let's do it."

Gabe led the way. He studied the wood for a moment. "It's an old door. It probably was brought from Nauvoo."

"Maybe traceable," Bronwyn murmured, mostly to herself.

He put his gloved hands underneath an end of the door. The women each took a side, and moved the heavy wood to one side of a shallow grave.

Again, an overpowering stench filled the air.

Bronwyn turned her head away. She noticed Mary Rose had done the same and stepped back, her complexion sallow.

Bronwyn's curiosity overcame her revulsion. She stepped closer, and her heart constricted. The shape of the head, the arms, hands, fingers. "It's human," she said. Unable to stand the condition of the body, she looked away as Enid bent closer.

"A young man, maybe five feet tall," Enid said, "and I believe he's been dead at least two weeks, judging from the temperature, weather conditions, and the rate of decay."

Bronwyn felt bile rise in her throat again and, turning away from the sight, breathed deeply in an attempt to calm her stomach. "Cause of death? Is there any sign?"

She turned to look back just in time to see Enid and Gabe exchange glances. Enid had gone entirely white.

For a moment neither of them spoke, then Gabe said, "The boy's throat was slit."

TWENTY-FOUR

Bronwyn climbed the stairs, weary from her all-night vigil. Cordelia had retired to her bedroom for an afternoon nap, and Mary Rose had gone to hers to write in her journal. The children were downstairs with Gabe. He read a book of nursery rhymes to Joey and Spence, both sitting on his lap, and the twins giggled over a boy they'd met the Sunday before at the meeting-house.

She gave Mary Rose's door a quick rap, and when bidden to come in, opened it and entered. Mary Rose sat at her desk, her journal open before her. She turned and smiled softly as Bronwyn came over to sit beside her.

"I've been thinking about the boy in the garden," Bronwyn said, "and a mother someplace who's missing her son. A father too, and maybe some brothers and sisters. A grandmother or grandfather."

"The boy in the garden." Mary Rose searched Bronwyn's face. "I haven't wanted to think about this, or even consider it, but are we certain it's not Coal?" Her eyes filled and she reached for her handkerchief. "You got a better look at him than I did . . . could you make out his features?"

The boy's image flashed before Bronwyn and she closed her eyes briefly to keep the memory of his face, the stench of the rotting flesh, from making her sick again. She didn't want to tell Mary Rose about the swelling, the condition of the tissue.

"I wondered the same thing," she said, "though I didn't want to say it for fear that might make it real." She reached into a pocket and pulled out a small cloth packet. She unwrapped it and held it out for Mary Rose to see. Inside were the squares of cloth from the boy's trousers and shirt and a strand of hair.

Mary Rose took the cloth from Bronwyn's hands almost reverently. "It's the wrong color," she said. "The hair, I mean. He could have been wearing different clothes—if by some miracle he followed us here. But he couldn't have changed his hair color."

"Coal's corn-silk hair is as shiny and bright as the rising sun," Bronwyn said, picturing the boy. "And this is dark brown and curly. I think if we held it in the sun, it might have an amber tint." She held it to the window, and smiled. "It does. Look at this." Still turning the small curl, she said, "I wonder what his mother thought the first time she saw those curls in the sun. I bet she tousled those curls the way we used to tousle Coal's hair."

She paused, staring at the piece of hair and thinking about Coal. "I want to find her and talk with her." She looked up at Mary Rose. "Our escape . . ."

Mary Rose moved closer and nodded. "It's more important now than ever. The danger is greater than we thought."

"I can't leave," Bronwyn said. "But I want you to take the children and meet the wagon train as we'd planned."

"You surely know I won't allow it—allow you to stay here in the midst of danger."

"We need to get the children out." Bronwyn stood and went to the window, pulled the curtain back, and looked out. "This was a young man. A boy, really. Enid said probably no more than fourteen. Possibly as young as thirteen."

"Coal's age."

The hot sting of tears threatened, and she swallowed hard. "I know."

She turned back to Mary Rose. "Put that together with the teaching of blood atonement, the rise of the Danites, and a ritualistic throat cutting . . . and what do you get?"

"I get that we must leave, all of us. As soon as we can make arrangements."

"I have reason to suspect that Gabe is caught up in this somehow."

Mary Rose blanched. "No, not Gabe." She closed her eyes as if praying for strength, and when she opened them, tears brimmed. She shook her head. "No, he can't be." She went back to her desk, and Bronwyn pulled up a chair to sit nearer.

Bronwyn leaned forward and dropped her voice as she told Mary Rose that Gabe tried to get her to move with him to a new settlement in the south. "He said the move had the prophet's blessing. He so much as said that my outspoken ways cause trouble among the other wives."

"If Gabe wants you to go with him," Mary Rose said, "maybe he's trying to protect you."

"Why not take all of us, then?"

Mary Rose hesitated, her gaze drifting to the window. "I can't answer that."

"I caught him putting away some papers this morning. He was visibly shaken when I came to the door. It was obvious he didn't want me to see what he'd been working on." She pictured the body and shuddered. "You don't know how much I don't want Gabe to be mixed up in this. But I think he is. The prophet has adopted him as his spiritual son, which now gives him even more authority over Gabe than before." She leaned forward. "Don't you see? Gabe is somehow trapped by those who would do him harm, do us all harm. For that reason, we can't trust him to protect us."

"That doesn't make him untrustworthy," Mary Rose said, dropping her head into her hands. "And aren't we rushing to judgment about the prophet himself?" She looked up. "Do you have any proof that he's involved with the Danites?"

"He was when we were in Nauvoo."

"That was different. That was after Joseph Smith had been killed. There was good reason to suspect the Gentiles were out to kill us all. The militia was formed to protect us, not to scare us into submission." Her words were strong, and she stood and paced the room. "Are we getting excited over something we can't prove? Even worse, are we making false accusations against the prophet and president of our church?"

Bronwyn sat back, stunned.

Mary Rose came back over and sat opposite Bronwyn. "I still have as many doubts as ever. But don't you see? That's the argument against our way of thinking. How certain can we be that we're right?"

Bronwyn bit her lip. "I can't leave until I find out whose child has been buried in our garden."

"Gabe said that as soon as he rides back to town, he's going straight to the prophet and Brother Foley. He'll tell them what has happened, and let the police take it from here."

Mary Rose's calm assurance helped Bronwyn relax. "If they can tell us who and why, then I'll agree to leave." She glanced at Mary Rose's journal. "Until then, I think we need to have a provisional plan ready."

Mary Rose followed her gaze and blanched. "Oh, no. I hope you're not thinking what I think you're thinking."

"You've written everything that's gone on since we joined the Mormons in Nauvoo. You've detailed what's been done against us, the good and wonderful things within the Mormon Church, the love we have for each other, the way we care for our own, the love we have for our children."

She nodded.

"You've written about the good, the bad, and everything in between. Our lives are within the pages of your journals, our heartaches and fears. Even what we're going through now." Bronwyn wiped the tears from her eyes. "You have a gift, Mary Rose. You've always wanted to write something that would change the world."

She picked up the journal on the desk, closed it, and hugged it to her heart. "This is it. This is your opus. Perhaps even more important than getting our family out, is getting this out—getting them all out."

Mary Rose swallowed hard and took the journal from Bronwyn, clutching it close, and closing her eyes. "I'll write about what we've found in the garden. I'll describe our terror. I'll tell about how we've become prisoners, fearing for our lives if we dare to disagree with Church teachings or disobey our leaders, or even our husbands. I'll tell what it means to be well on the road to apostasy, knowing that by stepping onto that road, we may lose everything we cherish—our children, our own lives."

Bronwyn bit her lip and nodded. "Do it quickly. I don't think we have much time."

"How will we get them out?"

"I don't know, but we'll find a way."

The sound of heavy footsteps ascending the stairs carried toward them. A moment later, Gabe knocked lightly on the door.

"Come in," Mary Rose called, and reached for a handkerchief to dab at her nose.

He stepped inside. "Did I interrupt something?"

Mary Rose shook her head. "No, please come in."

He stood in the doorway, leaning against the doorjamb, his legs crossed at the ankles. "I've made a decision. I can't let you stay out here all alone, not after what's happened. For now, I plan to move back to the ranch and bring Enid with me. We'll have to do some bedroom shifting, but I think it will be better for us all to be together. I have some things to take care of in town this afternoon—and Enid is probably still at the Ellis farm, but we will be back in time for supper tonight."

The set of his jaw said there would be no discussion. He gave them each a steady gaze and then turned and headed back down the stairs.

"How will we manage to work out our plans?" Mary Rose gestured heavenward and then surprised Bronwyn by chuckling. "Just when I thought things couldn't get worse."

Bronwyn noticed her cheeks held a bit more color, her eyes a bit more sparkle, and when she stood to walk over to the window to watch Gabe ride away, her step held a bit more spring.

"As for me," Bronwyn said to Mary Rose a moment later, "I'll also be back by suppertime."

Mary Rose didn't appear surprised. "You're not giving him much of a head start."

"I'm counting on Gabe's business lasting long enough for me to see what he hid in his desk this morning."

"You're going to break in?"

"I don't consider it breaking in."

"Don't forget that Enid could return any time. She could walk in on you rifling through the treasured Chippendale desk."

Bronwyn lifted her chin. "Gabe is my husband as much as he is hers. Maybe I'll exercise my rights and tell her since she's moving here, I'm moving to the town house. My first act as mistress of the establishment is to clean out the desk." She folded her arms. "And anything else I fancy to clean." She grinned. "That's where I got my start in life as you remember—housekeeper and nanny."

Mary Rose laughed. "That's not a bad idea. Maybe we both

should move there with the children and Cordelia and let Gabe and Enid have the ranch."

Bronwyn hugged Mary Rose. "I'm glad we can laugh, at least once in a while."

"Otherwise, there would be far too many tears."

TWENTY-FIVE

A breeze kicked up from the west, bringing with it the scent of blooming sage and wild lavender. Just outside the corral, dust devils spun, touching down here and there and then wandering off again as if in search of where they belonged.

Bronwyn and Mary Rose looked to Cordelia, whose idea it had been to commemorate the boy's life and untimely death before the police arrived to take away the body. She stood at the head of the grave with Mary Rose's family Bible open, and then, looking down, she read:

> *Fear thou not; for I am with thee: be not dismayed; for I am thy God: I will strengthen thee; yea, I will help thee; yea, I will uphold thee with the right hand of my righteousness . . . For I the* LORD *thy God will hold thy right hand, saying unto thee, Fear not; I will help thee.*

> (Isaiah 41:10, 13)

Cordelia, in spite of the toll the harsh years had taken on her, held her shoulders back with strength of conviction. Her voice, steady and clear, seemed to ring out across the landscape. Bronwyn imagined it carrying on the wind, causing even the birds to stop their singing to listen.

As Cordelia continued, Bronwyn clutched the boy's dark, curly lock in her hand, thinking about the child's last moments on earth. She hoped the end had come quickly and that he didn't suffer. Was he aware that no matter what he faced, God held his hand? Was he aware, somewhere in the depths of his heart, that no matter his darkest fears, God was with him?

If his death was carried out as part of a blood atonement ritual, could he have known it was by order of man, not God?

She shivered even in the warmth of the sun.

A new thought struck her with such clarity she almost stumbled backward. She'd been dwelling on the similarities between Coal and this boy—the age, the fact that both had disappeared—but it hadn't hit her until now that Coal's disappearance was a result of trying to save a young bride from being married to an older man, a girl he was sweet on.

She rubbed the boy's lock of hair between her fingers, pondering the thought and only half listening to Cordelia's readings of Scripture.

Could it be that anyone who took away the right of an apostle to marry as he thought God directed him was considered an enemy of the Church?

The idea took her breath away.

Was this what blood atonement was all about? Had she understood Brother Foley correctly when he spoke of enemies of the Church, of saving their eternal souls by killing them on earth? Was this boy considered so vile?

She stared down at the grave, feeling sick again.

What if his death was just the beginning?

Mary Rose sensed her distress and looked over at her.

Cordelia stopped reading midsentence as Bronwyn fell to her knees. She dropped the boy's piece of hair and placed her hands on the old wooden door.

"He got in the way . . ." she whispered, looking up at the other two women. "It's clear to me now." Icy fear sliced into her heart. "The same thing may have happened to Coal." She put her face into her hands, scarcely able to breathe.

Cordelia knelt and put her arm around Bronwyn. Mary Rose did the same on the opposite side.

She looked with tear-filled eyes from one to the other. "What if we find out he was sweet on some young girl wanted by an apostle or someone else higher up in the Church . . . ?" Mary Rose handed her a handkerchief, and she dabbed at her eyes. "If that's what happened, think about Coal's disappearance . . . it's too similar."

Mary Rose's voice was little more than a whisper. "We can't believe the worst happened to Coal. We can't give up hope that he'll return to us."

Cordelia nodded. "I pray that's not what took this boy's life. All we know for certain is that this wasn't accidental. And pray, we shall—for the repose of this one's soul and for our boy, wherever he may be. We can't know, but I know One who does."

As the fragrant breeze fluttered the leaves of a nearby cottonwood and a sparrow sang, she prayed, "Lord God, Father Almighty, we thank you for this child's life, and we give him back to you this day on behalf of those who love him. We commend him to your spirit. Help us find his loved ones so that they may be at peace, just as you have welcomed this child into your kingdom. Your Son once said to bring the little children to him to bless. He also condemned those who did not welcome them in his name.

"We'll let you do the sorting out of the righteous and unrighteous, Father, for we can't imagine where we might begin. Keep us in your peace, even as this child rests in your eternal peace. Give us strength and wisdom to do as you would have us to do.

"Be with our boy Coal, wherever he is. So many things are out of our control, and too easily we can become overwhelmed by the darkness around us. Help us find the light.

"Most of all, give us your peace.

"In the holy name of Your Son, our Savior, Jesus Christ . . . Amen."

The women hugged, and as Cordelia and Mary Rose headed into the house, Bronwyn stooped to retrieve the lock of hair. She wrapped it again, and placed it in her pocket with the bits of fabric from the boy's clothing.

She looked at the gravesite, longing to spend a few minutes alone, honoring the boy somehow. She thought of the things that Coal once treasured—a collection of pretty stones he'd found, a well-worn book of an account of the Lewis and Clark expedition, a box of dead insects he thought interesting.

She thought about asking Mary Rose if she had kept them, then thought better of it. Burying such things with a boy who likely had collected similar objects would be like admitting Coal would never come home.

Reluctantly she turned from the grave. Drawing a deep breath, she thought of the task before her. She couldn't let another moment go by before being on her way. As it was, she was leaving later than planned.

Her preoccupation with the child's death had let time slip away from her. She glanced up at the angle of the sun, and her heart raced. Above all things, she couldn't allow herself to get caught by Gabe, or Enid, at the town house.

She raced to the barn, saddled and mounted the mare, and headed toward town. She urged her to a trot, and then to a canter. The big mare loped along on the hard alkaline ground. Bronwyn closed her eyes, enjoying the feel of the wind on her face, the knowledge that perhaps she would find some concrete answers, no matter how difficult they might be.

The emotion inside settled, and she breathed easier than she had since Gabe's proposal the night before. After a moment, she opened her eyes. Three riders, hats pulled low, horses galloping, a cloud of dust rising behind them, approached her at an angle.

She held her breath—a challenge since she trembled like a leaf—slowed the mare and watched as they drew nearer.

It hadn't occurred to her until this moment that she should have brought Gabe's pistol.

Mary Rose sat at her desk, her journal open in front of her. A breeze came through the open window, fluttering the curtains and rifling the pages. She touched them with her fingertips to keep them still, taking pleasure in the feel of the thick paper, the smell of the ink, even the formation of her letters and words.

This leather-bound book, and those that preceded it, chronicled her life. She had filled five since the day she stepped aboard the *Sea Hawk* in Liverpool and now this journal, her sixth, was nearly complete.

How could she bear to let them out of her sight? What if they were lost, or stolen, or simply tossed away with someone's garbage along the trail?

The thought of such a thing happening to her words brought an almost physical pain. The books held her deepest, most heartfelt thoughts about her hopes and dreams—dreams about the novel she wanted to write someday. The pages were sprinkled with outlines of her book, with scenes and character studies, story ideas and dialect studies for character dialogue. The journals were filled with details of dreams she'd never expected to share with anyone, dreams she'd sacrificed when she married Gabe, dreams that faded in the harsh reality of her new, closed world.

But Bronwyn was right. If these chronicles could be published, they might save lives . . . like the one of the child in the garden.

Rumor had it that Brigham Young would become Territorial Governor now that the Mexican-American war was coming to an end. Would things then become better or worse for the Saints?

The U.S. Government needed to know what was happening in this faraway place. Women caught up in polygamy, unable to get out, helpless to make decisions on their own because of the total dependency on husbands who controlled the terrain around them in this world as well as their fates in the next. And the children, how she wept for them.

She dipped her pen into the inkwell, and as she made her first stroke, she wondered if this might be the last time she would make an entry in this beloved book.

> *What follows may be difficult to read, but everything I am about to reveal is true.*
>
> *A child was found murdered in our garden today, his throat slit in a ritualistic manner. Bronwyn and I believe it is the result of a new teaching among the Saints: blood atonement, the taking of an enemy's life, the letting of his or her blood so that the sinner may enter heaven.*
>
> *When combined with the knowledge that there are those among us that make up a secret police force called the Danites (most commonly) or the Avenging Angels, who have carried out raids on apostates or other enemies of the Latter-day Saints as far back as our days in Nauvoo, it is easy to see that this new teaching can encompass a wide range of real or imagined sins against God's chosen.*

Mary Rose sat back and drew a deep, shaky breath. Her right hand, still holding the pen, trembled, and a drop of ink spilled on the page. She watched its edges spider outward as it soaked into the paper fibers.

She was about to commit to paper the names of those she believed to be involved in crimes. Some were the names of people she knew well, good family men who loved their wives and children, but who rode out at night in secrecy, carrying out orders of those they've believed heard the voice of God.

If, by some miracle, the journals made it into the hands of government investigators, these same men might be condemned and imprisoned. If they were discovered by Foley's men, she would be condemned for naming them.

She swallowed hard and bowed her head. Could she actually go through with this? Then she remembered the boy in the garden.

She squared her shoulders, dipped the pen in the inkwell, and again began to write.

> *First, I will identify the leaders in this secret vigilante group called the Danites. . .*

Mary Rose didn't how much time had passed, but when she'd finished she had filled two-dozen pages, front and back. She'd named names, given dates and places that had been only whispered about before. If events were rumors, she said so, but provided enough information that should a government agent want to investigate, he would have a starting place. If her information was based on real evidence, she wrote every detail she could remember. She didn't realize until she started writing just how much evidence she had, or how it all fit together.

When she finished, she sat back and reread her words for accuracy. She reviewed the dates, times, places of Danite attacks as far back as the dark days following the assassination of Joseph Smith and his brother. She paid attention, especially, to the people involved, based on their whereabouts before, during, or after the attacks, sometimes whispered by eyewitnesses, other times by not-so-tight-lipped wives.

Her third time through the list, she stopped, stunned, her heart pounding. One name seemed to crop up far more than any of the others.

Bronwyn was right. Gabe was involved.

"Mama?" Spence called from the doorway. He looked up at her with eyes so much like Gabe's they took her breath away.

She held out her arms, and he ran into them. She gathered him into her lap, and he snuggled close. A moment later, Joey trailed behind, smiling up at her. Laughing lightly, she lifted him beside Spence and gave them both hugs. The boys had grown so much their legs almost reached the floor.

They chattered happily as she reached over and closed the journal. Their lives would soon be an open book for the world to read.

Could she go through with the plan? Gabe was their father.

TWENTY-SIX

The three men halted their horses on the trail in front of Bronwyn. The rider in the lead, a sandy-haired man, surprised her by smiling and tipping his hat. "Ma'am," he said.

Behind him, an old mountain man did the same, though not before giving her a strange, lingering stare. The third, dressed in buckskins, wore his mud-colored hair Indian style, plaited at the back of his head with a leather thong. He turned his horse so his back was to her. All three wore dust kerchiefs that covered their faces, though when they intersected her path, the sandy-haired man pulled his down to speak.

"Nice day for an outing," he said, as if they'd just come from an English tea.

She nodded even as she fought the urge to grin at such an incongruous greeting. Suspicion won out. Any sense of humor she might have had in the past was gone. Especially today.

Her mare seemed as nervous as she did, took a few steps sideways, snorted noisily.

Surprisingly, the swayback nag the old mountain man rode matched the motion and sound of her mare with a precise imitation. Then he added what appeared to be a big yellow-toothed smile.

This time she couldn't help grinning. "Yes, 'tis," she said, and dipped her head slightly. Again, she noticed the open stares of the mountain man. Smiling horse or not, she still didn't like the fact that she was in the middle of desert terrain without protection, and three men on horseback blocked her trail.

"Well, ma'am," the sandy-haired man said, finally, "we'd best let you be on our way. We hope we didn't frighten you. There are some rather dangerous elements in this territory. But I don't suppose we're telling you anything you don't already know, considering you live here. "

The mountain man dropped his kerchief and gave her a friendly nod. "Speaking of that, would you like us to accompany you to town? Make sure you get there safe?" His manner of speaking held a slight Scottish brogue, not unusual in the Mormon community. Converts continued to arrive almost weekly from Britain. Brigham, like Joseph Smith before him, considered it fertile ground for recruits. Even her own fading Welsh accent was accepted without notice.

Something else about the man's tone, his commanding presence, even dressed as he was, caught her attention.

"Thank you for offering," she said. "I travel this trail often. I'm nearly there—to town, that is—and I'm certain I will be quite safe."

"Well, then," the sandy-haired man said. "You just holler if you need help. We're camped out over yonder—" he gestured toward a stand of cottonwoods by the river— "and we'll come running." He gave her a wide smile that seemed to light the sky and then retied his kerchief.

The old man on the swayback did the same, then he surprised

her further by adding, "Just consider us your guardian angels should you need us. That goes for anytime, night or day." His eyes met hers, and she caught her breath at their intensity.

"Guardian angels?" What a strange thing to say.

"'Be not forgetful to entertain strangers: for thereby some have entertained angels unawares,'" the man quoted, his eyes twinkling above the kerchief. By the crinkles at the edges of his eyes, Bronwyn was pretty sure a smile was also hidden beneath.

Throughout the exchange the youngest man said nothing. As they rode away from her, she realized he'd spent the entire time looking off in the distance, his horse turned away from her.

The few minutes spent with the group lifted her spirits—just when they needed lifting. She sighed deeply as she nudged the mare forward again.

God moments, Cordelia called such encounters. When someone touches your heart in an unexpected way or when the beauty of the world pierces your soul. The trill of birdsong. The color of a sunset. The scent of a baby at your breast.

An unexpected encounter with someone, a stranger, whose eyes reflected love. Not romantic love, but something else inside. An inner light perhaps?

Her thoughts went back to Cordelia's prayer over the boy's body. She had prayed for light in the darkness. Had this encounter been an answer to Cordelia's prayer? Perhaps she hadn't entertained angels unaware, but they had certainly entertained her.

Hosea halted his horse, and his companions did the same, watching as the young woman rode away from them.

The youngest of the three nudged his horse closer to Hosea's.

He looked into the young man's eyes and saw the pain there. "Something tells me this encounter was one of the most difficult in your life."

"Aye," the boy said. "I wanted to run to her, shout out, grab her hands and pull her from the back of that horse and then dance at her surprise."

"Her surprise might have been too great to bear," Greyson said, riding closer. "After all, she hasn't seen you since long before Gabriel's wagon train left Nauvoo. She may think you're dead."

Coal shook his head. "She would never think me dead. Neither would Mother Mary Rose. They would go on hoping above all hope to see me again, believing in me—that I would be clever enough to get myself out of any scrape."

"Ah, yes," Hosea sighed.

The boy looked stricken. "I'm sorry. I didn't mean that Sister Enid wouldn't believe in you . . . that you couldn't see yourself out of . . ." His voice trailed off. "I mean, maybe in her heart of hearts she believes that about you too."

Hosea threw back his head and laughed. "Different circumstances, indeed, dear boy. I was reported dead by my crew. They experienced the same storm's fury—the same that washed me overboard. No one dreamed I would survive such a thing." MacDuff danced sideways, whinnied, and shook his head. "You disappeared, and though they may have guessed the Dakota had something to do with it, their search came up with nothing—or so Sister Amanda told us." He paused. "I think you're right, though. Your mothers, I imagine, have never given up hope."

Coal nodded. "I just wish I could let them know I'm here. If it just weren't so dangerous for them . . ."

"You've chosen the right path, at least for now," Greyson said. "These are dangerous times. I've met with the courageous Sister Amanda and heard her stories. You are right to protect yourself—and your family."

"Seein' her just now, though"—Coal sniffled and wiped his nose on his sleeve—"made me want to forget everything about keeping us safe. I had to turn my back so I couldn't look into her eyes. That would've made me blubber for sure."

Hosea chuckled again. "You did fine, boy. Just fine. You've still got the look of the Dakota, just like you did the first time I laid eyes on you."

Coal brightened. "That was something, wasn't it?"

"One for the books," Greyson said, laughing with them. "And I intend to see it gets written."

By the time Bronwyn reached the outskirts of town, the streets were bustling, which allowed her to blend in with the knots of people. Again, she marveled at how much change had come in the short time the Saints had been there. For as far as the eye could see crops thrived, and within the town itself, businesses prospered—liveries, mercantiles, barbers, doctors, and even a yarn and fabric shop run by several wives Bronwyn knew.

She slipped from the horse in front of a mercantile, a distance from Gabe's house, let the mare drink her fill from a trough, and then tied her to a hitching post. She spotted Brother Brigham's large home rising above the others around it, and headed for it.

Minutes later, she stood in front of Gabe and Enid's town house. She studied the windows and watched for movement inside but saw none. So, shoulders back, she strode up the walk way as if expected.

She rapped on the door and waited a moment. When no one came, she pulled out a key that Gabe had left at the ranch right after the town house was completed. Quickly, she stepped inside.

The light was dim because of the shade trees in front, and she dared not light the lamp on the desk.

She sat and tried to pull out the drawer where Gabe had hurriedly folded the papers and then hidden them away. It wouldn't budge. She reached into her reticule for her nail file, jimmied the tip this way and that, but the mechanism stayed frozen in place.

Nibbling her bottom lip, she looked around, trying to think of something else that might work. Hairpin!

She reached up, grabbed one from her hair, and placed it into the keyhole. Again, she jimmied the locked. Again, to no avail.

She leaned back in the chair. Surely, she hadn't come all this way to be defeated by a small lock. She touched the desk, admiring its solid, beautiful lines. She opened other unlocked drawers, rifled around for extra keys or tools that might work.

Nothing.

The shadows grew longer; she was running out of time. She either had to open it now, or leave.

She didn't want to scar the desk and leave evidence it had been tampered with, but she was desperate to see what Gabe had hidden.

She held the nail file to the lock, lifted a paperweight, prepared to tap the file.

That's when she heard the distinct sound of hooves by the side of the house. The shadow of horse and rider passed by the window, and fear knotted her stomach. Gabe! She heard him ride into the barn, followed by the jangle of tack as he removed the saddle. She stood, trying to decide whether to run from the front door before he came in the back. Or to take a chance that he might come around to the front—which meant she should run for the back.

Gabe's shadow passed by the window again. Now there was no time for escape. She looked around wildly for a hiding place. Nothing. Just as the front door lock clicked, she ran for the dining room and stepped behind the long lace curtain.

If he so much as glanced her direction, he would see her through the lace. She tried to console herself with the fact that the dining room was likely the last place he'd enter this time of day.

The front door opened, and he went immediately to the desk. He reached into his vest pocket, pulled out the key, and opened the drawer. He reached for the papers inside, then he frowned. Setting down the papers, he picked up Bronwyn's nail file.

He turned it over. Once. Twice. Still frowning, he stood.

Bronwyn held her breath.

Studying the nail file, he walked across the room, coming straight for her. She closed her eyes, waiting for the awful moment of discovery.

Then she heard his footsteps on the stairs. "Enid," he called. "Are you home? I didn't see your horse . . ."

Bronwyn ran for the desk, grabbed the papers, and slipped through the door, not bothering to close it.

She lifted up her skirts and ran until she reached the end of the street, then clutching the papers close, she raised her chin as any lady about town might do and adopted a leisurely stroll, nodding her greetings to the other women she met along the way.

Once she reached the mare, she let out a deep pent-up breath, and put her forehead against the saddle for a moment to let her heart stop its racing. She then tucked the papers into the saddlebag, mounted, and with a few more friendly nods to passersby, nudged the horse back onto the road leading out of town.

As soon as she was clear of town, Bronwyn turned the mare toward the river. The papers in her saddlebag were too important to go unread until she reached the ranch.

She spotted a clearing, shaded by a stand of small cottonwoods and protected from sight by a mix of desert plants and succulents along the trail. She slid from the saddle, her fingers trembling as she pulled out Gabe's papers. The river was unexpectedly shallow in this spot. She stopped for a moment to listen to its burbling rush, breathing in the scent of moist soil and damp. It calmed her spirit somewhat, and after she led the mare to the edge of the river to drink, she spotted a decaying log nearby. She went over to it and sat.

She'd never stolen anything in her life, and what she'd done at Gabe's town house nagged at her soul as if she'd stolen gold from a bank. She dropped her head, and Gabe's image filled her mind. Would he ever forgive her once he found out what she'd done?

What if the papers were merely some innocent drawings of the temple? Perhaps even the secret places deep inside the temple, places where ordinary Saints weren't even allowed to go? She looked down at the papers in her hands. If they were innocent of all wrongdoing, she would have to confess what she'd done, and Gabe would consider her untrustworthy . . . just as he'd told her the others thought. And he had defended her.

She unfolded the first paper. It was a list of some kind. She spotted her name at the top, then Mary Rose's. She expected to see Enid's next as Gabe's third wife. A list of marriages, perhaps, though she couldn't imagine why they'd need to be written in such a way.

Then she noted that the names that followed were men's names. And boys. Sons of some of their friends.

Puzzled, she flipped the paper over. Her breath caught in her throat. The opposite side, it seemed had been written by someone other than Gabe, and it gave the reason for the list that "followed." It had just happened that she'd read the list first.

POSSIBLE APOSTATES, it read at the top of the page.

This was not a plan detailing the holy of holies. Far from it.

This was a list of people who needed watching. She turned the paper over again to be sure she'd read it correctly. Her gaze fell on the first name: Bronwyn MacKay. And then the second: Mary Rose MacKay.

She sat there, shaken and distressed, trying to take in what it meant. Gabe had told her that she was being watched, so that wasn't new. But Mary Rose? What had she done?

Bronwyn forced her breathing to slow, to calm herself so she could think clearly. She looked out over the river, watching the swirls of water rapidly move by, taking in the cruel and abhorrent meaning. And then went back to the list. Many of the names were familiar. Hers and Mary Rose's were the only two women's names.

Curiously, an entire paragraph had been written about one of the "possible apostates." She frowned at the implications as she read:

> *Andrew Greyson, eastern newspaper reporter, last known to be living outside the city. He stops by town to ask questions of innocent Saints, befriends them, wheedles information out of them. A report to* New York Chronicle *was intercepted by a Brother on the trail outside St. Louis. It is now in our possession. He condemns our prophet, asking the U.S. Government to intercede, to keep him from becoming Territorial Governor. This enemy of our people, of our prophet, of our Church must be stopped at all costs. "Blood atonement" is our cry!*

Below the description of Andrew Greyson, someone had drawn a crude map of the city, the lake, and the river leading to it. An *X* with a circle around it had been marked near a sweeping bend in the river. She stared at it.

The place was not far from where she sat. Not far from where she met the three men on the trail.

Two thoughts hit her at once: Could one of the men have been Greyson? If so, he had to be warned. And if she was right—her heart raced at the thought—he might the one who could carry Mary Rose's journals out of the territory.

She folded the paper and opened the second.

At first she didn't understand it, then she read it again, catching her hand to her mouth.

> *I, the undersigned, as legal guardian and parent of Ruby MacKay and Pearl MacKay, do promise them in marriage to one, Apostle Erastus Gibbons, on the day they reach their fourteenth year.*

Erastus Gibbons, one of the Forum of Twelve, a powerful man within the Church. Powerful, old, and the husband of some twenty-seven wives.

And then she read the signature.

Gabriel MacKay

She stared at the name, too stunned for tears, too sickened to move.

TWENTY-SEVEN

Hosea sat by the river a ways upstream from camp, trying to catch another rainbow trout or two for supper. He was lost in thought when Coal made his way almost silently through the willows, sat beside him, and handed him some wadded up balls of bread to use for bait.

He looked up at the boy and nodded. "Even though you turned your back today, I knew you wanted to talk to Bronwyn. Why didn't you tell her?"

Coal grinned. "Why didn't you—about who you are, I mean?"

Hosea laughed lightly. "My revelation has to wait until I tell Enid myself. I don't want her to find out about me from Bronwyn or anyone else."

Coal picked up a small, flat stone and skipped it across the water. "Did you see that? Seven."

"You're getting better. Trouble is, you're scaring off the fish."

"I got one to skip eight times last night." Coal grinned and sat down to bait his hook.

The sun slipped toward the western horizon. "You still didn't answer my question. Why aren't you anxious to go to your family?"

Coal stared at the water, his hands dangling over his bent knees. "I worry about putting them in danger. If it gets out that I'm back, Brother Riordan will come after me—and them too, especially Mother Bronwyn." He picked up his pole and tossed the line into the river. The bread bobbed along with the wavelets for a few moments then disappeared beneath the surface.

"What you did to stop his marriage to Sarah happened a long time ago."

"Some people have long memories." He kept his eyes on his line.

"Why do I get the feeling you're not telling me everything."

Coal sighed, and then faced him, a half-smile turning up the corner of his mouth. "Probably because I'm not."

Hosea looked at the boy's flushed cheeks and the way his gaze drifted nonchalantly off over the river. He and Greyson had both learned to read Coal like an open book.

"Is it Sarah?"

Coal nodded. "She saw me walking down the street while you were in the assayer's office last week. She ran after me, insisting that we talk. I was afraid for her safety. I told her she shouldn't be seen with me, but she just laughed and said no one would know who I was. Of course, I pointed out that she had figured it out. She said that was different. Then she got a funny look on her face, turned bright red, and didn't say any more about that."

He swallowed hard. "She led me to a place behind the livery, told me about something called blood atonement, a new teaching. She said that it means anyone who goes against the Church and the prophet's teachings is an enemy. They will be punished. She even made the sign of someone slitting her throat. She was crying when she told me. And she's scared. She said she'd do anything to get out, but she's afraid—not just for herself. Her pa said he'd kill her ma if she ever left the apostle."

Hosea's heart caught. He'd tried hard not to judge this group and their teachings. Much of it was biblical, and he saw no quarrel. They loved their families. They were hardworking and industrious. And he knew that men beating up on their wives could happen anywhere, not just among the Mormons.

But to teach something like what Coal was talking about . . . ? Surely, the girl had it wrong.

"Blood atonement?" He studied Coal's flushed face. "Are you certain that the teaching isn't about Christ's atonement? He bled and died for our sins. Maybe people didn't understand the teaching."

Coal shook his head. "That's what she said. She said I need to be careful, that her husband, the apostle, is still angry about what Mother Bronwyn and I did the day of their wedding." He fell silent for a moment.

"If I contact my family, they'll all be in danger." He sat down again. "I came all this way to find them. Today when I saw Mother Bronwyn, it was all I could do to keep from running up to that old mare of hers and pulling her down into the biggest hug you ever saw."

He sniffled. "All this time I've been trying to figure out what to do, how to get a message to Mother Bronwyn or Mother Mary Rose, but when it comes right down to it, it's them I worry about, not me. If I'm seen with them, if it gets out that I've contacted them . . ." He sniffled again. "And poor Sarah. I'd like to save her, give her a chance for a real life. It's a crime what's happened to her."

Hosea gave him a rough hug. "I don't believe in coincidences. I believe all that happened to you with the Dakota Sioux, how they happened upon my campsite—which brought us together—was no accident. Same thing about Bronwyn crossing our path today. It was also no accident you talked to Sarah and that she told you what she did." He fell quiet for a time, and they both just watched the river go by. "There's a Scripture verse in the second book of Chronicles that brings me solace when I think of the darkness around us, when I think of all that needs doing, and I know I can't do it alone, or perhaps at all.

"I don't remember the exact words, but it reads something like this:

> 'You will not have to fight this battle. Take up your positions; stand firm and see the deliverance the LORD will give you . . . Do not be afraid; do not be discouraged. Go out to face them tomorrow, and the LORD will be with you.'"

"Like officers and crew on a ship," Coal said with a grin. "We stand ready, waiting for the captain's orders."

Hosea laughed. "Something like that, yes."

"You think there's a chance Mother Bronwyn might've recognized us today?"

"Not you," Hosea said. "You had your back to her the whole time." He thought about the way she'd studied his face. There seemed to be something there that sparked interest in him. "But maybe she knew me."

Coal grinned. "Your whole face is different. Besides, you had on that kerchief to keep from breathing that dust." He shook his head. "That dust sure beats all. I've never seen anything like it. Did you hear them saying in town today that some of the farmers are having trouble with crickets and grasshoppers? Up north, apparently. There are thousands. Everybody's hoping and praying they don't come our direction. We'll need more'n kerchiefs to keep 'em off our faces."

"No, I didn't hear that. Might just be talk. Somebody exaggerating." Hosea thought he felt a nibble at the end of his pole and pulled up his hook to see that it was empty. He rolled another wad of bread, set the hook in it, and then tossed the line out again.

"I just want to go home," Coal said. "I want everything to be the way it used to be." He gazed at Hosea. "I know folks on the outside say that polygamy is of the devil himself, but we had a happy family—at least until En—" He turned red. "I'm sorry."

"That's all right," Hosea said. "I can't imagine that any two women can get along as the wives of the same man. And when you add a third to the mix, especially a fiery soul like Enid, there's bound to be fireworks."

"What about you? How long are you going to wait to tell Enid you're here?"

"That's the question of my heart," he said. He watched the river roll by for a moment. "Just about the time I think I'm ready, I either get cold feet or decide it might cause her too much distress to find out the husband she thought dead is alive."

"But you told me this is your Nineveh," Coal said, sounding wiser than his years. "That's what Greyson's always calling it."

"That's when we've got to think about the verse I just told you about."

"How can you be so patient? I'm about ready to jump out of my skin I want so much so badly. I want my family." He swiped at the tears that filled his eyes. "I don't like all this danger and secret stuff. I just want to be safe with the ones I love." His voice softened. "Do you remember Ruby from the *Sea Hawk*? How she used to lisp? It was the sweetest thing you ever heard. None of us wanted her to lose that ol' lisp. And that Pearl. She has a mole the shape of a heart just under her right ear. She used to cry if Mother Mary Rose didn't plait her hair just right so it showed. She was afraid it was the only way people could tell her apart from Ruby."

"I remember the twins quite well," Hosea said. "They were little ring-tail tooters aboard the *Sea Hawk*." He chuckled. "It was the talk at officers' mess when Lady Mary Rose decided to let them keep a pet lobster in her bathtub and the cabin boy had to bring fresh water every morning just for the lobster."

"Oscar the Lobster, or as Ruby would say, Othcar the Lobther." Coal's eyes filled again. "Mother Bronwyn—though she wasn't *Mother* Bronwyn then—called us her little lambs. No one had ever called us that before. I acted like I didn't like it 'cause I was too big for such a thing. But I'd think about it at night in bed, remembering way back to when my ma and pa used to tell us Bible stories. They talked about Jesus Christ being the Good Shepherd. And I'd think about Mother Bronwyn and how she called us lambs, her face so beautiful and full of love, like we really mattered, and decided that if Jesus Christ the Good Shepherd was like her, I'd like him just fine."

He looked up at Hosea. "I wish we were back there, that you were our captain, and Mary Rose and Gabe were there just starting to like each other, and you and Gabe were laughing and talking up on the bridge when you thought nobody was listening. And everybody was talking about the miracle of Little Grace, and Bronwyn and Griffin were happy as clams . . ." He turned away, embarrassed by his outburst.

His pole suddenly dipped. "You've got a bite," Hosea said. "Looks like a big one."

"Whoo-ee," Coal said. "She's a good'un, all right."

Hosea watched him fight the fish, set the hook, and pull the gleaming, silvery trout out of the water.

Coal held up a hand. "I hear voices," he said. "Coming from the campsite."

Hosea stood, now at full alert. "It's Greyson and someone else."

"A woman," Coal whispered, his face turning white. "I think it's Mother Bronwyn."

TWENTY-EIGHT

Bronwyn remounted and headed upriver, searching the thick brush and undergrowth for signs of a campsite.

Of course, anyone writing about the prophet with recommendations such as Greyson's knew enough to keep well hidden.

She kept the mare at an even walk. The sun had begun its descent, and she didn't have much time before she needed to head back to the ranch.

She'd gone only a half-mile or so when she heard the yipping of a coyote. She halted the mare and then realized the sound seemed more like that of a domestic dog than a wild animal. She urged the mare forward again, this time slower, scanning the brush on both sides of the trail.

The mare started and whinnied when a small black and white mutt came barreling out of the brush, yipping and wagging his tail so hard his entire rear end waggled with it.

Bronwyn couldn't help smiling. She dismounted and walked over to the little guy and patted him on the head. "I assume you belong to someone nearby," she said, and stooped to rub the soft fur under his chin.

"You assumed correctly," a voice said behind her.

Bronwyn turned and couldn't help smiling despite her low spirits and desperate mission.

The man who had suddenly materialized was of average height. She'd seen his face before, earlier on the trail, but now that she could get a closer look, she was quite astonished by it. It wasn't that he was extraordinarily handsome. His face was quite ordinary except for his gentle, intelligent hazel eyes and the laugh lines around them. He had sandy hair and sported a day or two's growth of mustache and beard that matched.

No, what struck her as extraordinary went beyond his physical appearance. His expression contained a sense of wonder, as if he looked upon the world with awe, ready to catch its miracles, its goodness, its beauty. His smile was boyishly affectionate, yet it seemed the kind of smile he would give anyone he met, not just her. She trusted him right away.

"My name's Bronwyn MacKay," she said.

"Good to meet you, Bronwyn MacKay. I'm Andrew Greyson."

"I'd hoped so," she said.

His laugh was easy, as if it was something he did often. "I must say, that's one of the most original greetings I've had come my way in some time."

"We met earlier on the trail."

"I remember."

She hesitated, thinking of all she had to reveal, and took a deep breath.

"You look like you could use a place to sit down. I don't have much in the way of furniture, but you're welcome to sit a spell if you like." He led the way back into the brush, his little dog prancing along behind him. Leading the horse, Bronwyn followed him until she was sure the animal was hidden from the trail, and then wrapped the reins around the branch of a nearby tree. She reached into the saddlebag for the papers, and then followed Greyson to a large clearing.

The campsite consisted of a fire pit, long cold, a couple of logs pulled toward the pit, and farther out, some bedrolls. Sacks of food hung from tree branches. "Bears," he said when he noticed her quizzical look. "It seems they like our food as much as we do." He pointed to the logs. "A settee, m'lady, or a wingback?"

She grinned as she sat on a log opposite where he'd been working. Papers were scattered here and there, covered with neat lines of writing. Packets stuffed with other papers were stacked nearby. His fingers were stained with black ink.

Greyson looked at her curiously, his head cocked. The little dog sat near him, his tail wags sweeping the soil beneath him.

"I've discovered you're a newspaperman, a reporter. You've come here to learn about the Mormons and write to your newspaper about us."

He blinked in surprise. "You're absolutely correct, but may I ask how you found this out?"

She handed him the list of Danite names. He blanched as he read through it, and she could hear his breathing. He looked up when he'd gone through the names.

"Turn it over," she said.

He flipped the paper, and turned white. She hadn't noticed his freckles until his skin turned lighter than their darker pigment. He stared at the indictment for several moments and then looked up.

"Where did you find this?"

"In my husband's desk."

He listened quietly. "Thank you for coming to warn me. I'm sure it's at great risk to you personally."

"I have other reasons for seeking you out—though I would have warned you anyway," she said. "It's become increasing obvious to my sister wife and I that we need to get word out about what is happening to the wives and children in this community. My sister wife, Mary Rose, has kept detailed records with names and events of Danite offenses through the years. This militia—the Danites—were formed years ago for our protection, but their power has now moved far beyond what was originally intended. We fear for our people and for our families. We fear for the good people who are among us."

"I can understand why," Greyson said. "Your name is at the top of your husband's list."

"And Mary Rose's is second." She paused, choosing her words carefully, wanting to be as precise as possible. "A boy was killed, his throat slit, and he was buried in our garden. I need to find out why. I have my suspicions, but I won't stop until I get to the bottom of this."

"You've just answered my next question . . ."

"Which is . . . ?"

"Do you, your children, and Mary Rose want to leave with me? My friends and I could I get you out, get you to safety. There's a wagon train approaching. I met the captain. He's a good man. The company is made up of families from Arkansas. But there are enough men and firearms to protect you and get you to California."

"Yes," she said, "we must leave. Our lives are at stake. But we would only slow you down. You must go without us. I promise we'll follow as soon as we can."

He studied her face for a moment. "You don't have long—they are due to leave within days, possible hours. And your sister wife Mary Rose . . . you said she's on the list."

"Yes. She won't leave her children, any of our children."

He huffed out an impatient sigh. "Think of your own children. Their lives."

"I am. We'll get them to the wagon train. But you must leave first—go directly to Fort Bridger."

"You've done some studying of the route."

She nodded. "We've planned to leave for some time. We just didn't think it would come at a time of such urgency." She hesitated, then went on, "It's not just a matter of discovering who the boy is—though that is important. This may be part of a ritualistic bloodletting called blood atonement. More young men will die, if that's the case."

He visibly blanched. "There's no time to go into that now, but if you need information—and it appears you do—I have a friend among the people here. I met her at Winter Quarters, and I've run into her in town a few times since. She's helped me with information for my articles. She's a good woman. A brave woman."

"What is her name?"

"Sister Amanda Riordan. Though when she communicates with me in writing, she uses her maiden name—Beatrice Leverton. As did so many, she came into this 'new religion' never expecting what has happened."

"I know her. Not well, but I know a young girl who was forced into marrying her husband."

He gave her a steady look, and Bronwyn had an eerie feeling he already knew that, somehow.

"Go to her," he said. "Find out if she knows anything about young men and blood atonement. Use her maiden name, if need be—she'll know we've talked."

"You don't seem surprised," Bronwyn said. "About blood atonement."

"I've heard of the practice in my travels, mostly rumors."

"Will you take the journals?"

"Of course. You must get them here right away. From the looks of this missive, the Danites may strike any time. It's obvious they know where to find me." He paused, looking at her with such admiration and kindness, the sweetness of the moment made her want to cry. "I—we, those who are with me—will do anything possible to help you. No matter what happens, don't forget that."

"My guardian angels," she said, standing. "I remember what your friend said."

His eyes crinkled into a smile. "My friend might be one, sometimes I think he's got hidden wings. But as for me"—he patted the top of his head— "no halo here I'm afraid." He chuckled as he escorted her back to the mare.

He started to hand the list to her, but Bronwyn shook her head. "Keep it for evidence. There's something else you need to have." She handed him the agreement Gabe signed to give the twins away in marriage. "This is also evidence of giving young girls in marriage to old men in powerful positions."

He read the statement that Gabe had signed. When he looked up, his expression was filled with white-lipped anger.

"You're certain this is his handwriting . . . his signature?"

"I'm sure."

"This man is your husband?"

She nodded. "Until now, I thought he loved all our children so much he would give his life in exchange for any one of them." Her eyes filled with tears and she looked away from him. "I never expected this of Gabe. Ever."

"You all should get out now—before anything else can happen."

"I'll bring you the journals tonight. I beg you to get them to the proper authorities. The evil must stop."

He sighed. "I'll be prepared to leave as soon as you arrive."

She gave him a quick nod. "Thank you."

Bronwyn mounted and nudged the mare to a walk. Going over Gabe's list of apostates and enemies made everything acutely real to her. Rereading the promise of marriage Gabe signed appalled and sickened her. She didn't know if she could look Gabe in the face again without giving away her anger. And he and Enid were moving back into the ranch house this night.

Maybe Greyson was right. Maybe she and Mary Rose should get out with the children. Now. They had spent months planning their escape. Everything was ready.

She and Mary Rose had talked about the connection of the boy in the garden to blood atonement. It might seem a stretch to some, but they wondered if the men in high places might use the teaching to be rid of young boys or men who were competition for the young brides they themselves wanted in their bed.

What if the boy in the garden was just the beginning of such a blood bath. She shivered, thinking of it.

Could she exchange her desire to root out that evil for the lives of her children? Was she being unreasonable to expect that she and Mary Rose could protect the children, could protect the twins, when they were at the top of the list of apostates?

Should they pick up everything and run? Or stay and fight?

She halted the mare just before leaving the trail beside the river. She dismounted and walked along a narrow path to the water. She leaned against a cottonwood trunk and dropped her face into her hands.

"Oh, Lord. My sorrow is inconsolable," she whispered. "I've come to you before, telling you I don't believe you're real. And here I am again, still not knowing if you're listening, or if you care. Or if you're real.

"But I don't know what else to do, where else to go. My heart is heavy with worry—about my family, about the evil deeds being carried out in your name. I can't bear the heaviness anymore. I don't want to stay, neither do I feel I can go.

"I feel so alone. And scared. Not just for me. But for my family. Little Grace and Joey and Spence. For Ruby and Pearl. Oh, Lord, especially for them." She paused, letting the sounds of the flowing, bubbling water fill her senses, her soul. "For Coal. And for the family of the boy in the garden."

She fell to her knees and scooped up water with her hands, letting the cold liquid flow over her face. "Oh, God," she whispered. "Help me. Help us all."

PART III

Forgiveness is the fragrance the violet sheds on the heel that has crushed it.

~Mark Twain

TWENTY-NINE

Bronwyn knelt by the river's edge for several minutes, letting the sounds of the water bring peace to her troubled soul. A breeze rifled through the leaves above her, cooling her damp face, rattling the leaves. A few twisted loose and floated down beside her; a few others fell on the water and sailed downstream.

"They look like little boats, don't they?" a voice said from somewhere in the brush beside her.

She started, frowning. Then the resonance, the timbre, of a beloved voice filled her senses. She turned and peered into the tangle of undergrowth, but didn't see anyone.

"Once we made little boats with walnut shells and candle wax," the voice said, "a long time ago. You had me pick up pieces of straw and round leaves just big enough for sails. We melted the wax and filled the half-shell . . . then stuck in a piece of straw."

She squeezed her eyes shut as the memory flooded her heart. She remembered every detail, the look of wonder on a boy's face, the wonder of a mother's love as she watched him play. She caught her hands to her mouth, afraid to hope that the voice was real.

She took a breath and held it, waiting to hear the voice again.

"You told me that as long as I could dream dreams, I could sail anywhere in my mind. No matter where I was or what had happened to me, I could think of the good memories, of those who loved me and would never forget me, and that I would survive.

"You called me your little lamb . . ." his voice broke " . . . and though I thought of myself as much too big for such things, that's the memory I kept with me the whole time I was gone. I thought of those little boats and what you had said, and I didn't forget. Ever."

Coal stepped out of the brush.

Bronwyn drank in the sight of him. He was taller and something awful had happened to his hair. But his smile, his eyes, everything else about him . . . was just as she remembered. Just more of him and his voice had changed. Now, he sounded like a man.

He grinned at her.

"Coal . . ." she whispered, and opened her arms.

He fell into them, sobbing.

THIRTY

Bronwyn rode into the ranch, unsure how she would answer the question of where she'd been all afternoon. She was relieved to find no one outside the house. But as she rode by the garden, she noticed a gaping hole. Obviously, the body had been moved—by the undertaker, she assumed. Probably after someone from the police force had been out to investigate.

She dismounted, removed the saddle, and then took her time rubbing down the mare. She was still brushing the tangles from the old girl's mane when she heard the footfall of someone approaching.

She turned to see Gabe enter the door and willed herself not to recoil. He walked closer and she turned her head to avoid looking at him.

"You've been gone quite a long time."

"I—I took a ride . . . out by the river. It took longer than I expected. I needed to clear my mind."

She heard him sigh. "The boy was killed by the Paiute."

Her laugh was bitter. "I expected a more creative story from the Danites."

"What do you mean?"

She glanced at him. "Why would an Indian slit a boy's throat and bury his body under a door in our garden." She shook her head. "Why would anyone, for that matter?"

"Brother Foley isn't through with his investigation."

She stopped combing the mare's mane and looked up at him. Her gaze was piercing, accusing. She didn't care.

"Where else did you go this afternoon?"

She didn't answer.

"Someone said they saw you in town."

"It's time for me to go inside, Gabe. Would you please see to the mare for me?" She handed him the tool and brushed past him. She marched toward the house, still steaming. She did her best to put it aside before she reached the front door. She hesitated, her hand on the doorknob, and thought only about the children and her love for them.

How she wished she could tell them about Coal. But she couldn't. Not yet. She had kept Coal in the dark about Gabe's involvement with the Danites and the list she'd found. Even without knowing, he understood the danger he might bring to the family if it was known he was alive. He suggested before she could utter the sorrowful words that he needed to stay away for now.

Cordelia always said that love was the light that dispelled darkness. At this moment, she needed their love to dispel the darkness in her heart. As soon as she opened the door, children tumbled from every corner, running to hug her, shouting their joyful greetings, covering her with love and kisses. Joey and Spence grabbed her legs, hanging on as she tried to walk to a chair. She couldn't help but laugh and sit down on the floor, grabbing them and pulling them into big embraces. Little Grace came over and threw her arms around her shoulders, leaning against her back. "I missed you, Mommy." She snuggled her cheek against Bronwyn's neck.

"And I missed you, little lamb."

"Mother Enid has been reading to me all afternoon. She went to the mercantile and bought me a book about horses. It's beautiful."

Bronwyn exchanged a smile with Enid. The small act brought more peace into Bronwyn's fragile soul. Mary Rose came down the stairs, the twins trailing, chattering like little magpies.

Grinning, she came over to show Bronwyn a quilt that Ruby and Pearl were teaching her to sew. She never had gotten the knack of sewing, and the girls had taken it upon themselves to see that they taught her. Everyone seemed to be talking a mile a minute, and Bronwyn closed her eyes, relishing the sound. She again wished she could tell them all about Coal, and smiled, imagining the day they would see him.

Cordelia had been busy out in the kitchen and came through the door just then. "I hope you all are hungry. I made chicken and dumplings to celebrate us all being together as one great big family tonight. And Little Grace made cornbread, best I ever tasted."

"Hmmm-hmm." Almost in chorus, the children hummed their hungry approval. The twins went out to help set the table, and Little Grace scampered along behind.

Bronwyn held Spence and Joey a few minutes longer, loving the puppy-dog smell of them. Then they too scampered off to see what they could get into in the kitchen. Clatters and bangs of heaven knew what soon followed.

Bronwyn asked Mary Rose if she could speak to her privately, and the two women climbed the stairs. Enid, left alone sitting in Cordelia's rocker, seemed lost in the horse book she'd bought Little Grace.

Mary Rose sat on the edge of the bed while Bronwyn washed

her face and hands, and then brushed her hair. When she'd finished, she sat down beside her friend and told her about Andrew Greyson, the newspaperman who was on a list of Church enemies, and about riding out to the river to speak with him.

"I need to take the journals to Greyson before dawn. Are you ready to let them go?" She knew what they meant to Mary Rose, and would have understood had she said no.

But after a quick intake of breath, Mary Rose said, "Yes, but I would like to go with you." She smiled. "I suppose I need to give them a little send off—plus meet the man who's taking them."

"He's a good man," Bronwyn said. "A very good man. You can see it in his eyes. He laughs a lot, a good hearty laugh, and he's kind and trustworthy."

Mary Rose squeezed her hand. "It sounds like he made quite an impression on you in a short time."

"He did." She hesitated. "There's something else."

"I told you about the newspaper man being on the apostate list . . ."

Mary Rose nodded.

"I didn't tell you about the two names at the top of the same list."

"I think I know," Mary Rose said. "I knew it the minute you told me about the list. I could see it in your face. Yours and mine?" Her face held a sadness that made Bronwyn want to weep.

"I wish I didn't have to tell you any of this."

"We're in this together," Mary Rose said, and surprised Bronwyn by laughing softly. "Sister wives . . . how much more 'together' can we be than that?"

"What I need to tell you next is even worse."

Mary Rose took a deep breath. "Tell me."

"It's about the twins. I found a note about them. They have been promised in marriage to Apostle Erastus Gibbons."

Mary Rose caught her hand to her mouth. "No, that can't be.

Gabe may have been given a list with our names on it. But he would never allow that kind of harm to come to his girls."

Bronwyn reached for her hands again. "Gabe signed the note. It's official. He's giving them in marriage to that old man as soon as they reach fourteen. That's not long from now . . ."

Mary Rose dropped her head into her hands. "It can't be. Surely, he wouldn't do that." Bronwyn gathered her into a hug as she wept. Her own tears fell as she thought about Gabe's treachery. Mary Rose's face was pale as she straightened. If ever she needed words that would cheer, it was now. She drew a breath. "Something wondrous happened today—and we do need some good news right now. But we can let no one know."

"What is it?" Mary Rose leaned in closer, her expression filled with such hope, it made Bronwyn's heart ache.

"It's about Coal."

"Coal?" Her eyes opened wide. "Did you . . . find out something about him? Where he is?" She grabbed Bronwyn's hands again and held on as if for dear life. "Is he safe?"

"It's much better than hearing about him," she said, barely able to contain her joy. "I saw him."

Mary Rose jumped to her feet, and her hands flew to her cheeks. "How . . . ? Where . . . ?"

"It's a long story, and we only had time to speak for a little while." She grinned. "But you know Coal, that boy has a way of getting himself into scrapes, and this one was the biggest scrape you can imagine."

"Tell me. At least give me a hint."

"He was captured by the Dakota Sioux right after we tried to save Sarah."

Mary Rose looked stricken. "Oh, dear. Was he hurt . . . is he all right?"

"Yes, he's better than ever. Quite the young man now. Nearly as tall as I am."

Mary Rose let out a pent-up breath. "I must see him. Where is he?"

"He's with Greyson the newspaper reporter, and an old mountain man. You'll see Coal tomorrow when we drop off the journals."

Mary Rose threw her head back, letting out a joyful laugh, and then covered her mouth, lest she be heard. "Coal! Can you imagine? And leave it to our boy to end up with a newspaperman and a mountain man." She grinned. "I wonder how that happened."

"He didn't tell me, but I bet, as Coal would say, 'it's a good'un.'"

Cordelia called them to dinner, and the women headed to the stairs. Gabe stood at the base, watching them in silence as they descended.

The children chattered through what seemed to Bronwyn to be an endless dinner, oblivious to the tensions between Mary Rose, Bronwyn, and their father. Every time Bronwyn looked at Gabe, she lost her appetite. All she could think about was that note that signed away the lives of their precious twins. She pictured Ruby and Pearl in wedding gowns saying their vows to the apostle. She struggled to draw a breath but felt her throat constrict with anger, disappointment, and sorrow.

Cordelia glanced from one adult to another around the table, her expression curious, and then went back to chatting with the children, telling stories about her escapades aboard the riverboat years before.

After dinner, Gabe took the children into the great room for board games, reading, singing, and his bedtime blessing.

Bronwyn was clearing the dining table and stood, frozen, as the twins came forward and, with a hand on each of their heads, he asked God to bless them mightily in all their endeavors.

Nauseated, she wrapped her arms around her stomach and ran for the back door. She was bent double, trying not to vomit when she heard the door open and close behind her.

Gabe came up to stand beside her, and a moment later laid his hand on her shoulder. "Are you all right?"

She straightened, brushed off his hand, and stared at him. How could eyes so full of caring hide the despicable actions of a Danite?

"I'm seeing you clearly for the first time in years, Gabe. Who you turned out to be isn't what I expected."

"What do you mean?"

"I think you know."

"Did you have anything to do with some papers disappearing from my desk today?"

"Would it make a difference?" She stared at him. "As a Danite, you'll simply investigate and prosecute the person or persons who did it. I'm sure you'll have all the resources, secret and otherwise, to do so."

He stared back at her with equal intensity. "You're playing a dangerous game, Bronwyn. I've warned you before. I've tried to protect you. But there will come a time . . ."

She waved her hand in front of him. "Don't bother. You've said it all before. I almost believed you. But now . . . ?" A sad and mirthless laugh escaped her lips. "I simply don't. Not anymore."

"I care about you," he said. "I can't explain why my feelings for you are different than they are for the others. They just are." He looked up at the stars that were just beginning to break through the darkening sky. "We should have remained friends, just friends." He looked back into her eyes. "I foolishly let other emotions rob me of something I treasured."

"It's over, Gabe. Everything that was ever between us is over. Including friendship."

"I know."

"It's Mary Rose who's loved you all along. We both hurt her."

"I know that too."

"She's got a bigger heart than both of us put together. She

knows the pain of extending mercy and forgiveness even when it's not asked for. Yet, no matter the painful memories, she does it anyway. She stands to one side while the rest of us barge ahead, not thinking of the consequences, especially not thinking of the pain our actions cause others, especially her." Another wave of nausea hit, and she stopped speaking until it passed. "Not once has Mary Rose condemned me for what I did. Not once has she spoken against me. Yet, I deserved her ire, her contempt."

"I should never—"

Bronwyn held up her hand. "What you did to break Mary Rose's heart is between the two of you. I have asked her forgiveness, and she granted it. Whatever you've done, you'll need to repair, that is, if the desire is there. No one can do it for you."

Gabe stood proud and tall in the moonlight. He raked his hair with his fingers, and gave her that half-smile she'd always loved. Until now. She wished he didn't look so handsome and caring. She was sorry that was the image that would stay with her even as she betrayed him. What she had to do would be far easier if she didn't care about what happened to him.

Then the twins' voices carried from an upstairs window. Pearl giggled, and Ruby snorted over something funny. Little Grace put in a word or two and they all laughed again. Such innocence. And trust. She thought of the fatherly love she'd always seen in Gabe's actions toward them. Images of him from the early days, his laughter and song, his prayers, his fatherly advice. He was never too tired to give them his full attention.

Bronwyn stared at Gabe, her anger simmering just below the surface, simmering now but threatening to come to full boil if she didn't walk away from him. "How could you?" she whispered, and then turned and ran back in the house.

THIRTY-ONE

The household slept as Bronwyn and Mary Rose led their horses from the barn. They walked them around the back of the ranch to avoid being heard. The full moon was close to setting and in the east a hint of a silver-gray dawn outlined the mountains.

As soon as they were out of earshot, they mounted. They rode side by side while the trail was wide enough, but when they turned toward the river, Bronwyn took the lead.

The sky turned pale pink above the mountains and then faded to blue. The first rays of sunlight soon cast bars of light across the valley floor. As Bronwyn and Mary Rose neared the river, stands of trees rose before them, their leaves glistening in the morning light.

Soon they came to the place where Bronwyn had met Greyson the day before. She drew the mare to a halt, and behind her, Mary Rose halted her gelding. She listened for the telltale bark of the little dog, but heard nothing. Not even the sound of a human voice.

She told Mary Rose to wait, and then she pulled back the brush and, recognizing trail markers, walked along the same path she trod yesterday with Greyson.

When she reached the clearing, it was empty. All signs of anyone having been there were gone, even the fire pit.

Bronwyn emerged from the thicket of tall grass and undergrowth to find Mary Rose still astride the gelding, white-faced and shaken.

"I hear a rider coming," she said, inclining her head downstream. "And I take it, you didn't find Greyson . . ."

Bronwyn shook her head. "Quickly, follow me." She mounted her horse, and then nudged it with her knees, reining it back through the thicket to the clearing. She heard the gelding crash through just moments later.

A lone rider came closer, keeping to the trail they'd just left. Bronwyn held her breath. A lot could have happened in the hours since she last saw Greyson and Coal. They could have been caught, made to tell their business, and now the vigilantes planned to spring on Bronwyn and Mary Rose at the same spot. . .

She shook off the terrifying thought, and drew herself up tall as the rider came closer. And halted.

Afraid to breathe, she waited for what seemed to be an eternity. Finally, the rider moved on. Then, just as she was about to relax, she heard the soft footfall of someone approaching from the riverbank.

"I thought you'd never get here," a voice said from behind a thicket of wild roses and young oaks.

Mary Rose put her hands to her cheeks. "Coal?"

He stepped out, his whole face spreading into a smile. "Mama . . ." He ran over to the gelding, reached up, and swung her to the ground.

"Look how tall you are," she said, her eyes bright with moisture. "Just look at you . . ." She stood back, looking him up and down, biting her lower lip. "You look good . . . so good!" Now her tears spilled. She didn't bother wipe them away. She just held open her arms and Coal stepped into them.

"Why didn't you let us know you were here?" Mary Rose said after a moment. "We've all thought . . . the worst."

"I know, and I'm sorry. But the danger is too great. I didn't want it to happen until I knew I wouldn't bring greater danger to you."

"It's not dangerous now?"

He grinned. "It's worse than ever now. But yesterday, when I saw Mother Bronwyn crying by the river, I couldn't help but go to her." He gave Bronwyn a shy, affectionate look. "But no one must know I'm here."

"Does Sarah know?" Mary Rose studied his face as she spoke.

Bronwyn smiled. She loved Coal like a son, but Mary Rose knew his heart better than anyone. She had guessed long ago that his heart had broken over Sarah James. It might have been puppy love, but to Coal it was real. And watching them talk about Sarah now, watching Coal's face, she knew the puppy love hadn't slipped from his heart.

And the look of love on his face as he talked to his mama Mary Rose made Bronwyn's heart ache with the precious beauty of it. And the look on Mary Rose's face! Sorrow had carved a deep cavern in her heart, but having her boy come back to her was already filling it with hope and joy. She utterly glowed.

"She guessed who I was the other day," he said to Mary Rose. "I was outside the mercantile, and she spotted me, followed me so we could talk. I didn't think it was safe for her, but she did it anyway."

"When did you see her last?"

He shrugged. "Maybe four or five days ago."

"She used to ride out to our ranch almost every night, but we haven't seen her lately. I've been worried."

"I'm worried about her too," Coal said. "If anybody had seen us talking, it could be bad for her. Really bad. If you see her, will you tell her for me that . . ." He blushed and turned away.

Mary Rose hugged him, and Bronwyn said, "We know what you'd like to tell her, and we'll tell her for you."

He gave them both another shy smile and nodded. "Greyson said we can't dilly-dally. He needs to be on his way. He's worked it out so he can take a different route than the usual one to Fort Bridger."

Mary Rose frowned. "There's a wagon company approaching. Wouldn't joining up with them give him better protection?"

"They're heading to California," Coal said. "Greyson meets up with folks heading east at Bridger. He needs to get his writings to New York." He gestured toward the river. "Follow me, and I'll lead you to him."

Coal disappeared, almost silently, into the brush.

Mary Rose led her horse to the water, and then looked around for Coal. Bronwyn did the same, frowned, shrugged, and chose what appeared to be a trail. "The boy does have a way of disappearing . . ." she said with a sigh.

Moments later they came to another clearing. Greyson had saddled his horse and packed his gear, bedroll on back. Bronwyn made quick introductions, and Mary Rose handed the journals to him. She had wrapped them in heavy paper and tied them with twine.

"I'll take good care of them," Greyson said, meeting her worried gaze. "And if you've written intimate passages, I'll make sure they do not get into print. You have my solemn word."

"As you read them," she said, "you'll find that I've named names. Most of our people are good and kind and industrious. But there are others who are power hungry and abuse that power. It's that abuse that is troublesome. The killing in our garden may be the first of many blood atonement killings."

"The U.S. Government may have to send troops to take over," Greyson said.

Her eyes widening, Bronwyn exchanged glances with Mary Rose. "Take over?" she said to make sure she heard him right.

"That would be the only way to stop the abuses."

Bronwyn moistened her suddenly dry lips. "That is akin to declaring war against the Saints."

"I understand."

Her heart pounded wildly. "That's an even greater reason for the Danites to stop you."

His face turned solemn. "I understand that as well." He stepped closer to Bronwyn. "You are in this as deep as I am, even deeper. I plead with you to come with me—bring the whole family and get out now."

Bronwyn shook her head. "I told you yesterday why I can't." Then she turned to Mary Rose. "Why don't you go and take the children—?" She looked to Coal to see if he agreed, but the set of his jaw said he didn't. She wondered if Sarah was the reason.

Mary Rose shook her head. "We're in this together. We'll solve it together, and then we'll get them out."

Greyson tucked the paper wrapped journals in the saddlebags. "As soon as I get the journals into safe hands—someone traveling east—I'll come back. If you've got more for me about the boy's death, I'll turn right around and hightail it back to Bridger. The information must get published. Things must change."

He stepped into the stirrup and swung his leg over the saddle. He tipped his hat to the ladies, smiled, and urged the tall horse forward.

"I usually go with him," Coal said. "But this time I can't."

"Because of Sarah?" Mary Rose asked.

He nodded. "I still want to get her out."

Bronwyn took his hand. "I'm going to see Sister Riordan this morning. I'll find out what I can."

Just then a yipping little bundle of black and white fur spun into the campsite from the direction of the river. Coal squatted, patted his knee, and the dog jumped into his arms and licked his face.

"Name's Chuck," Coal said. "Short for Chuck Wagon."

When Bronwyn raised her eyebrows, Coal laughed. "Has to do with the Dakota. They were going to eat him for dinner. But we saved him."

The mountain man followed the dog into the clearing a moment later. His gaze met Bronwyn's and he nodded. Then he seemed to study Mary Rose as if he knew her. Coal watched them all with sharp curiosity.

"I told your . . . sister wife . . . yesterday and I'll tell you as well, if you ever need anything, you know where to find us. Greyson told me what's happened in your family, about all you're going through. It cannot be easy for you, especially when you think that someone you love has betrayed you."

Again, Bronwyn noticed something familiar about his brogue. But she had no recollection of seeing him before, and he would obviously have been memorable with his bent, crippled body hunched over with an ailment or injury that surely brought him much pain.

Using a walking stick, he hobbled over to Coal and rubbed the dog's head. "I see you've met Chuck." Coal met the old mountain man's eyes and grinned. There was obvious affection between the two.

Bronwyn noticed that Mary Rose also stared at him with unusual intensity. She hadn't said a word since he stepped into the clearing.

"That is true," Mary Rose walked closer to the mountain man. "What you said about betrayal. You sound as though you know from personal experience."

For a moment the only sound was that of the rushing river and a few songbirds.

"I do," the mountain man said. "But it was long ago."

"'Tis a difficult thing indeed."

"'Tis," he said, smiling again. His eyes seemed to brighten as they bored into Mary Rose's.

"You seem familiar somehow," she said. "It's as if we've met before." She hesitated. "It's your voice."

A hush seemed to fall around them. Even Coal caught his breath.

Mary Rose's gaze was locked on the man's eyes, and his on hers.

"Aye," he said, "we have."

THIRTY-TWO

Hosea looked from Mary Rose to Bronwyn, and then back again. His heart ached when he thought of the love he'd witnessed between Mary Rose and Gabe during the ceremony on board the *Sea Hawk*. They hadn't been able to keep their eyes off each other, so taken they were with the magic of their shipboard romance, the magic of their love, the magic of knowing that they would spend the rest of their lives together.

By following Enid's trail, he'd also followed Gabe and Mary Rose's. He knew what happened in Nauvoo, how Griffin died, and that Gabe took Bronwyn as his second wife. He knew about the friction caused by Enid when she arrived, how neither Mary Rose nor Bronwyn wanted Gabe to marry again.

Hope remained in their expressions, but it seemed fragile. Would it strengthen that hope if he told them his story? Told them why he'd come?

He'd followed the leading of his heart. Finding Enid had

become his quest. His obsession. Now, here he was, so close, yet separated by the inherent danger in this wild place.

He had determined long ago that he wanted to meet Enid on his own terms; he didn't want her to hear the news second hand that her husband did not die in that storm.

Should he tell the women his identity? Coal knew the truth, and he'd proved to be trustworthy.

His inclination was to keep quiet, at least for now. After all, he was the one who'd traveled from one end of the continent nearly to the other, endured challenges beyond all he'd thought possible, given his limitations. He deserved to take charge of this one thing—the time and place when Enid would find out his identity.

He chided himself for thinking of his revelation in such a way.

He studied their faces, their eyes. Mary Rose, once so pert and energetic, now appeared bone weary, as if she carried the cares of the world upon her shoulders. And Bronwyn, beautiful Bronwyn, looked as though her heart might fly into a million tiny pieces any minute.

Would it give them hope to know what happened to him? Hope that sees beyond the immediate into a future that knows God's loving and tender care?

Perhaps it was time. Maybe not his timing, but maybe it was God's timing.

Hosea hobbled to a stump and with a heavy sigh, sat, keeping his balance by leaning on his walking stick. Chuck jumped from Coal's arms, trotted over, and hopped in his lap.

Hosea smiled at Mary Rose and then at Bronwyn. "Since my accident," he said, "I don't have quite the stamina I once did. Someday I'll tell you my story." He gave them a gentle smile. "What I will tell you now, however, is who I am. Before I do, I only ask that you abide by my wishes to say nothing to anyone else until I'm ready."

Bronwyn tilted her head, quizzically, in that way she had; Mary

Rose watched him with an intensity, a knowing, that touched his soul and almost took his breath away. He knew before he spoke the words, that she had already guessed . . . and that without being told, she understood everything. His crippled body told one story; his close proximity to Enid told another.

Mary Rose had known deep heartache, and she recognized the same in him. She had looked into his eyes that day aboard the *Sea Hawk* just before she said her vows to Gabe. Her joy had known no bounds. Love and promise shone in her eyes, a promise that gave every bit of her soul to her beloved.

To have and to hold, she said, looking into her beloved's eyes, *from this day forward, for better or for worse, for richer, for poorer, in sickness and in health, to love and to cherish; from this day forward until death do us part. . .*

Hosea saw something reflected in Mary Rose's eyes that told him, without a word being spoken, she understood a love that would bring him across the continent to find Enid.

That intense moment passed between them, and then Mary Rose gave him a slight smile. "Captain," she whispered, "I'm so happy to see you again."

THIRTY-THREE

Bronwyn and Mary Rose borrowed Enid's buggy to ride out to the Riordan ranch to ask questions of Sister Amanda. Enid seemed happy to switch to horseback. She was headed to some outlying ranches, which required crossing some rugged terrain. Seeming unusually concerned about the new reports of stillborn calves, she asked if they would check with Sister Amanda about any new cases at their ranch. She also mentioned the reports from the north, now seeming more than just rumor, about the exploding populations of grasshopper and crickets.

The Riordan ranch was a much larger spread compared to the MacKays' and encompassed several outbuildings to accommodate the apostle's thirty-six wives and dozens of children.

To Bronwyn, the ranch looked more like a small town. The apostle had been more industrious than most Saints since arriving in the Valley. Acres of healthy corn, potatoes, and wheat extended as far as the eye could see. Several hundred head of cattle grazed peacefully in verdant pastures near the mountains.

The women parked the buggy and walked up to the front door of the main house. A young woman that Bronwyn remembered as one of the apostle's wives opened the door. She was quite pregnant but seemed happy about her condition. "We've come to call on Sister Amanda," Bronwyn said.

The girl smiled and invited them in. "I'll see if I can find her." She waddled off, leaving them standing in a large hallway with a view into two other large rooms.

Children seemed to occupy every free space in those rooms, and from the bounces and thuds it seemed, they trampled around on the second floor as well. It was a surprisingly happy place, filled with singing and laughing and the pounding of feet as children chased each other. Bronwyn spotted two little boys sliding down the banister, whooping and hollering. Three others stood on the landing, impatiently waiting their turn.

It appeared the apostle's first wife believed in letting children be children. Bronwyn grinned at Mary Rose and whispered behind her hand, "The more I find out about Sister Amanda, the more I like her."

Mary Rose whispered back, "Maybe Apostle Hyrum believes in a large family with a multitude of wives because he loves the happy chaos."

Bronwyn laughed. "I wonder how long it takes to tuck each of them in at night."

"They've got a multitude of mothers," Mary Rose said. "They probably take turns."

"Think of the meals . . ."

Just then Sister Amanda bustled around the corner, wiping her hands on her apron. Her face, smudged with flour, was red from the exertion of trotting from the kitchen.

"Hello, hello," she said. "Sister Mary Rose, Sister Bronwyn, please come in and sit down—if you can find an empty spot." She laughed. "What brings you out to the Riordans today?"

"Do you have a minute to talk?" Mary Rose said. Then she laughed and glanced around the house. "Do you ever have a minute to talk?"

Sister Amanda smiled. "Not often. That's why I'm happy to take a breather. And I've always got a minute for you two." She led them into what was likely once a parlor. But the furniture was covered with wooden blocks, homemade dolls, and an array of tiny tin dishes from a child's tea set.

Sister Amanda swept some toys off a couple of chairs and indicated that the women take their seats. She did the same for herself, sitting across from them.

"It's not so happy business that we've come about," Bronwyn said.

Sister Amanda stood and closed the doors to keep the children from entering the room. "Go on." She acted as if hearing such an announcement was commonplace.

"You may have heard by now that we found a young man's body in our garden."

"Yes, I did. Hyrum told me about it. He said the Paiutes are to blame."

"I've never heard of any Indian group burying someone under a door," Bronwyn said.

Mary Rose leaned forward. "And why would the Paiutes kill any of us, door or not? They've been friendly and helpful since we came here. And say they did, why bury the body in our garden?"

Sister Amanda sat back and studied their faces. "It happens."

Bronwyn shook her head, frowning. "It doesn't make any sense."

Sister Amanda continued to stare at the two women as if trying to make up her mind about something.

Bronwyn and Mary Rose exchanged a glance. Finally, Bronwyn said, "A friend said that a brave woman named Beatrice Leverton might help us with some answers."

Sister Amanda brightened, and then she nodded. "There are those who don't want innocent blood on their hands, so they get the Paiutes to do the unpleasant work for them."

Bronwyn frowned. "Do you think that's what happened this time?"

"I do."

"Do you know who the boy is?"

"I know of a missing boy. His mother is beside herself with worry. I've recently begun to wonder if the boy in your garden might be him."

"What is his name?"

"Robby Teagarten. His father works in the livery, and his mother and sisters run the cloth and yarn shop. Their names are Ruth and Zacharias Teagarten." She moved her gaze to an open window, looking terribly worried.

"Is Sister Ruth in her shop most of the time?"

Sister Amanda nodded. "Yes, with her daughters, Iris and Rose. Last week at the Relief Society meeting Sister Ruth asked us to pray for the return of her son. She said he'd been missing for several days."

She stood. "I really must get back to my bread making. I'm teaching some of the younger sister wives how to do it. It seems they were never properly taught." She shook her head and smiled. "Can I do anything else for you young ladies?"

"It's nice to be called that," Mary Rose said. "I feel anything but young these days."

"Life on the frontier isn't easy," Sister Amanda said, her eyes full of understanding.

They walked with her to the front door. "There's one more thing," Bronwyn said. "About Sister Sarah?"

"Yes?"

"She was coming out to the ranch several times a week, teaching our twins how to play the fiddle . . ."

"Oh, yes. She learned it from Naomi," she said. "And I remember her saying just recently how she enjoys those visits."

"We haven't seen Sarah for several days. Is she ill?" Bronwyn hoped she wasn't pregnant again.

"That girl . . ." Sister Amanda sighed and rolled her eyes. "She comes and goes, though I know Hyrum isn't exactly pleased with her actions and would rather have her stay here with the rest of the family. She's had trouble adjusting to our life here." Then Sister Amanda hesitated, her hand on the door handle. "Come to think of it, I haven't seen her for quite some time. I'll ask Hyrum if he knows."

She walked with them for a ways outside. "How are you getting along with Enid?" she asked, quite suddenly.

Bronwyn and Mary Rose exchanged glances. Bronwyn said, "Quite nicely, thank you."

Mary Rose murmured much the same.

Sister Amanda seemed to study their faces for a moment, and then smiled. "Back in Winter Quarters, I thought perhaps that was a wedding that might not happen . . . for a lot of different reasons."

"In the end, we do what all good Saints do," Mary Rose said. "What our good husband's direct us to do."

Sister Amanda winked. "That's all any of us can do," she said, and the three women laughed together.

Bronwyn and Mary Rose climbed up into the buggy, and Sister Amanda waved them off, still chuckling.

An hour later, Bronwyn and Mary Rose parked the rig outside the livery. Bronwyn gave the interior a quick look, and Mary Rose headed round back, both hoping to see Brother Zacharias.

Mary Rose shook her head when she saw Bronwyn. "No one here."

They walked across the street to the cloth and yarn shop. Bronwyn spotted the closed sign in the window when they were still several feet away.

When they reached the shop, Bronwyn knocked on the door, hoping someone in the family might be inside, even though the shop was closed. She waited a few minutes and knocked again.

Finally, she shook her head.

Two women approached them, lost in a whispered conversation behind gloved hands. As they drew closer, Bronwyn recognized them as two sister wives—Marie Sue and Martha Chamberlain—who'd traveled with them in the MacKay wagon company.

The women nodded as they neared Mary Rose and Bronwyn. They started to pass, their demeanor curt, but Bronwyn stepped in front of them.

She greeted them with a smile. "Marie Sue, it's a pleasure to see you this morning."

Mary Rose gave her a puzzled look, and Bronwyn shot her a "trust me" look in return. Neither Bronwyn nor Mary Rose had much use for the Chamberlain wives. All seven were known to be gossips, Marie Sue and Martha the most vicious of all. During the wagon travel out of Winter Quarters, Bronwyn and Mary Rose did their best to keep their distance.

Once, on a lark, however, they'd started a juicy rumor about a fictional member of the wagon train just to see how far it would travel. They told Martha first, asking her to promise she wouldn't tell a living soul. The rumor returned two days later, the poor fictional character's reputation ruined by innuendo and exaggeration.

When the Chamberlain sister wives discovered they'd been tricked, they'd turned icy cold shoulders whenever they crossed Mary Rose and Bronwyn's paths.

"Hello, Martha," Mary Rose said, who obviously understood Bronwyn's tactics. "How are you this fine day?"

The ladies gave them a sniff and tried to pass again.

"What a shame to see the shop closed," Bronwyn said, sighing. "I'm so disappointed."

"I didn't know you could sew," Martha said.

"It's Mary Rose who couldn't make a straight stitch if her life depended on it," Marie Sue said. "She grew up in the lap of luxury, household servants, on a large estate—don't you remember?"

She spoke as though Mary Rose wasn't standing next to her. Bronwyn felt her cheeks start to burn with anger, but she couldn't let the women get her goat.

She forced another smile. "We're both just learning." She laughed easily and waved a hand. "In fact, the twins are teaching us both how to quilt. They're quite the little seamstresses." She looked at the closed sign again. "Pity. I'd so hoped to see Sister Teagarten and her girls this morning."

"It is a pity," Mary Rose said with a tsk-tsk. "And so unusual. I can't remember the last time I noticed a closed sign on this establishment . . ."

"I suppose everyone needs a day off from time to time," Bronwyn said. "I know I could, even from the humdrum of everyday life, raising children and the such. Nice seeing you ladies. We really must be on our way . . ." She took Mary Rose's arm and the two women stepped into the street.

"Well, apparently, you haven't heard the news," Marie Sue said, following them and dropping her voice.

"What news is that?" Bronwyn feigned indifference, while Mary Rose feigned impatience . . . which made the ladies all the more anxious to halt their progress across the street.

Martha raised both eyebrows. "About their boy."

"I knew they had daughters—Iris and Rose . . ."

Martha stepped closer and, behind her gloved hand, whispered into Bronwyn's ear, "They are in mourning."

The reality of why they had come here in the first place hit Bronwyn again, and though she had no more tears to cry, moisture filled her eyes once more. "What happened? Do you know?"

Martha shook her head. "Apparently, he was on his way to meet someone—a girl—a ways out from town. The Indians wanted his horse, and he didn't want to give it to them. At least that's what we heard. They slit his throat and left him for the buzzards."

Sister Marie Sue dropped her voice and stepped closer. "It was that young wife of Apostle Riordan's. The one that he married in Winter Quarters."

Bronwyn's heart dropped. "Sarah . . . ?"

The sister wives nodded. "One and the same. Sister Quigley told me they were meeting regularly, but no one could figure out where."

"But Sarah's already married," Bronwyn said. "I don't think she'd do such a thing . . ." But she was thinking about Coal and the fact that if the young woman was sweet on anyone, it would be her son.

The sister wives exchanged a glance, their brows lifted high, noses in the air. "Well, we heard she asked Brother Riordan for a divorce. Can you imagine such a thing?"

"We also heard that her father—who's a wife-beater, you know—threatened to kill her mother if she so much as thought about leaving her husband, that nice apostle." She shook her head, her lips puckered. Something in her eyes, despite her gossipy nature, told Bronwyn she understood the heartache and horror that Sarah's mother faced. And even that of Sarah herself.

Marie Sue elbowed her way closer to Bronwyn. "Do you know what I think?"

Bronwyn didn't know if she could take anymore news of this nature—it hurt to know about others' suffering—but she said she wanted to know.

"This all has to do with all those other disappearing boys . . . you've heard about them, right?" Marie Sue's expression had turned serious, her eyes full of sadness and confusion.

"We've heard rumors, but nothing concrete," Sister Martha said, her demeanor changing as well.

"We hear that young men, sometimes boys, have been run off because they're a threat to the old men who want to take the comeliest young brides for themselves. If they see a young man taking a fancy to a younger woman, they run that poor young man out of town."

"We heard from Sister MacDonald, who heard it from Sister Baggins, who heard it from an apostle's wife, that blood atonement will soon be used as punishment for those who go against the prophet's edicts."

"We heard Brother Foley speak about that in church," Mary Rose said.

Sister Martha raised an eyebrow. "Well, so you did. I guess I'm not telling you anything new then, am I?" With a humph, she took Sister Marie Sue's arm, and with noses in the air, the two marched back to the boarded walkway.

Mary Rose drove the buggy back to the ranch, Bronwyn sitting beside her lost in thought. They reached the fork in the trail where the road turned toward the river. She thought about Coal wanting her to tell Sarah he was thinking of her. Coal had also said that he and Sarah had talked to each other in town. What if someone had seen them? Had reported it to Brother Hyrum?

Blood atonement.

"It's just as we thought. If it's announced that God has revealed to the prophet that a man and a woman will marry, anyone going against that announcement is going against God's will."

Mary Rose looked over at Bronwyn. "So it follows that if a young man courts a girl who's spoken for, he's an enemy of the Church. He has sinned against God and the prophet."

"And now we hear the men who order it done are too cowardly to carry it out themselves. We hear they order the Paintes to do their dirty work."

Mary Rose looked as shaken as Bronwyn felt. She halted the horse, and the two women just sat there for a few minutes in silence.

"It's as if everything we feared is a reality . . . and it's bigger, much bigger than we thought," Bronwyn breathed.

"And it may be just the beginning," Mary Rose said.

"And then we come again to the question: Why this boy? Why our garden?"

"Mistaken identity?" Mary Rose flicked the reins again, and the horse started forward. The buggy swayed as they hit a deep rut.

"When I saw Robby's body, my first thought was to look for proof it wasn't Coal. All I could think of was his corn-silk hair. It didn't match, so I dismissed the idea. Robby's hair had been coarse and brown, but now that we've seen Coal . . ."

"Two boys around the same age," Mary Rose said, "about the same size, same height."

Bronwyn leaned forward. "Sarah had been coming to our ranch quite often. Maybe Brother Hyrum's suspicions were aroused, and he had her followed."

"It still doesn't make sense. She came out to visit us—we saw her ride onto the ranch and ride off later, heading straight home." She flicked the reins to keep the mare moving. "She never met anyone there. Coal said he couldn't come near us—or her—for fear of causing us harm." She glanced at Bronwyn. "Do you think they spoke to each other only the one time?"

Bronwyn nodded. "That's the only time he mentioned. And she sought him out, not the other way around. They're sweet on each other. So I don't believe she would have wanted to see or talk to anyone else."

They rode along in silence for a few minutes, and then Mary Rose slowed the mare. "What if Robby was sweet on Sarah? Maybe he'd been following her. Maybe she didn't want his attention, but he kept at it anyway. Or maybe she didn't even know."

"Someone found out and told Hyrum," Bronwyn said.

"Even if they didn't, he would still have wanted the boy out of the way."

"What if the Chamberlain sister wives are right? Maybe Sarah told Apostle Hyrum that she wanted out of the marriage? Maybe after Sarah saw Coal, she asked for a divorce."

"Too many troubling questions," Mary Rose said. "And so far, no clear answers." They were nearing the ranch. Mary Rose flicked the reins urging the mare to a trot.

"Whoever killed Robby must have left evidence," Bronwyn said, turning in the seat to face Mary Rose.

"We're back to where we started," Mary Rose said. "Sister Amanda said it likely was the Paiutes acting on someone else's behalf."

"I don't think the Paiutes had anything to do with this one," Bronwyn said.

"Why?"

"It has to do with the door." She fell silent as they rode onto the ranch. They'd almost reached the barn when she said, "I keep coming back to it, why it was placed above the body at all . . ."

Mary Rose halted the mare, and the two women stepped from the buggy. Mary Rose looked troubled. "We put ourselves in grave danger when we gave the journals to Greyson. But we have no proof that Robby was a victim of blood atonement—proof that younger men are being run off or killed." She shuddered. "If that's what this is all about—the trouble here, the darkness, goes far beyond the Robby's death."

"We have to find evidence," Bronwyn said. "Solid evidence to connect blood atonement with his death."

"I know, dear friend. I know."

As they were leaving the barn, Bronwyn glanced at a piece of wood propped against a wall just inside the door. The dank air smelled of hay and manure, and the cavernous room seemed eerily dim. As she passed by the plank, a series of dark smudges caught her eye.

It wasn't until she reached the house, however, that she realized the piece of wood was the same size as the door that covered the boy's body.

And the smudges were the color of blood.

THIRTY-FOUR

By the time it occurred to Bronwyn that the piece of wood in the barn was not only the same size as that which had been placed over the boy's body, it *was* the door—it was too late to run back to examine it. She was already in the house being covered with hugs and kisses from the children. Even so, her thoughts were glued to the image of the bloodstains.

Were they fresh? Why hadn't she seen them before?

She went over in her mind how she and Mary Rose helped Gabe move the heavy door. They lifted it and placed it to one side of the shallow grave. They didn't turn it over. Just lifted it and set it down, right side up.

When the police came to have a look, and later the undertaker, they likely did the same. Whoever moved it to the barn hadn't noticed the smudges. Why not? Had it been too dark in the barn?

She heard Cordelia bustling around in the kitchen with help from Ruby and Pearl. Gales of laughter exploded from time to time . . . a bittersweet sound. Mary Rose had gone upstairs to clean up for dinner, and Little Grace said that Sister Enid was doing the same after an afternoon of "taking care of everybody's cows."

She headed to the kitchen, gave Cordelia a hug, and was rewarded with a wide smile. Cordelia patted her cheek. "What have you and Mary Rose been up to all day? If you've been out on some grand adventure, I'm disappointed you didn't take me with you." She winked and then went back to supervising the biscuit making.

"Trust me," Bronwyn said, "we'll have plenty of adventures to come."

Ruby and Pearl showed her how they'd learned to roll the dough and cut the biscuits with a tin cup. She asked them about their day, and they told her about starting a new garden on the far side of the barn. "Enid brought us some new seeds from the mercantile," Ruby said. "Once the soil is ready, we're going to plant squash."

"And corn," Pearl added. "Except I don't like the worms that get in the ears." She shuddered.

After a time, the girls headed off to find the others, and soon happy chatter drifted through from the great room to the kitchen.

Bronwyn stepped over to the brick oven where Cordelia stirred a pot over open coals.

"Do you remember what time of day Brother Foley's men were here?" she said.

Cordelia nodded. "Late afternoon. I remember because I was plucking a chicken for dinner and one of 'em made a joke about apostates," she said. "They said they might need the feathers for some tarrin' they were hankerin' to do."

"I thought that might have been the case."

Cordelia gave her a sharp look. "It sounds like you're onto something." Besides being the most loving person Bronwyn had ever known, she was also one of the most intelligent. She wouldn't be surprised to find out that Cordelia already knew about Hosea and Coal.

"I noticed blood on the door. Someone moved it to the barn and left it standing on its side—a different side than what we'd seen before."

"And you think there's blood on it?"

Bronwyn nodded.

"Don't you think you ought to get out there, then, and take a look?"

"Can you make sure the children don't follow me?"

"Of course. The lantern's by the back door."

Bronwyn grabbed the lantern and then hurried across the yard to the barn. She knelt beside the piece of wood, first examining the smudges. There was no doubt that it was blood, but how could she know for certain that it was Robby's?

She moved the lantern from one end to the other and then back again.

She sat back, studying the marks. They seemed to form letters or stick figures . . . then she realized they were letters, but upside down.

With a shudder, she sat back, feeling the blood drain from her face.

Crudely written, likely using the boy's own blood, were words and numbers she didn't understand. COL318. Underneath were several more smudgy letters. She couldn't make them out.

She picked up the lantern and ran back into the house, doused the flame, and then headed into the kitchen.

"It is blood, probably the boy's," she said, keeping her voice low so no one else would hear. "But I don't understand what this could mean—COL318.

"Someone's name?" Cordelia checked the oven to see how the biscuits were coming along.

"Not with numbers."

"Maybe COL is supposed to be COLT, as in the pistol." She shrugged. "But that doesn't make sense."

"The boy's throat was slit. There wasn't a firearm involved."

Then another thought occurred to Bronwyn that nearly robbed her of breath. "Coal," she said. "Surely it wasn't because they thought the boy was Coal. Many people don't know how to spell his name."

A moment of stunned silence followed, and the two women stared at each other. Then Cordelia bowed her head, almost as in prayer. When she raised it, she said, "Can you bring down Mary Rose's family Bible for me? I have an idea, but it may be far-fetched."

Bronwyn hurried up the stairs to find Mary Rose. Breathlessly, she told her what she'd discovered, then both women returned to the kitchen with the Bible.

"Turn to Colossians 3:18," Cordelia said. "And read to me what it says."

Mary Rose rifled through the pages and then, finding the passage, read, *"Wives, submit yourselves unto your own husbands, as it is fit in the Lord."*

"It is as we thought," Mary Rose said. "But was it because of Sarah . . . or was it meant for us? We certainly haven't submitted ourselves to Gabe."

"We just don't know if the boy was mistaken for Coal," Bronwyn felt a sting behind her eyes. "We may never know."

Cordelia had tears in her eyes as she closed the Bible. "How can God ever forgive us for what we do in his name?"

The twins helped Cordelia put a large bowl of stew in the center of the table, and then the family gathered round. "Where's Papa," Joey asked.

"We can't eat wifout him," Spence said, sticking out his lower lip.

"He had some business in town," Enid said, "but he'll be back soon."

Bronwyn and Mary Rose exchanged a glance.

Hosea.

What would Enid do when she found out he was alive? What would Gabe do?

Cordelia said grace, and then asked Enid to ladle stew into their bowls. Ruby gave everyone a proud smile as she passed the biscuits.

Enid talked about her visits to the outlying farms, the growing numbers of sick cows, and the reported swarms of insects approaching town.

Mary Rose and Cordelia had fallen quiet, and Bronwyn, still sick at heart over the discovery in the barn, had a difficult time chatting with the children. She met Enid's gaze with a smile of gratitude for keeping the conversation light and for keeping the children engaged with anything other than the bizarre findings in the garden.

After supper, Enid took it upon herself to read to the younger children while the twins helped Cordelia clean up the kitchen.

Mary Rose pulled Bronwyn aside. "I'd like to see what you found on the board in the barn."

Bronwyn nodded and led the way, lantern in hand.

"Is that a *B*?" Mary Rose asked. "And an *L* beside it?"

"It's so crude it could almost be anything."

"No, look at the next letter. I think it's a *U*."

"BLU . . ." Bronwyn bent lower. "What could that mean?"

Just then, a distant sound rumbled toward them, so faint at first it didn't register.

Then it became apparent. Horse hooves. Thundering. The riders coming fast.

The raid on the ranch in Nauvoo flashed before Bronwyn's mind. On full alert, she reached for the lantern.

"Wait," Mary Rose said. "Blood atonement."

"I know. That's what I'm afraid they're after."

"No, I mean the words on the door. Someone can't spell, so it probably reads *B-L-U-D*, and I can barely make out an *A*, though it looks a bit like a *D*."

"That's all the time we have," Bronwyn said, snuffing the light.

"That's got to be it," Mary Rose whispered. Then as the riders came closer, she said, "Shall we try to get to the house?"

"It's too late. They're almost on us. I want to wait to make sure who it is."

Whoops and hollers rose as the riders drew nearer. Bronwyn's heart threatened to pound out of her chest. Her children were in the house . . . she should never have left them.

"Lookee here what we found!" someone shouted. "Whoo-eee! Lookee here!"

Mary Rose reached for Bronwyn's hand and squeezed it.

"Come on out, ladies. We know you're here and we know what you done. Come on out, and we'll be easier on you. Otherwise, you don't want know what's going to happen."

Bronwyn stood, but Mary Rose pulled her down. "Don't," she mouthed.

They heard the front door open. Cordelia called out, "What do you thugs want? What are you here for?"

"Hey, boys," someone said. "The little lady thinks she can scare us off with a rifle."

"You shoot it, ma'am," said a more reasonable voice, "and we shoot this here newspaperman from New York City. You don't want innocent blood on yer hands, now, do you?"

Bronwyn's heart twisted, and it seemed Mary Rose had forgotten to breathe.

"All we want are two people, then we'll go away nice and quiet-like."

Someone shouted, "Hey, boys. Listen to this." And he started to read from one of Mary Rose's journals in a singsongy nasal voice.

August 7, 1844

> *But the child's sob curses deeper in the silence*
> *than the strong man in his wrath.*
>
> —Elizabeth B. B.

We tried to save a young girl today. Most in this community, the men at the least, would perhaps not consider Sarah a child. They call her a young woman, and they praise her and her family for the great honor that was to be hers this day.

Her name is Sarah James, fourteen years of age. The prophet and president of the Church ordained that she marry Apostle Hyrum Riordan, a man in his seventies. She is the youngest bride to be chosen for what the prophet calls the greatest privilege bestowed on womanhood. Though I fell ill nearly a week ago and still hovered near heaven's gate until this morning, Bronwyn and young Coal carried out our plan—devised weeks ago. All went well, but now the community is up in arms and demands they both be returned—Sarah to marry the old apostle, and Coal to be punished. As I write this, I fear Bronwyn will not escape punishment. At the very least, she will be reprimanded. Many convicted of apostasy are expelled from the Church, the family, the community. I've seen it happen before, though not to a woman.

Mary Rose let out a soft moan.

Bronwyn felt the sting of tears at the back of her throat.

"We're about to have ourselves some fun with this newspaper-man. He thinks he's so high and mighty with them fancy words he's been writing about us . . . telling the whole country how bad we are with our strange ways. A little hot tar will teach him what blood atonement really means before we carry out the act to save his eternal soul."

Cheer and whoops rose.

"We come to arrest two people who are in cahoots with him," another speaker said.

"You send out the two MacKay women, Sister Mary Rose and Sister Bronwyn, and we'll leave y'all alone. Send 'em out now, little lady, and watch where you point that rifle."

"You'll be sorry when Brother Gabriel finds out about this," Cordelia said, her voice even. "You're trespassing on his property. Get off, now." She fired.

For a moment, the crowd fell silent.

Then another voice came from the back of the crowd. "Saying Brother Gabriel will do anything to save his women or his property won't do you any good, ma'am. Now put that firearm down, or we'll set the barn on fire right now."

Bronwyn gasped.

The front door of the house opened, and a moment later Enid called to the posse, "They're not here. We don't know where they are. You'll have to take that up with my husband."

"I think we ought to have a little look-see for ourselves," a gruff-voiced man said.

"You get off this land right now," Enid said calmly. "Mother Cordelia is a good aim. She'll take down at least three of you before you can load. Now, get out of here."

"You'll be sorry if you're hiding fugitives, Sister," another voice said. "Your sister wives are wanted to appear before Brother Foley. If you see them, you tell them that for us."

"You talk to Brother Gabriel," Enid said again. "I'm sure he'll straighten you out. You're looking for the wrong people. I'm sure somebody stole those journals."

Coarse laughter rose even louder along with some yee-haws and more whoops. "Tell Brother Gabriel?" one man guffawed. "Why, ma'am, he's the one who sent us."

Still laughing, the posse turned and headed back down the road.

Bronwyn and Mary Rose stepped out and caught a glimpse of them just before they disappeared. Andrew Greyson rode toward the rear, a guard on either side. His hands were tied behind him, and his head hung low.

THIRTY-FIVE

What is this all about?" Enid's face was red, her hands shaking, when Mary Rose and Bronwyn reached the house.

"How are the children?" Mary Rose started up the stairs to get to them.

"Thank goodness, they slept through it all." Enid put her hands on her hips and glared at Bronwyn. "What happened out there?"

"You're going to have to trust me," Bronwyn said. "And you must—we all must—get ready to leave. Immediately. I will explain on the way."

Even as she said the words she wondered how she could she explain it all. And Greyson, how the thought of him cut her to the core. All was lost, the journals—all the evidence against the secret militia, the Danites, had been in his hands. Now he was taking their punishment. Her heart ached for him.

"Get the children," she cried. "We've got to get out of here fast."

"Leave? Where are you thinking of going?" Enid said.

She took Enid's hand, exasperated. The woman obviously wouldn't budge without at least some explanation

She sighed. "I promise to give you details—everything we've found out—later. But for now, believe me when I say Gabe is up to his neck in this vigilante group activity. The man was telling the truth. Gabe sent them for us.

"The boy in the garden, his death was the work of the Danites. I found proof. I also found a list of apostates in Gabe's desk at the house in town."

Enid's mouth gaped open, but she clamped it shut as Bronwyn continued.

"My name was on it. Mary Rose's too. Also Andrew Greyson, the newspaperman, and where he was camped. That's how we found him to get the journals out. We did it because of the boy's death. We need to get word to the outside about the group and the horrific acts they're carrying out against those who disagree with them."

"Does Brother Brigham know?"

Bronwyn let out another exasperated sigh. They didn't have time for this. But one thing she'd discovered about Enid: she liked to know details; and she was stubborn. Without answers, she might not go. If she didn't, she might endanger them all.

And there was Hosea. Waiting.

"I don't think the prophet knows how far they've gone with this. I can't believe he knows. It's his teaching, but others are taking it perhaps more seriously than he intended."

Enid took a shaky breath. "Where will you go?"

"I'd hoped you'd say 'we.'"

"My name isn't on the apostates list."

"True, but can you stay here, living with a man you know is a killer?"

"I'll never believe that about Gabe. I know him better than you or Mary Rose do. Better than anyone."

Bronwyn bristled. Enid may have known him as a child, but she didn't know him now. At least she didn't want to believe that Enid's words held any truth.

Mary Rose came down the stairs carrying a load of blankets and clothes. "I don't believe it either, not in his heart of hearts. But he's caught up in something bigger than he is. It's mean and dark and done in the name of God. He may not see it yet, but I hope and pray he will someday."

Bronwyn took Enid's hand again. "Please come with us. We don't have time to argue. And if you stay, you will be expected to tell where we've gone. They might not be easy on you, trying to get the information."

"For one thing, I won't know where you've gone, so what can I tell them? And truly, I don't think Gabe would let them hurt me . . . and I can't believe he would let them hurt either of you."

"Think about his allegiance to the Church. It comes first. The prophet's word is law. Where do you think his heart is?"

She studied Bronwyn for a moment, and then nodded. "I'll ride with you. I'm not sure I'll go with you the entire distance . . ." She opened her eyes wide as a realization came to her. "The wagon company that's south of here. That's where you're headed, isn't it?"

"Just get your things. We haven't much time."

Mary Rose trotted back up the stairs and a moment later returned with Joey, still asleep in the crook of her arm. She repeated the action to retrieve Spence, the second time a sleepy Little Grace trailed behind. Cordelia hurried up and down several times bringing satchels of clothes and a stack of blankets.

"I have no more time to talk," Bronwyn said, starting up the stairs. "We've been expecting this for weeks, and now it's time. If you're with us, we'll be happy. If you stay, you'll be in our prayers."

The children, not things, were most important to Bronwyn. While others gathered supplies, she checked on each of the little ones, making sure they were dressed for the journey, making sure their sleeping pallets were in place, favorite child-sized blankets near each.

Shoes! Did her little lambs have the shoes they needed for walking the trail, which they most certainly would have to do by journey's end? She looked under beds and in trunks, searching for a left shoe here, a right one there, of varying sizes.

From the top of the stairs she looked back to see Enid pick up the Hawken and boxes of ammunition, put them by the door, then climb the stairs, appearing at the top a few minutes later with two large medical books, a satchel, and the book about horses she'd bought for Little Grace at the mercantile.

Within minutes, the children were piled in the back of the wagon with the blankets and food. Just as when they made their exodus from Nauvoo all those years before, Mary Rose drove the team with Cordelia and Bronwyn sitting beside her. Enid rode beside them, her expression unreadable.

Bronwyn swallowed hard as the little band started across the moonlit terrain.

If she let herself think about it, she thought she might drown in her own sorrow.

Gabe! What have you brought upon us all?

THIRTY-SIX

Hosea and Coal sat near the campfire, Chuck curled up in the crook of Hosea's arm.

"What're we going to do when it comes time to go our separate ways?" Coal grinned at Hosea. "Who does he go with?"

Hosea chuckled. "Maybe we'll just let him choose." He paused, looking up at the starlit sky. "Either that or we'll have to stick together."

The boy got a dreamy look on his face, and Hosea was almost sorry for mentioning it.

"All of us together, one great big family," he said. "I can see it now."

Hosea stood and placed Chuck on the ground. He grabbed his walking stick, went over to the fire, and stoked it. Then he tossed on another couple of pieces of oak. The sparks flew.

Chuck trotted to a clump of cattails near the river, raised his leg, then trotted back and curled up beside Coal.

"Have you decided when to go see Enid?" Coal said as Hosea hobbled back to the stump he'd occupied earlier and sat.

"Boy, you're pushing because you want to see fireworks better than those sparks I just stirred up." He laughed. "Now that I told Bronwyn and Mary Rose, I need to tell her as soon as I can find her. I'm worried that now the cat's out of the bag, it's only a matter of time before she hears."

"Tell me again how they took it."

Hosea sat back and grinned. "I could tell your mama Mary Rose had it figured out somehow before I said my name."

"She's smart that way."

"Yes, she is. Very smart."

"Tell me about Mama Bronwyn."

"Just when I think I have this whole polygamy thing figured out, you get to talking about your mothers and sisters, and I can't figure out from your perspective what's wrong with it," Hosea said. "I've never known anyone with two mothers before who loved them both the same."

"Then what's the ruckus all about with Gentiles when they get up in arms over polygamy? I've seen 'em ready to go to war with us because of it."

"It's different with men and women," Hosea said. "Not as easy to share affection, I suppose. People don't consider it natural, and sometimes it's used as a way to wield power over women."

"It's in the Bible. King David had, well, hundreds of wives, didn't he?"

"I can't remember exactly how many, but a lot. I always figured that though God permitted it back then, it's not what he knows is best for us, then or now. Like a lot of things. He gave mankind a gift called free will. Sometimes we use it in the right way, even to God's glory. Other times we use it in a way that can cause us and others great pain."

A balmy breeze came off the river, fluttering leaves, and bringing the sound of frog song closer.

"I know I wouldn't ever want more than one wife," Coal said, his expression serious. "I just wish that . . ." He didn't finish, and Hosea knew he was thinking about Sarah. "You didn't finish about Mama Bronwyn. What did she say when she found out your name?"

"She said I had the same beautiful, intelligent eyes that she remembered, and that she should have recognized me right off. She also said she likes the beard, that it gives me a scholarly look."

Coal grinned. "That sounds like her." Then he sobered. "When you tell Mother Enid who you are, what if . . . I mean, we were just talking about free will and all." He looked worried, which touched Hosea.

"You're wondering what if she turns away from me?"

Coal nodded.

"You've come all this way, thinking it was God's will for you to do it. So, even if you do what you think is God's will, what if she just goes ahead and does what she wants?"

Hosea gave him a gentle smile. "I've had the same questions in my own heart. Enid will go ahead and do what she wants. That's the kind of person she is."

Coal leaned forward. "How could you stand something like that happening? After everything you've been through . . ."

"I wouldn't want her to pity me because of what I've been through."

"I wouldn't either," Coal said. "I mean, if what happened to me the same as happened to you."

"If she loves me for who I am, I'll see it in her eyes. If she doesn't, or if she pities me, I'll know that too."

"I hear something," Coal said, and stood up. "Horses maybe. They're not coming fast, whoever it is."

Frowning, Hosea grabbed the stick and hoisted himself upright. The fire popped and cracked, the frogs raised a fuss, and the wind grew stronger, rattling leaves and branches. And his hearing wasn't what it once was. He cupped his ear, and then nodded. "I hear horses, maybe a wagon."

"It's them. I know it is," Coal looked ready to dance. "Do you think they're ready? To leave, I mean? Maybe that's why they're coming."

Hosea kept a calm exterior, but he was as ready to dance as the boy was.

And then he remembered.

He'd said to the women that he would be there for them if they ever needed him. They'd said they had to stay to find out who killed the boy and what it had to do with blood atonement.

This was too soon.

All thoughts of dancing disappeared as he watched the river road for the first sign of the travelers' approach.

Bronwyn spotted a distant campfire through the trees and prayed that it was Hosea and Coal's. The moon was higher now, helping to light their way.

Each creak of the wagon wheel, each step of the horses, brought them closer to safety. Hosea and Coal would take them to the wagon company, but could they get there in time? She shivered.

Wagon travel was slow at best, and with all the children and their supplies in back, plus three women riding, the two-horse team struggled on flat terrain.

Behind them, somewhere in the valley, the vigilantes met, probably planning to fan out and look for them. Would they go back to the ranch first? She hoped so. The more delays the better. She needed to put a greater distance between them and the Danites.

She didn't like to think about the impossibility of their situation. A slow wagon trying to get away from a fired up, fast-riding posse of vigilantes, hell-bent for revenge?

The prophet might be reading the journals right now. And she shuddered to think what might be happening to Andrew Greyson, that good man with the gentle eyes and ready smile.

Her thoughts returned to what he'd done for them by carrying Mary Rose's journals. Was there a way to rescue him? Where would they have taken him before the vigilantes carried out their threats? A shack somewhere? Someone's barn? They might as well try looking for a needle in a haystack.

Enid rode up beside her. "Why are we coming here?"

"We met some people who said they would help us."

"Can we trust them? "

"Yes."

"How did you meet them?"

"They were with Andrew Greyson. I told you about finding the map with his name." Enid deserved to know that Coal was there. She'd kept his secret as long as she thought it would protect him and the family. Secrecy was no longer needed. Besides, it would be enough of a surprise to see Hosea after all these years.

"One of them is Coal," Bronwyn said.

Enid's jaw dropped. "Our Coal?"

She smiled. "I know it's a shock but, yes, our Coal."

"How did he get here and why didn't you tell me sooner? I am part of this family, you know."

Bronwyn smiled to calm her down. "That's why I'm telling you now. And truly, I didn't know until recently. He met up with Greyson and . . . well, Greyson, back at Winter Quarters . . ." She filled Enid in on the rest of the story, though she had to admit, what she knew was sketchy at best.

She nodded and rode along in silence. Then she said, "Having Coal with us makes it even more dangerous. He's been a hunted young man since Sarah's wedding day. If that apostle finds out he's here . . ."

"That's why he kept his presence a secret even from us," Mary Rose said, leaning forward. "He knew that we'd be in danger if he was seen with us."

"That does it, then. I'm not coming with you. I'll see you to the camp to make sure the people you trust are there, then I'll double back."

Bronwyn stared up at Enid, remembering what she'd said years before about intending to become Gabe's first wife. Had she been biding her time, waiting for just this opportunity to make her dream come true?

And now that they were in greater danger because of Coal she decided to call it quits?

"I have to go back," Enid said. "Please don't try to talk me out of it."

Bronwyn turned forward, working through their situation in her mind. She knew where they were going, the route they were taking, and now had the power to betray them all. Would she use that power?

"I see the campsite up ahead," Enid said. "I'll go in first to see if it's Coal, and if not, if we can trust whoever it is." She dug her heels into the horse, and took off down the road.

Mary Rose and Bronwyn looked at each other. It seemed neither one could stop their smiles, despite their dire circumstances.

"She's going to see who it is?" Mary Rose said in wonder, and then laughed. "See if we can trust them?"

Bronwyn rolled her eyes heavenward. "God help us," she said, meaning it. "Does she always have to be first?"

"I'd certainly like to know what you two are up to," Cordelia said. "But from the sounds of it, it may be more entertaining to just watch it happen."

Hosea watched as Enid rode into camp. She slid from her horse, looked Hosea up and down, and then turned her focus to Coal. He tried to contain his disappointment.

She stared at Coal, and he just stood there grinning at her.

She frowned and moved closer. "Coal?"

He nodded. "It's me."

"I just found out that you're here. My goodness, child, you have grown."

"That's what everybody keeps saying."

She opened her arms and hugged him.

Hosea could see there was more emotion in her actions than she let on. When she stepped back, she said, "What did you do to your hair?"

"I tried to fit in with the Dakota . . ."

"Now, that must be some story."

"It is."

She glanced at Hosea, a frown crossing her face for an instant, and then walked from the campsite out to the road.

Hosea and Coal followed.

A heavy-laden farm wagon creaked and swayed along the road. It was covered with white canvas, and drawn by a team of two. They would be better off with oxen, and Hosea hoped to buy or trade once they reached the wagon train.

Mary Rose halted the team, and Hosea stepped up to help the women down as best he could. Mary Rose gave him a warm smile, Bronwyn did the same, hugging him before stepping away. When he reached for Cordelia, she gave him a coquettish nod. "Well, sir, it appears this trip is getting more interesting all the time."

Mary Rose and Bronwyn filled Hosea in on what had happened at the ranch, and Enid pulled Coal away from the others, speaking to him earnestly. He noticed that Coal nodded several times as she spoke, but Hosea couldn't overhear what she said.

She strode back over to the others. "I've already told Mary Rose and Bronwyn that I'm going back," she said.

Hosea's heart froze.

How could she? After what she'd just found out about Gabe? Did she love him that much? Of course she did. Why else would she return?

He found it difficult to breathe, and even as she spoke, he turned away from her and stared at the fire. His dreams had been just that. Dreams. Easily burned to ashes. He was weary, so weary. It was time to go home.

The children were waking now, and Mary Rose said they needed to be on their way. She asked Hosea if he was coming with them.

He drew a deep breath and turned back, a smile fixed in place. "Coal and I will go with you all the way to California. And Chuck, of course." He tried to meet Enid's eyes, but she was getting ready to mount her horse and head back to town.

He concentrated on her face, so familiar, so beloved, yet different somehow. There was a new sharp angle to her demeanor, a bitterness, perhaps. Yet still he loved her—oh, yes, he loved her. He longed to take her into his arms this moment.

But their time was over. Their chance for love in the past. He smiled at her and gave her a little salute.

She frowned briefly and turned the horse to head back down the road.

"You must tell her." Bronwyn now stood beside him. "There may never be another time you can. You must tell her now. Hurry!"

Still, he didn't move.

"If you don't, I'm going to run out there and scream to the top of my lungs that you love her and she's a fool if she doesn't love you too and that she'd better get that horse turned around and hightail it back here."

Hosea grinned. "I don't think I've ever heard you scream."

She poked his chest with her index finger to emphasize her point. "Then you just listen, mister, because you're going to hear the loudest—"

He held up a hand. "No screaming, please. I'll do this my own way."

Hosea walked out to the moonlit road. "Enid," he called. "Enid, come back. There's something you must know."

She halted the horse, and for a moment just sat there, still as a marble statue, in the moonlight.

"Enid," he cried again, and he threw down his stick and limped as fast as he could toward her. "There's something I forgot to tell you in my last letter."

She turned then, and watched him walk toward her. For several heartbeats she didn't speak. Just stared. "Your letter?" she said, frowning. "What letter."

Then she blinked and caught her hand to her mouth. He could see that she was crying.

"Hosea?" she whispered. She slid down from the horse and ran into his arms. "Oh, my darling," she cried. "Is it you?"

"I forgot to tell you," he said, holding her tight, "I forgot to tell you I love you. I always have, and I always will."

THIRTY-SEVEN

Enid rode for an hour before she came to a rise and looked down to see the ranch before her, bathed in moonlight.

She halted the roan and bit her bottom lip, trying not to think about what lay ahead. She was riding headlong into danger, more than she'd ever encountered in her life.

For once, she put away her own desires and thought about those she loved. None of them knew how much they meant to her or to what ends she would go for them.

Her gaze took in the barren ranchlands, the barn, the garden, and finally the house itself. It reminded her of bones without flesh, gray in the pale light, bereft of lamplight, of children's laughter, of wafting scents of Cordelia's cooking.

One way or another, this was the end of life with the Saints. Her greatest discovery had been of herself, though she would be the first to admit she had a long way to go.

She followed Gabe to Nauvoo for selfish reasons. She needed him. Needed the challenge of proving that, though Hosea had rejected her in the end, she could still snag Gabe right from beneath Bronwyn and Mary Rose's noses. It was a matter of pride.

Bronwyn and Mary Rose didn't want her to marry Gabe; she'd known that from the beginning. But she was determined to have him anyway, no matter the cost.

Yet in the end, they had included her as part of the family. The children adored her. She never let on how much their love healed her, how something deep inside her came alive again because of it. When Little Grace adopted her as her favorite "mommy"— even though she knew Grace told Bronwyn and Mary Rose the same thing—her heart rejoiced.

She had come to the MacKays believing that life owed her. She'd known too many heartaches. Gabe left her young and pregnant to pursue his career; she'd lost their baby, a baby he didn't even know about. Hosea had ridden into her life as if on a white steed, tall, handsome, the captain of the whole world in her eyes, and she'd found what deep and abiding love between a man and a woman was meant to be. She'd known what it meant to be cherished.

And then lost him.

And turned into a bitter and angry woman, not caring if she made everyone around her as miserable as she felt.

Hosea. . .

It warmed her to think of him, but she scarce could take it all in. They hadn't had time to talk. And if she told him, or told any of them, what she planned, she knew she would break down in tears and never set foot outside their protective circle.

How she'd longed to stay in Hosea's embrace. Her determination had wavered, but only for a moment when he held so tight she felt the beat of his heart. Stepping back before her resolve faded, she had kissed him and held his gaze with hers in the moonlight, wanting to memorize the love and forgiveness she saw there. Then she ran to her horse, mounted, and rode away without looking back.

She urged the roan down the slope, and within minutes rode through the gate to the ranch house. She tied the roan outside, visible to anyone coming by. She let herself inside and lit every lamp so the windows glowed and light spilled out for anyone and everyone to see.

Enid MacKay had come home, and she wanted everyone to know.

And then she sat in Cordelia's rocking chair and waited. And tried not to think of how alone she was. How vulnerable.

How much she wished the Hawken lay across her lap.

An hour passed. And then another. Then she heard the thundering of hooves, the shouts, angry shouts of men out for blood.

"See who it is inside," a gruff voice yelled.

"I see someone."

"Go get Greyson," someone shouted. "We'll tar and feather them together."

"The tar's nice and hot," cried another. "Boiling hot."

"Hot enough to kill him. Dead or alive, we'll carry him through town hogtied on a pole. Send his body back to New York. Teach Gentiles a thing or two about writing about us."

The door flew open. Gabe was the first to enter. A dozen others crowded into the room around him.

All of them looked wild eyed, worked into a frenzy. Even Gabe.

"Where are they?" Gabe demanded when he saw Enid. "Where's my family?" His face was wild with rage. "Answer me!" he shouted. "Where is my family?"

She stood, hoping her trembling knees didn't show underneath her skirts. "If you'll settle down, I'll tell you," she said, attempting to smile.

"Bet you can't trust her either," one of the men muttered.

"I don't know why not," Enid said with a sweet smile. She went over and took Gabe's hand, leaning against him lovingly. "After all, I'm here and the other wives aren't."

She took a deep breath. "Gentlemen, would you like some hot cocoa? I have a lovely recipe . . ."

Gabe gave her another stern look and drew a deep breath. "Tell me where they are. Now."

"Have you tried the house in town?" She kept her sweet smile in place.

"Of course, we just came from there."

"Well, that would have been my first guess." She shrugged. "Now, how about the cocoa?"

Some of the men actually looked tempted. If she hadn't been so scared, she would have laughed.

"There's a search going on right now," Gabe said, his voice calmer. "They will be found, you can count on that. But I need to find them first so no one will get hurt." He stepped closer and dropped his voice. "Please, I beg you, tell me."

Something in his eyes told her she'd been right after all. She sighed as if exasperated. "I thought you would have guessed by now, Gabe, you and your vigilante friends. Your family is on the way to Fort Bridger. They plan to head east, back to England, last I heard Mary Rose say. She still has the deed to her family's manor house, you know." She hesitated, and then added. "With riches like that, why would she head anywhere else? Young women don't inherit property like that every day."

She smiled at the men. "Can you blame a woman for wanting to take the fastest way home?"

Gabe stared at her, working his jaw, then he turned to the other men. "Find the others and tell them they're headed to Bridger. I'll be behind you." Then he grabbed her arm firmly and pulled her through the doorway. As soon as the other men had ridden off, he released her arm. His face softened. "Now, tell me where they really are."

"How do I know I can trust you?"

"You don't."

She studied his eyes in the moonlight, and thought of their childhood together. How they played along the seashore on Prince Edward Island, built castles in the sand, and rode their horses in the shallow waves, letting the water splash over them. They'd made sand angels, and then lay still as the water pulled the sand out from under them, threatening to pull them with it, out to sea.

Who had Gabe run to when the news reached him that his family perished at sea? He had run to her and she'd held him while he sobbed. He had lived with her family, taken in as a son when he had no one else.

Had she ever known him to be cruel, or even harsh? Never. He'd been her friend, the best she'd ever had. When she followed him to Nauvoo, he hadn't wanted to marry her. She realized now, looking into his eyes, that friendship was really all he ever wanted. And perhaps, because of the Church's influence, a spirit baby or two born of her womb.

Even that didn't ring true. He knew because of his friendship with Hosea that she was barren. When he married her he had done what he thought good and honorable at the time. He didn't love her with a romantic love. He loved her as a friend. Why hadn't she seen that all along?

She smiled, finally.

"Your family is waiting," she said. "If you want to come with us to California."

"That's all I want," he said. Something new shone in his eyes.

Her smile widened. "And you won't believe how it's grown since the last time you saw us."

He cocked his head. "What do you —?"

"You'll find out."

Laughing, she stepped into the stirrup and swung her leg over the saddle. Gabe did the same. "I'll race you to the top of the rise," she called back to him, riding on the wind. "And I'll bet you ten sand dollars I win."

"Yee-haw," he cried, waving his hat in the air. "In your dreams."

They were children again, riding in the moonlight, following their hopes and dreams, following their hearts. "This way," she cried. "Follow me!"

And he did.

EPILOGUE

Be not disheartens'—Affection shall solve the prob-
lems of freedom yet;
Those who love each other shall become invincible.
—Walt Whitman

Mary Rose urged the team up the final hill between her rig and the wagon company in the valley below. When the weary horses reached the top of the incline, she halted them for rest before starting the treacherous journey downward.

The wagon train's cookfires had long ago died, but scattered here and there coals glowed, breaking up the darkness and competing with the pinpoints of starlight in a sky just beginning to fade to dawn.

The children had fallen asleep again—Ruby, Pearl, and Little Grace under the canvas cover; Joey and Spence on Cordelia's and Bronwyn's laps. Through the long night of travel, the conversation had been hushed, though lively, as Coal and Hosea caught the others up with their stories, and she, Bronwyn, and Cordelia told theirs.

Now dawn was about to break, and Mary Rose looked out over this small western valley and the wagon train that would lead them to California, her thoughts turned to what they were leaving behind, a life that she and Gabe had once thought full of adventure—beginning their married life in a new country with an exciting new frontier religion. Heady with a surety of purpose, they'd felt invincible. What could possibly come between them? she remembered thinking. They held a deep and abiding love for each other, a love that she was certain would not die.

Her soul felt battered, and worse, betrayed. Especially this final betrayal. She hadn't spoken of it, but when Enid rode off— even after a show of affection for Hosea—she wondered if the two of them had planned the final betrayal.

Her heart twisted. How desperately she wanted to believe in Gabe.

Hosea came up on the horse he affectionately called MacDuff, and halted beside her.

"If you look back, you might turn into a pillar of salt," he said, guessing her musings.

She gave him a soft smile. "I try not to. But Gabe keeps crowding into my thoughts. I'll never know what happened in the end. It's like a death, only worse."

"Don't give up hope," Hosea said.

She looked at him and nodded. "You're a living example of that, Hosea. Your story . . . your heart of forgiveness and mercy and love . . ." A sting of tears filled her throat. "I don't know if I could do what you've done. Keep loving no matter what. Follow my beloved to the ends of the earth—not even knowing what I'll find when I get there."

"That's how God is with us," he said. "He never gives up, no matter what we've done. Remember the story of the ninety-nine sheep?"

She nodded. "From my childhood. The shepherd leaves the ninety-nine to search for the one lost sheep."

"That story is a portrait of God's undying love for us. We may take paths that He would not have us choose, paths that lead us into sin and temptation, cause us greater heartache and pain than we can imagine . . . but He comes to find us, not matter where we stray."

Bronwyn, sitting next to Mary Rose, spoke up. "You've just said that He finds us, not the other way around." Her voice held a sense of wonder. She cuddled Joey close, resting her cheek on the top of his head.

"I remember aboard the *Sea Hawk* how you called your little ruffian wards—"

"Be careful how you refer to us," Coal grinned from where he was letting the pinto graze a few yards ahead. "We weren't that bad."

Hosea laughed. "It was in the eye of the beholder, son." Then he turned back to Bronwyn. "You called them your little lambs and no matter how they were acting, what antics they were up to, they responded to the love in your voice, to that word *lamb*."

Bronwyn's eyes filled. "Unearned love," she said. "Being loved for . . . just being."

"That's the profound simplicity of God's love," Hosea said. He turned to look out in the distance. "Nothing can get between you and the One who loves you, not principalities with their powers, not institutions and rules made by man."

"Those things we've done that have hurt others and shamed us . . ." Bronwyn whispered. "Unforgivable things."

Hosea nudged MacDuff closer. "That's called grace," he said. "Sometimes it's difficult to believe that God extends it to us freely. But He does."

He rode off a short ways, and in the light of breaking dawn, his silhouette made her think of him again as their captain. He sat tall in the saddle, his back straight, his face forward. His profile exuded strength. And now that she knew what he'd endured—and overcome—when he was swept overboard and washed up on the shores of Maine, she was in awe of the man. Master and commander, some called the captains of sailing ships. He had been that indeed, when she first met him.

Now his strength rose not from that commanding presence, but from a strength and peace that came from his heart.

Just then Coal shouted, "Riders approaching!"

Mary Rose heard the children wake and scramble to the rear to peer out. She looked around the side of the long canvas cover and grinned. "Bronwyn," she said, almost unable to contain her joy. "Bronwyn, get down and look at this."

Bronwyn watched the approaching group of riders. It was light enough now that she could make out Gabe and Enid on separate horses. It appeared that someone rode on the saddle behind Enid. And a third horseman beside Gabe.

She glanced over at Coal. He'd noticed the rider in back of Enid. Red hair, a face wreathed in smiles as she peered out from behind Enid, a pretty face with large eyes that sought out his. He blushed and kicked the soil with his foot, but Bronwyn had never seen him look happier.

The group came closer now, and Bronwyn gasped. The third horseman was Greyson. He lived!

Oh, Father, she breathed, *Thank you!*

She moved her gaze to Gabe and looked into his eyes as he drew nearer. He searched hers, and it seemed, even from a distance, that he asked for forgiveness.

So much to say, so much mercy and forgiveness needed among them all. Where would they begin?

Hosea came up to stand beside her. "It begins with one step, one day at a time," he said. "Forgiveness doesn't come all at once. It's part of a journey. But when you begin it, you'll never be sorry. Neither will you be alone."

Mary Rose came up to stand beside her and Bronwyn reached for her hand. Around them, the children cheered and carried on, waking the birds in the trees overhead.

Then the two women stepped out to meet the riders.

Gabe spotted the wagon first, off in the distance, touched by the first rays of the rising sun. He called back to Enid to take a look. Her horse trotted slightly behind, slower than his now because she rode double.

Gabe looked over at the rider beside him and raised a brow. "You ready to meet my family?"

"You forget I've already met a few of them." Greyson grinned. "And I liked what I saw. Plus I spent a lot of time with your son. He's a fine young man. I doubt that he would've made it through his ordeal with the Dakota if you hadn't taught him how to survive."

"I didn't ever think I'd see him again." Gabe's heart skipped. He couldn't reach his family fast enough, but neither did he want to leave the others in his dust.

"Sometimes we don't know what's around the next corner." Greyson laughed. "Like last night when it was you coming for me instead of the mob with a pot of hot tar."

"I'd planned it all along, but didn't know if I could pull it off. Enid's the one we need to thank. I couldn't have gotten you out— or Sarah either—without her help." He slowed his horse so she could catch up.

She looked over at him with an expression of pride, then shaded her eyes. "They're here," she said, "all of them."

"You said our family had grown," Gabe said. "I know about Coal finding us, but who's that on the swayback next to him."

"Hosea," she said, her voice soft.

He drew in a breath of utter astonishment. "You can't mean it."

Without bothering to explain, she took off at a gallop toward the wagon. Hosea dismounted and opened his arms. Enid fell into them. He held her as if there would be no tomorrow, and then he looked up, his gaze seeking Gabe's.

Gabe halted his horse, dismounted, and for a moment didn't move. Then slowly Hosea smiled and inclined his head. Gabe stared at him, and then, slowly, smiled in return and nodded.

Children spilled from the back of the wagon, shouting and laughing and hanging all over Gabe and Enid. Everyone seemed to be talking at once.

Even as the cacophony continued, Gabe went over to Mary Rose and pulled her aside. "I would never have allowed the twins to marry," he said.

"I should have trusted you."

"I hadn't earned your trust," he said. "You had a right to believe what you did, to take the actions you did. I had my plan to save us all"—he smiled—"but I didn't expect you and Bronwyn to come up with your plan." He searched her eyes. "I have a gift for you if you'll come with me."

She followed him to his horse. He opened the saddlebags and pulled something out, and then turned to her.

"One is a bit smudged," he said, "from the thug who got to it before I did. But I was able to save the others before any harm came to them . . . or anyone read them." He placed the first one in her hands.

Her eyes filled as her fingers touched the leather cover. She stared at it for a moment, and then clasped it close. For a moment, they looked at each other.

Then he said, "I don't know if we can start over, if we can recapture what we once had . . ." He looked toward the sunrise. "Or if you can ever forgive me. If anyone can . . ."

He reached for her hand, and she let him hold it. "I would like to try," he said.

The sun now shone bright on the wagon company below them. The cattle were starting to move, and wagons lurched forward as the cries of the wagon master carried in the air. Children played alongside the wagons, some women drove their wagons, others walked alongside.

"It's time to go," the captain called out, grinning at Gabe. "Let's get this prairie schooner on its way."

Gabe gave him a salute, mounted, and rode up beside him.

AUTHOR'S NOTE

Dear Reader:

The Betrayal came from a deep place in my heart, perhaps more so than any of my other two dozen works of fiction. The plot was not one I had to mine. It found me.

This doesn't mean the subject wasn't a challenging topic to tackle. It was. *The Sister Wife*, book one in the series, was difficult enough to write as I plotted the journey of Mary Rose and the heartbreaking circumstances she faced. But as we moved geographically and emotionally deeper into the story—this time telling it through Bronwyn's viewpoint—I realized that the questions raised held an acute truth not only essential to my story . . . but also essential to our faith journeys today.

These questions have to do with who we are as beloved children of God, with the choices we make, with the wrong turns we take on our life's journey, with the consequences we pay as a result. They also have to do with God's forgiveness, mercy, and grace—and that always, no matter how often we fall or mess up our lives or the lives of others, there is never a moment that His love for us falters.

J. I. Packer says in his classic *Knowing God*:

He knows me. I am graven on the palms of His hand. I am never out of His mind . . . He knows me as a friend, one who loves me; and there is no moment when His eye is off me, or His attention distracted from me, and no moment, therefore, when His care falters.

There is unspeakable comfort . . . knowing that His love to me is utterly realistic, based at every point on prior knowledge of the worst about me, so that no discovery now can disillusion him about me, in the way I am so often disillusioned about myself, and quench His determination to bless me . . .

There is, however, equally great incentive to worship and love God in the thought that, for some unfathomable reason, He wants me as His friend, and desires to be my friend, and has given His Son to die for me in order to realize that purpose.

Packer's words go right to the heart of Bronwyn's journey in *The Betrayal.* And to the heart of my own journey. Perhaps yours as well. All of us have taken wrong turns in our lives; we've been headstrong, ignored God's truths, and hurt others, perhaps betrayed those we love most in the world. Some of us have made what we think are irreparable mistakes—betraying God, betraying our best selves.

Bronwyn struggles with the betrayal of her dearest friend, Mary Rose, in *The Sister Wife.* She struggles throughout *The Betrayal* with feelings for Gabe that she doesn't understand, yet knows are wrong. She is tempted to give in to these feelings, knowing full well that if she does, she will again betray her friend.

If we "listen" carefully to her words and thoughts as she tries to convince herself that she has every right to act on those feelings, we might be surprised at how similar her argument is to those we've either used ourselves or heard others use to justify their choices.

Have you ever struggled with past actions you thought unforgivable . . . with choices you knew were not God's best for you? I encourage you to lay down the burden of past wrongs at the foot of the cross, ask God's forgiveness, and then, if possible, go to the ones you have hurt and ask their forgiveness, and if possible, prayerfully do your part to restore the relationship. It isn't easy. Asking forgiveness makes us vulnerable. It opens our hearts in ways that are unfathomable. Sometimes painful.

God is in the business of healing, but he waits for us to take the first step. When we do, we'll find Him lovingly waiting to go with us on this journey. He will dry our tears and give us the strength to do what needs to be done.

I love the promise He gives us in Psalm 86:5 (NIV):

> You, Lord, are forgiving and good, abounding in love to
> all who call to you.

I want to add a note to sharp-eyed readers. Utah did not become a U.S. territory until 1850. When referring to "the territory" in this work, I am using it as a generic term. Also, though I refer to *blood atonement* as being discussed in 1848, historically the theology wasn't openly preached by Brigham Young until closer to the time of the Mountain Meadows Massacre in 1857 (as portrayed in my novel *The Veil*).

I would love to hear from you. I invite you to drop by my website—www.dianenoble.com—where you will find photos of our research of old emigrant trails, a list of my previous books, recipes, journal entries, and more. Don't forget to sign my guestbook. You can also look me up on Facebook and Twitter. I read and respond to every e-mail and value each letter or note I receive.

With all joy and peace,
Diane Noble

DISCUSSION QUESTIONS

1. What are your thoughts about polygamy? Do you believe that religious groups have the right to practice plural marriage in today's society? Why or why not?

2. How do you feel the practice relates to freedom of religion? Should there be limits? Why or why not?

3. Why do you think it was practiced by the patriarchs of the Old Testament? What verses of Scripture can you find to support your view? Did the practice please God? Did he condone it?

4. How do you think individual women in a plural marriage feel about themselves, e.g., what do you think happens to their self-esteem when another woman is brought into a marriage? Is there a difference between polygamy practiced by fundamentalist LDS sects and Muslims in this country or elsewhere?

5. Fundamentalist sects say a polygamous lifestyle is more stable for children than multiple marriages and divorces within their family. What do you think? Statistics show there is a higher percentage of cases of anxiety and depression among women and children in plural marriage relationships. Why do you think this is the case?

6. Bronwyn is in a "legal" polygamous marriage, according to her Church and the society she lives in. Why is she torn between remaining chaste and giving herself physically to Gabe? Would this be a difficult choice for you if you were in her circumstances?

7. Do you think Mary Rose is right in her bahavior toward Bronwyn and Gabe as she watches the emotional interplay between them? How would you describe her attitude (in one word)? How about her attitude toward Enid (again, one word only)?

8. What is Gabe's driving force as he embraces the practice of polygamy? Do you think he loves any of his wives more than the others? Which one, and why? Or does he love himself? Do you see any act of sacrificial love toward them?

9. Bronwyn longs for someone to love her as if she is the only one in the world to love. She thinks that human love can fill this void. Do you see this as a metaphor of human longing, male or female, for the all-encompassing, unconditional, sacrificial love of God? Why, or why not?

10. If Gabe were to come back to Mary Rose and ask her forgiveness, do you think she should or could forgive him? In your own life, if someone you love betrayed your trust, is

it possible to extend forgiveness, grace, and mercy to that one—no matter the offense? Does it matter if you are asked for forgiveness? Can you forgive anyway?

11. If you are the one who betrayed another, do you think it's necessary to go to that loved one you betrayed and ask for forgiveness, even if considerable time has passed? Why, or why not?

12. Consider the words from the Lord's Prayer, *Forgive us our trespasses, as we forgive those who trespass against us.*

Take a few minutes to think of someone you need to forgive . . . or of someone you need to go to for forgiveness. Consider God's mercy, grace, and deep love toward you and ask him to help you extend that same compassion toward the one he has brought to your mind, or the strength to act if you are the one in need of forgiveness.

ACKNOWLEDGMENTS

Throughout the days and months I worked on *The Betrayal*, I have been blessed by many who encouraged, supported, and cheered me on, especially the following:

Cynthia DiTiberio, my editor at HarperOne, who remains passionate about The Brides of Gabriel. Her editing skills brought *The Betrayal* to life, and she is such a joy to work with. It's with a heart of gratitude that I thank her for her patience and grace! Cindy, you are a treasure!

Joel Kneedler, literary agent extraordinaire, for his encouragement, insightful direction, and godly grace. He keeps the world at bay while I work (a major feat!) and has a special knack for keeping me focused. As always, you're the best, Joel!

Lorin Oberweger, editorial consultant, cheerleader, and book-in-progress angel. Lorin, what would I do without your incredible insights, fiction expertise, and unwavering support? Thank you once again for being there for me.

Jan and Jack List, who provided a little bit of heaven on earth and a place of inspiration for my muse while I worked on *The Betrayal*. Thank you, dear friends! Big hugs, too, to friends who generously helped us furnish our "nest"—especially Dona annd Larry Burns, Betsy and Bob Clopine, and my "lil' bro," Jim Thomas.

It was a joy to add the name of a special character, Beatrice Leverton, to my cast of characters. The name was provided by Dorina Sleep, who during a charity fund-raiser drawing won the chance to become (or to provide the name and characteristics of) a character in this work. Big hugs to Jim and Tori Thomas for naming "Chuck Wagon" and providing the description for Hosea's furry sidekick to honor their beloved pet.

A special thanks to my family and friends, prayer warriors all, who encouraged and supported me during the writing of this book, especially Dennis and Kathi Hill, Kristin Hill, Melinda Head, Amy Martinez, Linda Udell, Marihelen Goodwin, Tom and Susan Johnson, Flo Smith, Sharon Gillenwater, Annie Jones, and Lynn Bulock; my online Facebook family—those related by blood and those related in "spirit," especially Papa Gene and Linda Newcomb; and to my St. Hugh's family in Idyllwild.

To Dan Rondeau, my spiritual director, whose godly wisdom, thoughtful guidance, and joy- and peace-filled presence always lifts my heart and gives me new truths to ponder. Dan, when we've been together, I never fail to come away feeling that I've spent time sitting at the feet of Christ. Thank you for reflecting his peace, joy, and love to me.

Biggest hugs of all to Tom, my resident historian and chef extraordinaire. Your expertise in the area of American history, especially the history of the American West, is so appreciated when I'm working on a series such as this! Thank you for your kind patience and immense unerstanding during the long months of my "hermitage" while I worked on *The Betrayal*.

© Scott Campbell

Diane Noble

Award-winning novelist **DIANE NOBLE** writes stories that tap into the secrets of the heart. Whether her characters live in twelfth-century Wales, nineteenth-century America, or in today's world, Diane explores their secret longings and loves, their heartaches and triumphs, and, ultimately, their redemption. She brings them to life, drawing on her own experiences and observations and digging deep into human emotions common to us all.

Beloved for her heartwarming novellas adapted to stage (*Come, My Little Angel,* and *Phoebe*) and acclaimed for her award-winning novels (*The Veil, When the Far Hills Bloom*), Diane's works include romance, mystery, suspense, and historical novels.

Diane and her historian husband enjoy exploring rugged nineteenth-century immigrant trails in their Jeep and "African safari" tent trailer, and they belong to various organizations that support the exploration and preservation of these trails. Diane is also member of Women Writing the West, an organization dedicated to the celebration of the role of women in the American West, yesterday and today.

Visit Diane's website at www.dianenoble.com and write to her at diane@dianenoble.com. You can also follow her on Facebook and Twitter.